The Chimera Strain

Kevin Lee Swaim

PUBLISHED BY: PICADILLO PUBLISHING
COVER DESIGN BY: THE COVER COLLECTION
PROOFREADING BY: DONNA RICH
ISBN: 978-0692356227

Also by Kevin Lee Swaim

Project Strikeforce

Project StrikeForce

The Chimera Strain

Project StrikeForce: Exodus

StrikeForce Reborn

Sam Harlan, Vampire Hunter

Come What May

Hard Times

Damned Cold

Deal with the Devil

ACKNOWLEDGMENTS

Thanks to my beta readers. Your feedback was invaluable.
Special thanks to all the active and retired military members who helped
with this endeavor. Any mistakes contained herein are entirely mine.

DEDICATION

To my family, for bearing with me while I spent so many days and
nights working on this novel.

CHAPTER ONE

Syria

JOHN FRIST HURTLED to the ground near the Iraqi border at over one hundred miles per hour, his head protected by his Visual Improvement System for Optical Recognition. The VISOR's electronics quieted the rush of air to a barely audible whistle while his HUD displayed the rapidly decrementing altimeter. The C130J Hercules he had jumped from was a quickly moving red dot in the HUD as it disappeared into the night.

Below, his VISOR showed a ghostly overlay of information. The roads were highlighted in yellow, the vehicles in blue, and his main objective, the series of low stone buildings, blazed in red.

He grimaced. In two years, he had gone from soldier to terrorist to guinea pig. The Office of Threat Management had recruited him, experimented on him, and turned him into a technologically enhanced killing machine. He was stronger and faster than before, and his Battlesuit and VISOR were just the beginning. The Implant in his abdomen provided a steady stream of drugs to enhance his musculature and his brain, even painkillers to numb the dull throb from the prosthetic where his left foot had been blown off in an explosion caused by a terrorist, Abdullah the Bomber.

It had taken six months after the mission in New York City, six long months of surgeries and physical therapy, to heal his wounds. It had taken him that long just to relearn how to walk, to run, to fight with his prosthetic.

Damn thing still hurts.

A voice broke the whisper of air. "Mission is a go. Prepare for deployment."

The voice belonged to Eric Wise, the leader of Project StrikeForce and Assistant Director to the OTM. Eric was a former Delta Operator, one of the hardest and toughest men John had ever met.

Eric also knew John's terrible secret.

John had blamed the Red Cross for misplacing his emergency leave paperwork, causing him to miss his parents' funeral. After his discharge, he had moved to Washington, then bombed the Red Cross building in Fairfax, Virginia. Five hundred and twelve people had died in the blast.

The OTM had identified him and kidnapped him from the street in front of his apartment. He had been renditioned to Guantánamo Bay and interrogated for months by the CIA in the secret part of the base, Camp 7. When there was nothing further to glean, they'd transported him to Area 51, where the scientists working for the OTM had wiped parts of his memory, replacing others with false ones, before experimenting on him.

They had injected him with nanobots and woven his bones with carbon graphene. They'd removed his gallbladder and replaced it with the Implant. They'd pumped him full of drugs and worked him over, all the while under the impression that he had no memory of what he had done.

Only Eric knew the truth.

The same drugs used to heal his body had also healed his mind, reconnecting neurons, giving him back his memories.

John remembered *everything*. He remembered the bombing. He remembered the bag being placed over his head when he was taken from the street while opening the door of his pickup truck. He remembered waking as nanobots crawled through his body, weaving graphene, causing an excruciating pain worse than the torture he had endured at Guantánamo Bay.

If John slipped for a moment—if anyone found out—he was a dead man. The OTM couldn't allow him to live. He was too great a risk, too great a threat.

He'd had plenty of time to think during his rest and rehabilitation after the events in New York City. There was only one conclusion—the only reason the OTM would bother mind-wiping a terrorist was because the process wasn't safe. He had no family, no friends. No one would miss him. If Project StrikeForce failed, if the tech proved unsafe, they could safely dispose of his body and no one would be the wiser.

The OTM hadn't counted on the drugs. The drugs had repaired the damage done to his brain when his Humvee had been hit by an IED in Iraq. They had repaired the damage, and his mind was finally clear, his misplaced anger and obsession with the Red Cross gone. He was horrified at what he had done. He wanted to atone for his crimes but was forced to fight for the OTM.

He had grown *weary* of it.

None of it mattered. He was just a machine, preparing for battle. The ground quickly approached, and he steeled himself for the jerk of the parachute.

When it came, the Battlesuit slammed against the cords as his body decelerated. He felt the whine of the servos as the VISOR's computer manipulated the lines to steer him to his destination, three thousand feet below. "Chute deployed."

"You'll be landing hot."

Half a world away, Eric watched the VISOR's telemetry and video from the drones flying overhead. Below, all was quiet as the people inside the houses went about their business, plotting terror attacks against the United States.

They weren't innocent. Eric had walked him through the mission profile. The men and women below were plotting something big. The first step in halting that plan was to eliminate the terrorists and gather intel.

Eric was right, he *was* coming in hot.

He concentrated and the VISOR's night vision blinked on. He saw the ground rapidly approach, and when he hit, the shock ran up his legs and jarred him hard enough to make his vision swim. He collapsed to the ground, a stabbing pain in his leg where the prosthetic was bolted to the tibia, then turned and grabbed the cords and pulled hard, wrapping them in his arms until the black parachute fabric was bunched up tight.

"I'm down."

He placed the parachute material on the ground and weighted it down with several rocks. He glanced around and found the nearest guard a hundred yards away. He watched the VISOR's split screen as the guard to the south strolled past a stone hut and around a corner.

He removed the oxygen bottle from his belt harness and disconnected the hose from the VISOR, setting it under the edge of the parachute. There was a soft beep as the VISOR began filtering the night air, then he removed his HK MP5SD. The VISOR blazed to life, showing his estimated current ammo count.

"Ready to proceed."

"Copy that. Activating the Implant."

He felt a surge as the Implant dumped the highly experimental drugs into his bloodstream, and he gasped for breath, his heart pounding in his chest. Concern over the mission faded until all that was left was the urge to act.

"Implant activated. I'm going in."

He raced across the loose rock, footsteps sure and light, prosthetic springing wildly as he covered the twenty yards to the first house. It was no bigger than the small apartment he'd lived in after his discharge. He came around the corner and spun into the thin wooden door, tearing it off its hinges. Thermal vision from the drones showed eight occupants in the house, six men in the front and two women in the back.

He barely had time to register their surprised looks as his suppressed HK cracked. He spun it ruthlessly and efficiently, catching the first man in the chest, then moving on to the second. They fell where they sat, but the third man was grabbing for his AK, his long gray beard whipping madly, then John's bullets tore through the man's side.

He moved on to the next three as they scrambled across the room for a table loaded with rifles against the far wall. They never made it. John mowed them down, their bodies shuddering under the hail of gunfire, collapsing to the floor as bullets ripped through them.

In less than five seconds, he had taken out six men, all of whom were dead or dying. He gritted his teeth as he ran across the room and kicked in the bedroom door. Two women cowered next to the bed. They never stood a chance. Darkness provided no cover as he emptied the rest of his magazine into them. Their chests bloomed with red in his thermal vision, and he dropped the magazine and inserted a new one, then cycled the bolt.

"The guard is coming back," Eric said.

"I see him."

"You've got two more on the west and four in the other house."

"I *know.*"

He ran out of the house and headed west as one of the men in the house opened the door. He caught the man with his HK, and the man registered shock, his bearded mouth opening wide, then collapsed as the bullets tore through his chest.

Bullets pinged around him. He pulled a grenade from his harness, yanked out the pin, and tossed it through the open door. The men inside dove for cover, and he cut loose with his HK, killing the second man, who stood over the body of his friend in the doorway.

The bullet ripped through the man's face, entering one cheek and exiting the other, spraying blood and teeth against the doorsill. The grenade exploded, and he heard shrieks from inside. The overhead thermal vision bloomed red inside the room, then faded away. He saw the outlines of the men inside, convulsing, and knew they were no longer a threat.

That left three guards, two running toward him from the west and one approaching from the south. They were shouting in Arabic and firing wildly.

His black Battlesuit made him no more than a shadow as he ran at them. He fired on the run, killing the guard on the left. The guard on the right, a short man wearing a patuu, ducked behind a low stone wall, screaming incoherently.

He barely registered the man approaching from the south before he felt the impact to his leg, like a baseball bat against his thigh. He grunted in pain and dropped to the ground, then carefully shot the man, center mass, with his HK. The man fell in the dirt, his legs spasming.

The last guard was still shouting from behind the low stone wall, but John didn't care. He stood, picked up a stone the size of his fist, and tossed it a dozen yards behind the wall. The guard popped up, turning to face the other direction, his AK-47 hammering away.

John took the opportunity to put a burst of rounds through the man's back.

In less than two minutes, he had cleared the compound. He shook his head in disgust and went back to the first house. A lamp in the room cast a dim glow, but he didn't need it. The VISOR turned night into day.

He removed a black nylon bag from his hardened backpack and placed two laptops, found on the wooden table, inside it. He inspected the rest of the room, rolling the dead men over, methodically going through their robes. He found a notebook and tossed it into the black bag, a USB thumb drive from another man joining it. He grabbed the computer on the corner desk and kicked it open, exposing its guts, then yanked the hard drive free of the enclosure and placed the drive in the black bag.

He glanced around at the men splayed across the room. Their clothes were stained with blood, and their bladders and colons had emptied and filled the room with an unbearable stench that even the VISOR's filters couldn't mask. He searched the dead women in the bedroom, as well, but found nothing. The room was empty except for an RPG in the corner and cases of ammunition stacked between two beds.

He tried and failed to ignore the women's glassy eyes, which appeared hollow and accusatory in his night vision.

"The site is secure, and I have the merchandise."

"Copy that. Extraction is inbound."

John nodded to himself. The Sikorsky UH-60 would be there in moments. The gunfire had surely been heard in the town to the west, and fighters would soon investigate. He exited the house and ran east, his legs pumping hard. A faint thrumming grew louder, then suddenly intensified as the Black Hawk descended.

The helicopter was quiet and sported enough stealth technology and electronic countermeasures to make it invisible to radar. The side door opened, and a tall black man waited, his HK 416 at the ready as he scanned the area to the west.

John dove into the helicopter. "Make it rain."

The black man nodded and signaled to the pilot. John's stomach fell away as the Black Hawk soared into the sky. The black man grabbed him by the shoulder to steady him and grinned. "Welcome back," Taylor Martin said.

John nodded to him. "Thanks, TM."

The other Delta Operator, Mark Kelly, a short man with sad brown eyes, helped haul him into the seat, grabbing the nylon bag with the recovered evidence. "Good work, John."

John fumbled with the restraints before managing to secure them. He glanced back through the open door and watched the houses turn red in the VISOR's thermal vision, then felt the distant whump-whump-whump of multiple missile strikes as the area was reduced to flaming rubble.

From half a world away, Eric's voice cut through. "Deactivating the Implant. Excellent work."

John said nothing. He knew from experience that he would crash as the drugs left his system, his brain working overtime to process the experience. He would watch in slow motion as he killed the men and women, grabbed the valuable intel, and made his escape. The flight back to the States would give him time to dream, to relive the horror of combat. It put his teeth on edge.

So much for their perfect killing machine.

* * *

Area 51

The chirp of wheels hitting the runway woke John from his restless sleep. He rubbed at the grit in his eyes, then nodded at Taylor and Mark. The Gulfstream taxied into a hangar where a Humvee waited.

The stench of jet fuel washed over him as he exited the plane, jolting him wide awake, and he shook his head. "God, I hate that smell."

Behind him, Taylor laughed. "Really? I always thought it smelled kinda sweet."

"That's because you're weird," Mark said.

John couldn't help but laugh. The past two years had brought an easy camaraderie with both men. Former Delta Force, like Wise, they were not only the most competent soldiers he had ever worked with but also genuinely *likable* men.

Taylor had suffered severe injuries in Texas, and they had bonded in rehabilitation. Mark had checked on them every day, helping them through surgeries and checkups, until they were fit for duty.

There had been days when he felt he could barely go on, days when Taylor was down, too, and Mark would offer some sardonic comment, usually directed at their nurse, Kara Tulli. It made the bad days better, and Wise was there too, coaching them, pushing them to get their medical clearance.

They loaded the Battlesuit and the weapon cases into the Humvee and drove west. It was another twenty minutes before they had entered the underground base west of the runways and hangars, cleared the checkpoints, and found themselves in the War Room.

The War Room was a large chamber a hundred feet across, carved from rock and lined with concrete and steel. Rows of desks neatly divided the room, and gigantic monitors hung from the walls. The place hummed with activity, and the officer on deck, Sergeant Todd Clark, led them to the conference room, where Eric waited with Nancy Smith.

Nancy greeted them coolly, her chilly blue eyes barely acknowledging their presence. "Gentlemen."

"Glad you're back," Eric said with a warm smile. Eric was the epitome of a Delta Operator, short brown hair just a little too long for regulation and sharp brown eyes that glittered with intelligence. "Karen's been analyzing the data you scanned and uploaded."

They took seats as Eric signaled for Karen Kryzowski, the OTM's lead data analyst, to join them.

Karen entered the room, coffee cup in one hand and a tablet computer in the other. She took a seat near the display on the front wall and fiddled with her tablet.

"Karen?" Eric prompted. "What have you found?"

She looked up. "We're decrypting the drives. The notebooks have already given *some* information. This group has access to something they consider a game changer."

Her fingers swiped around the tablet, and the scanned photos of the notebook appeared on the wall display. "See this section?" She highlighted the Arabic words. "This references a large financial transaction. *Serious* money. And this? It's planning. The drives should contain the operational details. Guys, for this kind of money, it *has* to be something big. Biological or nuclear, that's what I think."

John was suddenly aware of the chill in the air. "I thought Al-Qaeda in Iraq was bush league? Kinda like the JV team?"

"Not anymore," Nancy said, her usually calm exterior visibly shaken. "They think the only way to win Iraq is to carry out an attack in the United States."

John waited for someone to speak, but the room was deathly quiet. "What's next?" he finally asked.

"Go see the docs for your after-action checkup," Eric said before turning to Karen. "How much longer before you've decrypted the drives?"

"A day or two," Karen said. "I'm exploiting a flaw in the math behind the encryption scheme. It's a weakness that's never been addressed since the RFC. Plus, I have a *ton* of computational power to throw at it."

Eric smiled, shaking his head. "I don't think any of us really understand what you're saying, but a day or two is acceptable."

John almost missed the look Karen gave Eric. He had sensed something between them, and Nancy's body language spoke volumes.

It was no secret in the OTM that Nancy was interested in Eric, and even though she tried hard to conceal it, he saw it on her face. She wanted Eric and didn't like it that Eric had … something … with Karen.

Then again, who was he to throw stones? He had finally summoned the courage to ask Kara Tulli for coffee, and they had been on the equivalent of three dates. She was the first woman he had expressed interest in since before his deployment to Iraq.

They stood to leave, and Eric clapped him on the back. "Good job, John. I *mean* that. Take some time after you've completed your after-action report. You've earned it."

He gave Eric his best fake smile. "Will do."

* * *

John stripped to his briefs as Doctor Elliot placed lead wires on his chest and legs.

"Anything out of the ordinary?" Elliot asked as his massive black hands moved quickly and delicately to place the adhesive pads.

"No. The mission went off without a hitch."

Kara Tulli gave him a reassuring nod as she took a blood sample from his left arm, then placed the sample in a steel refrigerator in the corner. "Cold?"

He grinned. "It's a *little* cool."

She draped a thin white sheet over his chest as Doctor Elliot finished with the last of the leads. "Might as well cover up," she said. "You're going to be here awhile."

He sighed. He was used to the after-action physicals, but it didn't mean he *liked* them. He wrapped the sheet around his body and reclined against the lumpy hospital bed as Elliot ran the diagnostics. "Doc, with all the high-tech gadgets around here, can't you come up with a bed that's more comfortable?"

Elliot laughed. "Sorry, John, we *have* priorities."

He wanted to call them on *their* priorities, like experimenting on him, wiping his memories, and injecting him with billions of nanobots that crawled through his skin like an electric fire.

He gritted his teeth. There was no point in it. He could never express his true thoughts, to Doctor Elliot or to Kara.

Sure, she had agreed to have coffee with him, but that was only after she'd helped patch him up while he practically killed himself trying to atone for his actions.

She used to stare at him out of the corner of her eye, the hostility evident. The look had finally softened when he was recovering from losing his foot. He reached down and absently scratched at it with his fingertips.

Elliot noticed and raised an eyebrow. "The prosthetic bothering you?"

"Yeah. Even when I'm *not* wearing it."

"In a couple of years, this artificial prosthetic osseointegrated to your leg will be outdated technology. We've developed a way to print a foot out of bone using CNC, and next year we hope to print the arteries and blood vessels. As soon as we can figure out how to print and graft the nerves, we'll be in business. Think of what we will be able to do with the next generation of StrikeForce technology!"

John shivered, and it *wasn't* from the chill in the room. He could almost forget at times that he was the first generation of StrikeForce, but he also knew what happened to first-generation technology.

Old tech is routinely dismantled and destroyed.

* * *

Eric tried to hold Karen Kryzowski's arms, but she grabbed his wrists and pinned them tightly against the soft blanket on his cot. His eyes slid up her body, pausing at her naked breasts, and then he gasped as she ground herself on him, riding him as she orgasmed.

They were both panting from exertion, slick with sweat, and she laughed as he shuddered, his own orgasm bursting forth.

For a moment, he lost himself in her. His problems faded away, and he felt he could finally breathe. He closed his eyes, and when he opened them, she was watching him with a smile on her face.

"What?" he asked.

"You really need to do this more often. The stress is eating you alive."

He shook his head. "I'm fine."

"No, you're not. Halfway through, I could tell you were still worried about the mission. About John. About Nancy." She rolled off and snuggled next to him, her sticky skin pressed against his flesh.

"Maybe I'm worried about sleeping with a married woman."

"You know that Brad doesn't mind. We have our arrangement. He takes care of *his* needs, and I take care of *mine*."

He stared in disbelief. "I don't get it. You don't feel *any* jealousy?"

She laughed hard enough to make her muscular belly shake. "Nope. Never have, never will."

"It goes against everything I know of women. I mean, sex should mean something, shouldn't it?"

She smiled lazily. "You're sweet. This isn't about *love*. I like you. You're smart and focused. Driven. But I *love* my husband. What we just did wasn't love. It was sex. You're wound tight, and it's seeping into your work. You don't have to feel guilty. You don't have to feel conflicted. That's why Barnwell set up the program. It lets people blow off steam."

Hearing her say it didn't make him feel better. "With sex."

She smirked. "It's good for you. He's got the data to back it up. Don't knock it."

He carefully extricated his arms and legs from her embrace, then stood and walked to his bathroom. He leaned over the steel sink and looked in the mirror, inspecting the bags under his eyes.

Karen is right, I am wound tight.

He poured a glass of water and took two ibuprofen. His knees were acting up, and the pain was distracting. As an Operator, he had jumped from his share of helicopters, ran through brutal deserts, and marched up rugged hillsides.

I miss it.

After all his years as an Operator, he hadn't fully understood what his current desk job would entail. Instead of fighting against terrorists, he was directing John and the rest of the OTM in a global war, entirely in secret.

His former Delta buddies had no idea—they thought he was home in Cincinnati, enjoying his retirement.

The Office of Threat Management did the dirty work that needed to be done, no matter how unpleasant, and he wouldn't have it any other way.

That didn't mean he enjoyed *all* of it. The paperwork never abated, and there were constant threats ready to erupt at any moment, each with the potential for another 9/11.

Not to mention John and the StrikeForce technology.

He took a deep breath. John's memories had returned, and only John and Eric knew it. If John's secret got out, that would be the end. Fulton Smith, the Director of the OTM and Eric's boss, would no doubt order John's immediate execution.

Smith *didn't* like surprises and *hated* insubordination.

At the least, it would end Eric's career. At the most, it would guarantee him a position next to John on the firing line.

If that threat wasn't enough, the StrikeForce tech was killing John. Eric kept the secret from him—Docs Elliot and Oshensker had already detected signs of tumor growth.

John's immune system—enhanced by the drugs they pumped into him—kept the tumors at bay, but Doctor Elliot assured him the cells would eventually survive. Thanks to the same drugs, the cancer would grow at an accelerated rate. They had a year, perhaps two, before the nanotech would cause an explosion of tumors.

John was dying.

"Eric? You finished in there?"

He jerked at the sound of Karen's voice and shook his head. He hated his lapse in morality, but he certainly enjoyed the sex with her. It was his only release, the only thing keeping him sane.

"Yeah." He stepped quickly over the cold tile and back into the bedroom.

Karen lay naked on the bed, as comfortable as a cat on a windowsill, and his eyes were drawn to her. Her skin was creamy white from long hours spent in the underground base, her breasts large enough that they lolled to the sides.

"How's Nancy?" he asked.

"Really? A naked woman in your bed and you want to ask about *another* woman? No *wonder* you have problems."

"You know what I mean."

She laughed, her eyes twinkling. "I *know* what you mean. I don't have to keep an eye on her, she's been on me like a hawk since we became friends. It gets awkward at times because she knows about us and she *clearly* wants to be with you."

"I can imagine."

"Her idea of bonding time is an evening at the gun range. I've gotten pretty good. Nothing like you or John, of course. She's … opened up about her childhood."

He joined her on the bed, wrapping his arm around her and pulling the blanket tight around them. "Oh?"

"Did you know she hasn't seen her mother since she was six? That she was raised by military couples around the world, but never stayed with any family longer than a year? The Old Man says it was for her protection. I think that's what made her the way she is."

He thought about that, then shook his head. "That doesn't fully explain it."

She rolled over, resting her head on his chest, and ran her fingers gently over his shoulder. "You know she's got a lover?"

"What? Who?"

She sighed. "Dewey Green."

"Dewey Green? The weird guy in the basement?"

"He's *not* weird, and that's *not* a basement. It's his office."

He exhaled slowly. "Right." He had forgotten that Karen had helped recruit Dewey Green from the NSA and that they shared an unlikely friendship.

"Okay," she admitted. "He comes *across* as weird, but he's got Asperger's. He's actually one of the smartest people you'll meet."

"I've read his file," he said grudgingly. "The thing he's doing with the NSA? The virus and the Iranian centrifuges? That *is* brilliant."

"Yes, it is. And don't forget, if it weren't for his code, the VISOR wouldn't work. His optical recognition software is already being used by other three-letter agencies. Dewey can be hard to deal with, but he's my friend, and I don't want to see him hurt."

"You've heard?"

"About Nancy's ex?" She nodded. "Nancy chews men up. Dewey can barely process normal emotions, let alone sex. With her? He probably doesn't understand what's going on."

"You think that's why she picked him?"

She stared at him. "She doesn't have to worry about commitment. She doesn't even have to pretend to be human. She told me she leaves right after sex. Poor Dewey."

"Uh-huh. Sounds terrible."

She slapped his chest. "Why do I *even* try? Men are pigs."

"I get your point. Mr. Green is a valuable asset to the OTM. We can't afford to lose him."

She hesitated. "What are you going to do?"

"I just *love* this job. I live to deal with *these* types of issues."

"You have to speak to her. You encouraged me to befriend her. I actually feel sorry for her, but Dewey and I go way back."

"Sure, I'll speak to her," he said. "You know, the woman whose father is my boss? The woman who has a serious lack of empathy and a predilection for firearms? The woman who would rather shoot first and ask questions later?"

She grabbed the pillow from under his head, yanked it out, then slapped him across the chest with it. "Fix it with Dewey, or you can go back to being all pent up inside, mister."

He rolled over and kissed the soft skin between her breasts. "I'll see what I can do."

* * *

Chicago

Deion Freeman slipped the key card into the hotel room door and withdrew it quickly. He turned the handle when the light turned green but didn't fully open it. He glanced down the hallway of the Hampton Inn, then quickly opened the door and stepped through, carefully shutting the door behind him as he moved quietly to the bed.

He wasn't quiet enough. The woman on the bed rolled over and pulled him to her, grabbing at him like a wild animal. He couldn't help but smile. "Jesus, Val."

Valerie Simon laughed. She wrapped her legs around him and rolled him onto the bed, straddling him. "I missed you."

"I wanted to check out the continental breakfast," he said with a smile.

Deion liked Valerie. He loved her, in fact, though he was hesitant to admit it. They had spent several years working together for the CIA, in the Afghanistan heat. Long hours and murky politics made the job difficult. Then, one day, they had found themselves alone. They were both at a point where they had no one, and before they knew it, that close working relationship had turned into something more. Their relationship had come to a sudden halt when one of his more unorthodox ops went bad.

He quickly found himself demoted to guarding prisoners at Camp 7 in the sweltering Cuban heat of Guantánamo.

Until Eric recruited him.

Before he had time to process it, he was back in Afghanistan and working with Valerie on the hunt for Abdullah the Bomber. Seeing her again, he realized how much he missed her, a fact that was only reinforced when they almost died in a firefight.

If not for Eric's quick thinking in rerouting a CIA Predator and the arrival of Delta Force Operators, they would have been killed by members of the Mujahedeen that wanted to stop them from interrogating a young man named Koshen.

Valerie had suffered a concussion and superficial scrapes and scratches but healed quickly. Deion was not so lucky. Just days after, he was almost killed in Dallas. He wasn't wounded as badly as Taylor Martin, but he lived, unlike their teammate Roger.

He took it as a good sign. After clearing it with Eric, he started calling and emailing Valerie. They carried on a long-distance romance, seeing each other over the ensuing two years, but now he was ready to introduce her to his family.

She noticed his sudden seriousness. "Uh-oh. Breakfast is that bad?"

"No," he said with a grin. "The breakfast is fine. They've got blueberry muffins. I know you like blueberry muffins."

"I *do* like blueberry muffins, but that's not what's bothering you. Is it your dad?"

He thought about it for a moment. "I just want everything to go well."

She frowned. "Is it because I'm white? Or because I'm ten years older than you? You think he won't like an old white woman dating his son?"

"It's not him I'm worried about. My brothers can be—"

"Jerks? Assholes? Racist, ageist, white-woman-with-a-few-gray-streaks-hating bastards?"

He bit his lip. That was *exactly* what worried him. Valerie was a decade older than him. Her short pixie-cut black hair was streaked with fine silver, and while he found it endearing, he could imagine his brother's jokes. As for her skin color?

"Let's just say I love them like brothers, and sometimes I want to smack the ever-loving *shit* out of my brothers."

"I can handle them," she said confidently. "I'm more worried about how you'll introduce me. You never read them in. They have no idea what you really do. Doesn't that concern you?"

"No."

"Why didn't you read your father in, at least?"

"Pops had enough to worry about after Mom died. Putting four boys through college on his salary was hard. Once I was an officer, I just never found the right time."

"Doesn't he wonder why you hardly visit? Doesn't he wonder what you do?"

He shook his head. "I work in the import-export business. I spend a lot of time overseas."

"Riiight. And *I* work for the State Department. You could have told him. At least given him an idea."

"I couldn't. He still had to look after my brothers. I was the lucky son, the one who got the scholarship to Harvard. They *expected* a successful businessman, not a CIA spook."

"If only they knew how important your work was. If only they knew what you did." She hesitated. "Come to think of it, *I* don't even know what you do."

He turned away and grunted. "Not this again."

"Damn it, I'm *not* a civvie. Something's *not* right. People have asked about you, and I can't tell them anything because I don't *know* anything. I've heard of off-book ops, but you're so far past off-book you couldn't see it in a mirror. You're in the deep black."

He took her face in his hands and kissed her softly. "I can't say, Val. Sorry."

She pulled back. "Can you *ever* read me in? Who is Eric? Is he your boss? Your teammate? What exactly do you do? Where do you work? I don't even know where you *live*."

He reached for the bottom of her gray T-shirt and pulled at the hem. "Maybe. Someday."

She yanked her shirt back down. "I think I want to get breakfast." She stood and wiggled a pair of faded blue jeans over her thin hips.

"You're right about one thing," Deion said. "You're *not* a civvie. Of all people, *you* should understand how this works."

She sat on the edge of the bed and pulled on her socks. "Let's just get breakfast."

* * *

Area 51

Karen sat across from Nancy in the cafeteria, a large room filled with bright white tables, acoustic tiles covering the ceiling. Technicians and soldiers were eating, and by the food on their plates, they were eating well. The OTM spared no expense to feed them, a sharp contrast to the well-maintained but decades-old Formica tables.

"You ever wonder where they got these?" she asked.

Nancy shrugged. "Surplus. You wouldn't believe how much of this stuff is laying around, forgotten. We found massive amounts of inventory just waiting to be destroyed. It was easy to have it trucked to the Groom Lake facility while the base was being refurbished and expanded."

Karen nodded. She knew the underground base had once housed a vast collection of stolen military aircraft, and that as the world's military powers had shifted from stealth fighters and bombers to drone technology, the OTM had repurposed the underground base. The Groom Lake facility was still in use and still testing aircraft, but Karen knew most of the new aircraft were American-designed, stolen and modified by the Russians and Chinese. The base no longer needed to maintain a standing fleet of Soviet MiGs.

She also remembered the awe she'd felt when she'd realized just how enormous the base *really* was. Nuclear-powered boring machines developed by the CIA had melted massive tunnels in and out of the base, then the military had blasted rock and hauled it away to create the vast chambers now occupied by the War Room and the StrikeForce labs.

"You never answered," Nancy said. "Do you have time this afternoon? We will have the shooting house to ourselves."

Karen tried not to sigh. "I know, but I'm waiting for a job to finish. It's scheduled to complete in a few hours." She hesitated. "Dewey is *trying* to free up more time on the mainframe cluster. If he does that, it might be sooner."

Nancy grimaced. "Dewey."

"You still seeing him?"

Nancy rolled her eyes. "Seeing him? What is this, the fifties? I *use* him."

"He's a nice guy, but Dewey is … different. Interpersonal relationships aren't his thing."

"That's exactly *why* I picked him. No entanglements. No expectations. He's adequate. Not clingy, or judgmental. I don't have to be myself with him."

"Aren't you *supposed* to be yourself during sex?"

Nancy laughed, which made a table of soldiers—three men and two women dressed in camo fatigues—turn and stare. Nancy met their gaze, and they quickly turned away.

"Myself?" Nancy asked, turning back to her and fixing her with a chilly stare. "*Myself* isn't likable. *Myself* is scary. Ask anyone."

You got that right, girlfriend. "I don't believe that's true. I think growing up the way you did makes it hard to relate to others. It didn't make you inhuman or a monster. Not like Frist…"

Nancy stared without blinking. "Barnwell would argue with that."

"Then Barnwell is an ass. You *can't* let others define you."

Nancy took a deep breath and exhaled slowly. "You're a good person. Like Eric. How is he?"

"He's stressed. It's a hard job, but I can't imagine anyone doing better."

Nancy finally blinked. "Barnwell agrees. He thinks highly of Eric, and he *would* know. He's been my father's right-hand man since … before I was born. I realize now that's why my father treats me as he does…" Her voice trailed off. "He's seen terrible things. My *head* knows that, but my heart still doesn't. I'm still angry with him."

"The Old Man loves you. You can tell whenever he's around. His eyes follow you. I didn't notice it at first, but his face lights up when you're near. He *cares* about you."

"I know he does," Nancy admitted. "I'm *trying* to be a better person. You're my first real friend. Someone I can let in."

Karen shuddered inside. While she had *some* affection for Nancy, she wouldn't consider it a *true* friendship. Then again, she wasn't sure if Nancy could ever have a true friend. "Thanks. I know that means a lot."

"Yes, it does," Nancy said. "That's why I don't hold sleeping with Eric against you."

"It's not like that," she said. "We're *not* together. I'm married. What Eric and I do is just … for fun." She was shocked when Nancy nodded.

"I believe you. I'm not jealous, or angry, or hurt. He needs a clear head, to perform at his peak. You help him do that. Dewey is the same for me. Sex with him is like releasing a pressure valve. It makes me less likely to do something rash. What I'm saying is, don't stop. Keep helping him. My father placed a lot of trust in him. The StrikeForce project is just the beginning."

Karen's cell phone beeped and she picked it up, read the message, then smiled. *Just in the nick of time.* "Dewey cleared up CPU time. The job just finished. The drives are decrypted."

* * *

Eric knocked softly on John's door.

John opened it and gave him a sour look. "I wondered when you would stop by."

"I had to wait until you were checked out," Eric said. "Can I come in?"

"You don't have to ask. You're the base CO. You can go wherever you want."

Eric sighed. "It's called being polite."

"I know," John said. "Doesn't change anything."

Eric waited patiently until John finally beckoned him in. John's quarters was a smaller version of his own, and he took a seat on the couch against the wall, motioning for John to sit next to him. "How was the mission?"

John stared at the wall. "You were watching."

He waited silently.

"I killed those women without hesitation," John finally said. "They offered no threat."

"You don't know that for sure."

"What were they going to do, cower in the bedroom until I dropped dead?"

"We couldn't leave witnesses. The US isn't authorized to be operating in Syria."

John sighed. "I'm the monster, but *you* authorized killing them."

"We went over this. They were terrorists, and the intel pointed to something big. We needed boots on the ground to get hard data. Those women? They were wives. Supporters. They wouldn't hesitate to kill Americans."

John slammed his hand against the couch's armrest. "That gives us the right to assassinate them?"

Eric waited for John to calm down, then said simply, "Yes."

John glared, then finally slumped forward, resting his face in the palm of his hands. "I *hate* this."

"I know you do. I'm sorry, but it's my job and it's your duty. You owe the country for what you did."

John looked up. "You think I don't know that? That was the *old* me. I'm a different man now, but I'm still paying that other man's debt."

Eric nodded. "Yes, you are. You'll keep paying that debt until you die. Damn it, we're making a difference. I *need* you."

"I'm not at the top, Eric. I don't see all that you see. To me, it looks like I'm an overtrained assassin."

"You're not. You're a soldier and a good man who's doing what he can to make the world a better place."

They stared at each other until John finally said, "I don't feel it."

Eric decided to lay his cards on the table. "If I didn't believe in you, would I keep your secret? Protect you? Would I risk *everything* if I didn't think we were doing the right thing?"

John's glare softened. "No. You're a lot of things, Eric, but you wouldn't lie to me about that."

Eric nodded, even though he *was* lying. John was dying, but Eric kept that to himself because the rest of what he told John *was* the truth. They *were* making a difference, and he needed John. He needed the ultimate killing machine if they had any chance of stopping the threats to the United States.

Eric's cell phone vibrated and he checked the message from Karen. "Looks like the drives from Syria are paying off. We're needed in the War Room."

CHAPTER TWO

ERIC NAVIGATED THE mantrap and entered the War Room as John followed close behind. The steel desks were abuzz with activity as the analysts typed furiously, and the collective noise as they discussed the drive decryption was a dull roar that echoed against the hard concrete walls of the chamber.

Nancy stood outside the front conference room, and he tried not to notice how her plain black outfit highlighted her shapely figure. She beckoned them to join her in the room with Karen, Taylor, Mark and Sergeant Clark.

He took the leather chair next to Taylor and nodded to Nancy. John slid in next to Taylor and gave him a fist bump, then nodded to Mark, Nancy and Clark.

Clark watched John, his expression neutral, but Clark's green eyes followed the young soldier with barely contained hostility.

Clark had run point on the operation to capture him after the Red Cross bombing. Clark would never forgive John, Eric knew, and he didn't blame him.

He turned his attention to Karen, who sat at the front of the room, loudly slurping coffee while typing on her keyboard, and asked, "You found it?"

"Yeah, yeah, yeah. It's all here." She stabbed at the keyboard, and a file appeared on the wall screen. "This is an encrypted email sent to an ISP in Nashville. It's about Al-Hakim."

"Al-Hakim the American?"

Al-Hakim was born and raised as Gary Hite in California. Hite was barely out of his teens before he was swept up in a tidal wave of resentment against the US forces in Iraq and Afghanistan. Al-Hakim had joined Al-Qaeda in Iraq and was now one of their trusted advisers.

"The very same."

"Why didn't we catch it before this?" Nancy asked, clenching her fists. "I thought we snagged a copy of all inbound and outbound emails to ISPs in the US?"

"We do," Karen said, "but you're talking about hundreds of millions of emails a day. We don't have the computing power to decrypt them all. We try and flag any coming from suspected terrorists, but I don't have to tell you how many of *those* there are. This email was sent by one of the men in Syria to Abduhl Sadir, a sheikh in Nashville. Sadir has no known terror ties, but I'm backtracking emails to and from him for the past year."

"What did this one say?" Taylor asked, pointing at the wall screen.

Karen glanced up from her keyboard, and her eyes were full of concern.

Something has her spooked.

"It's about a package Al-Hakim purchased from a North Korean agent," Karen said. "I *think* they bought an atomic bomb."

Eric's stomach sank. It was only through sheer luck that they had found an email trail referring to a meeting in Syria. That had been enough to convince the president to authorize their Syrian mission, but now it looked like they were on to something bigger.

It wasn't enough that they had stopped Abdullah the Bomber before he could set off a dirty bomb in Times Square.

Now they were faced with a *real* atomic weapon.

"Does it give more details?" he asked.

Nancy shook her head. "They talk about striking down America. Establishing a Muslim Caliphate. The same spiel."

Mark Kelly cleared his throat. "What do we know about Sadir?"

"Emigrated from Saudi Arabia in his twenties," Karen said. "His family is well off, they have friends in the royal family. Spends most of his time at his mosque. Nothing indicates he's involved with terror."

"*Now* there is," Nancy said. "We need surveillance on him."

Eric nodded. "I agree. Sergeant Clark, where's Deion?"

"Still on vacation."

"Contact him. We'll pick him up in Chicago on our way to Nashville." He noticed the look on Nancy's face. "What? We'll be going that way. I have to brief the president."

Mark smiled and spoke before anyone else could. "You miss this. Tell me you *don't* miss this."

"There's no need," Nancy said. She nodded at Taylor, Mark, and John. "*They* can pick Deion up."

He glanced from Nancy to the rest of his team. "I'm just there to supervise."

Even John rolled his eyes and muttered, "Good luck with that."

Nancy shrugged. "You're in charge," she said in a voice tinged with disapproval.

* * *

Honolulu, Hawaii

Huang Lei sat in his penthouse apartment, staring at the azure-blue ocean in the distance. He could almost convince himself the sea was a gentle and unwavering sheet stretching beyond the horizon. He knew better. The Pacific appeared calm on the surface, but its deep currents could be treacherous.

Those currents swirled below the surface, driving weather patterns, the ocean stretching for thousands of miles with only small islands to offer refuge. A man could get lost out there, never to be found. The ocean would destroy all evidence of him.

It was vast and uncaring.

There was a barely audible ding from his computer. His laptop rested on a magnificent desk of antique koa harvested from a plantation on the island and crafted by the finest woodworkers. The laptop contained its own ocean of data, as vast as the Pacific that stretched to the horizon. He had spent much of his life developing tools to move that trove of data around the world, accumulating his fortune.

His wealth stripped away civility and the rule of law, allowing him to acquire enormous amounts of information, and as his father had always reminded him, information *was* power. He sighed and pressed a button.

The man who answered was an old friend, one of his first employees, and his most trusted adviser. "Mr. Huang," the man said, bowing his head deferentially.

"Yes, Liu Kong."

"There has been a complication. I'm uploading the data."

"Very good." He opened the folder and viewed the contents. Things were moving in the ocean of data, eddies and currents whose origins were still hidden. He had ideas—guesses, really—

about those forces, but if his plan was to succeed, action was required. "Make the necessary arrangements."

"Yes, Mr. Huang," the man said, disappearing as the video call ended.

He sat back in his chair and turned his attention back to the ocean, his mind carefully pondering what he had read. As much as he loved his penthouse apartment and office in Hawaii, he would trade them in a moment for his plan to bear fruit, and for his father to finally be avenged.

* * *

Chicago, Illinois

Deion tapped his fingers on the kitchen table of his father's condo, watching the old man prepare sandwiches. Even after all he had seen in the CIA, he still felt like a little kid in his father's presence. The old man was big and broad-shouldered, with thick arms still heavily-muscled from years of tossing airline baggage.

Deion's father glanced down the hall. "What's she doing in there?"

"Making herself presentable, I suspect." An old painting of flowers hanging on the far wall and a rickety pinewood wine rack on top of the refrigerator were all that remained of his mom. When his father had moved in, the condo had been a wreck. But, over the years, the dents and dings in the wall had been repaired, the light fixtures replaced, and new coats of paint freshened it up. The condo now held a little of his father's personality.

It was a far cry from the cramped apartment of his childhood.

His father glanced up from slicing tomatoes. "You know your brothers are gonna have words for you."

"I know," Deion said. "It's why I *didn't* want to introduce her."

Valerie emerged from the bathroom. He knew she was uneasy, afraid to say or do anything to blow the opportunity to meet his family.

"Thanks, Mr. Freeman."

"Call me Oliver, honey. You're practically part of the family."

Deion almost spat out his coffee. "Pushing it, aren't you?"

The old man gave them a devilish grin, the whites of his teeth contrasting against his deep ebony skin. "Got to push you a *little*," he said with a wink. "Sometimes a man don't see what's *right* in front of him."

The doorbell rang, and Deion's father stepped through the living room to open the front door.

Deion's youngest brother, Kelvin, stood with his wife, Tonya. They were dressed casually, but Deion did a mental tally on the cost of their clothes and came up with a figure that indicated his brother still hadn't gained control of his wife's spending. They stepped inside, and Deion noticed the way that Tonya entered first, Kelvin following behind.

Time hasn't changed a thing. Tonya is still clearly in charge.

Kelvin spied him. "The prodigal son returns."

Deion was glad to see Kelvin, but Tonya was another matter. He just didn't *like* her. "How was the drive?"

"The usual," Kelvin said. "A hassle driving all the way down here just to see your sorry ass."

Tonya pointed one of her carefully lacquered fingernails at Valerie. "This your girl?"

Deion introduced them. He caught Tonya's quick glance, scanning Valerie's face, her clothes, and how she presented herself.

"Nice to meet you," Tonya said.

Valerie gave Tonya her best smile. "Likewise. I've heard *so* much about you."

Tonya's eyes grew wide. "Really? Because we haven't heard *shit* about you. Isn't that right, Kelvin?"

Kelvin nodded absently. "Yeah, Deion, we haven't heard shit."

"How did you two meet?" Tonya asked.

"Through a friend in Washington," Valerie said.

"Through his company?"

Valerie nodded. "I work for the State Department. He came asking for help with some import fees."

"You're in the government?" Tonya asked.

"Just a little cog in a giant machine," Valerie said. "What do you do?"

"I'm a paralegal."

The doorbell rang again, interrupting Tonya's inspection.

Deion's father opened the door and Darrell, Deion's middle brother, sauntered in wearing a red tracksuit, head shaved and a thick gold chain around his neck.

Deion bit back a laugh. Darrell had always wanted to be a rapper, even when they were kids dancing around to Grandmaster Flash, but the irony was that Darrel was anything *but*. Darrell had graduated from the UIC with flying colors before passing the bar and handled probate law at Tonya's firm.

"What's up?" Darrell asked, raising an eyebrow.

"Just waiting for you and Jamal," Deion said. "I thought he was coming with you."

"He can't make it," Deion's father said. "Just going to be *us* for lunch."

They entered the kitchen, and he caught his brothers glancing discreetly at Valerie. They took seats at the kitchen table as Deion's father prepared their lunch, and the talk soon turned to Deion and his childhood.

"Deion was smart," Darrell said. "We all knew he was gonna amount to something. We just never thought he'd wind up working at an import business."

"We can't all be lawyers," Deion's father said with a smile. "Some of us got to work for a living. With that fancy degree and all those languages he speaks, I expected him to go into politics. Valerie, did you know my boy speaks five languages?"

Valerie smiled. "So I've been told."

"He was a *smart* boy," the old man said, "not like these two lunkheads."

Darrel and Kelvin shot their father a dirty look, but the old man appeared unapologetic.

"You and Mom *never* stopped talking about Deion," Kelvin said. "*Deion* did this and *Deion* did that. Oh, Deion got a scholarship. Deion—"

"Give it rest," the old man barked, his smile fading. "You boys done good, all of you, 'cept for Jamal, and there ain't *nothing* wrong with bartending." He placed plastic trays of meats and vegetables on the table, followed by soft baked buns. He smiled at Valerie. "Help yourself. We don't stand on ceremony here."

The trays were soon passed around as everyone assembled their sandwiches while the old man poured them glasses of soda.

"What do you do for the government?" Darrell asked Valerie between bites.

She shrugged. "I work with small businesses. Most of the time I'm emailing and faxing secretaries, trying to clear up shipping or sales problems. It's *very* boring."

Tonya gave her a toothy smile. "I'm sure it's *fascinating.* Deion was one of those problems?"

"Yes," Valerie said. "A problem with export paperwork. Signatures in the wrong place, the wrong form, that kind of thing."

"Did you know Kelvin works for the government?"

"Really?"

"He's a manager at the post office and a member of the APWU. He's moving up in the world. Isn't that right, baby?"

Kelvin shrugged. "Doing all right. What about you, Deion? You moving up? You must be, 'cause you don't ever come home. Must be that's why you're so busy."

There it is. "As a matter of fact, I *am* moving up. It's not that I don't *want* to come home. I don't live here like you, Kel. I can't just drop by."

Kelvin glared at him. "You had no problem swinging by when Mom died, but as soon as you helped Dad move, you took off again."

"He's got a point," Darrel agreed.

Deion turned from Kelvin to Darrel. "You too?"

Darrel smiled, but his mouth was pinched. "I know you're too *busy* to come home. I know we have to look out for Dad while you get to live your life—"

The old man interrupted. "Don't you bring me into this. I know Deion's doing what he's got to do. A man has to make a living. No shame in that."

Darrel snorted. "What about the shame in dating a white woman?"

"Darrel," the old man said, slamming his fist against the wooden tabletop hard enough to make the glasses shake. "You *don't* insult a lady in my house."

"What?" Darrel said, raising his hands. "I'm just saying what we're *all* thinking. He comes home, the first time in a year, and he brings a white woman?"

"Apologize to Valerie," Deion said, "or I'm going to wipe that smirk off your face."

He felt Valerie's hand on his arm, and when he turned to her she was still smiling, but there was a hard glint in her eye.

"Don't worry," Valerie said, "I don't mind. I can understand how this might be upsetting. It's not like you prepared them for this."

Tonya cleared her throat. "It's none of my business what you two get up to, but aren't you a little old for him?"

Valerie's grip tightened on his arm. "I don't think age is a number so much as a state of mind." She turned to his father. "I should be going."

His father smiled warmly, then turned back to the others. "That's a bunch of nonsense. You all done lost your manners. This girl is under my roof. You treat her as a guest, or I will, *by God*, knock you into next week. You understand?"

Kelvin and Tonya looked down at their plates, but Darrel spoke up. "We're not kids anymore. You got to stop treating us like that."

His father shook his head. This time, there was no disguising the anger in his voice. "I'll stop treating you like a child when you stop acting like one. I can't believe you act like this in *my* house. Lunch is over. Put your damned plates in the sink and be on your way."

There was an awkward pause before Tonya spoke up. "Nice meeting you, Valerie."

Deion wanted to believe Tonya meant it, but he caught the self-satisfied smirk she directed to Kelvin.

For a moment he considered taking his brothers outside and beating some sense into them. With his training, it would be easy to knock them around. They wouldn't stand a chance.

It wouldn't do any good. You can pick your friends, but you can't pick your family. Besides, they would want to know how a Harvard graduate with a gift for languages could manhandle them.

They stood and dutifully placed their plates in the kitchen sink before leaving. Deion sat next to Valerie while his father watched them leave.

When the door had shut, the old man sighed, then turned and winked at Valerie. "You have to understand. They're *knuckleheads*."

Valerie laughed. "I understand."

The old man's face lit up. "You're taking this well. Nice to see Deion found himself a level-headed woman. Must be you're in the same line of business."

"No," Valerie said. "I work at the State Department."

The old man stood and removed an apple pie from the refrigerator. "Darling, let me tell you something about my boy. He *ain't* in the export business."

Deion stood. "I'm not sure what you're saying—"

The old man waved for him to sit. He shuffled to the counter and brought back a stack of plates, then sliced a big piece of apple pie and placed it on one of the fine china plates and handed it to Valerie, then sliced another piece for Deion. He cut himself an even bigger portion, then took a bite.

His head rolled back, eyes closed, and he let out a satisfied hum. "Nothing like a piece of pie to make you forget your troubles." He opened his eyes and winked at Valerie. "Now, I was born at night, but not *last* night. Ain't no export business keeps you *that* occupied. After you graduated, you got snapped up. I never said nothing, because it wasn't my decision to make. It was yours. After 9/11, the world changed. I understand that."

Deion started to speak, but the old man chuckled dismissively.

"Don't tell me you weren't halfway around the world. I'm not blind. I'm *proud* of you, boy. I always *been* proud. You picked a rough life, but you did it for your country. Nothing wrong with that. This little lady, she got the same eyes you do. Always looking for the walls and doors. I figure it's to find a way out in case of trouble. No, you two *are* in the same line of work."

Deion started to speak, but Valerie shushed him. "Mr. Freeman?"

"I told you, girl, call me Oliver."

"Oliver? You're too kind. Thanks for having me in your home."

The old man's smile grew wider. "It's nice to have a *lady* in the house."

* * *

Arlington, Virginia

Smith watched from the backseat of his Lincoln as the Gulfstream G550 taxied to the hangar. The door of the plane opened and his daughter, Nancy, stepped out, followed by Eric Wise.

They approached the car, and Eric nodded to the Lincoln's driver, a former Ranger named Robert Growman, then slid into the front seat while Nancy took the back, next to Smith.

"Good morning," Smith said.

Nancy stared straight ahead. "Father."

Eric turned to squint at Nancy, then turned to him. "Fulton."

Smith smiled at the discomfort in Eric's voice. Even after two years of grooming, Eric still regarded him as the man who had commanded his father during Vietnam, the man who'd recruited him to the Office of Threat Management. He wondered how long it would take before Eric felt comfortable calling him by his first name. He nodded at Eric, then cleared his throat. "Robert."

The town car accelerated smoothly and headed northeast, toward the White House. Smith had considered moving the Gulfstream flights from the Ronald Reagan Washington National Airport to Andrews Air Force base, but he preferred the public airport's anonymity.

Still, Robert took a circuitous path through the heavy D.C. traffic and entered the underground parking lot blocks west of the White House. Robert nodded to the guard, who opened the steel gate, allowing them to enter the vault—a reinforced concrete bunker—where they exited and took the automated electric tram to the Eisenhower Executive Office Building, across the street from the White House.

As they rode the tram through the featureless gray tunnel, he pointed to the hardened concrete walls. "This was built at the order of Harry Truman, one of my first acts as director."

Nancy gave him an odd look while Eric squinted thoughtfully.

I'm repeating myself. The slips were coming faster, and it terrified him. He would have to call Hobert soon and schedule more tests.

They reached the Eisenhower Building and exited the tram, then entered the same style mantrap that guarded the War Room at Area 51. The doors sealed shut and they spoke their names, then waited as the guard behind the wall of bulletproof glass validated their biometrics.

The guard, a man that Smith had handpicked decades before, nodded to them and the far door hissed open. They walked through another gray tunnel of concrete, under Seventeenth Street, then made their way the short distance to the bunker under the West Wing. After they keyed their badges, the massive door finally trundled open.

The president of the United States was the lone occupant, and he sat with slumped shoulders at the conference table. He glanced up, and his dark skin did nothing to hide the bags under his eyes. "Smith."

They entered, and the door rumbled shut. "Mr. President," Smith said. "You remember Nancy and Eric?"

The president's eyes flickered over them. He nodded and said, "Let's skip the pleasantries. What do you want?"

They took seats at the table and Smith handed his metal briefcase to Eric, who opened it with his thumbprint. Eric withdrew a stack of papers and shoved them in front of the president. "We have a situation."

The president leaned back in his chair. "It's always a situation. I still don't believe I'm speaking with you. Your organization goes against everything I believe in."

Eric started to speak, but Smith raised his hand. "Mr. President," Smith said, "you know *what* we do and *why* we do it. Personal beliefs are … irrelevant."

The president glanced up, jaw working, then stopped. He sighed, and said, "What you've done over the years? It doesn't just violate the Constitution. It violates the people's *trust*."

"That didn't stop you from authorizing that thing in London last March," Eric said.

Nancy had sat quietly but finally spoke up. "Mr. President, the OTM has averted another world war. Numerous times. The men that came before you? *They* didn't like it, either. That didn't stop them from doing their jobs." Her pale blue eyes were like tiny chips of ice, but her voice was calm and reasoned.

"You're right," the president finally admitted. He picked up his coffee cup with trembling hands and took a sip, then made a face. "My predecessor made it clear to me before the inauguration that no matter my convictions, I would have to make hard choices. He said he would pray for me. I *finally* understand what he was talking about. What's the situation?"

Smith nodded. He liked the young man from Illinois, much as he had liked the young man from Texas before him, and the man before that, all the way back to Truman. Then he remembered the president from Texas, the man who had ignored so much of his advice, the *one* president he had wanted to throttle with his own hands. No, these young men were likable, which made it all the harder to watch as the weight of the presidency ground them down—until they barely escaped the office alive. "There's a possible *Empty Quiver*."

The president's jaw dropped. "A nuclear weapon?"

"A weapon, or perhaps just the material," Smith said. "North Korean."

The president opened the folder, flipped through the pages, then carefully closed it. "This came from the operation in Syria?"

"Yes," Eric said. "The intercepted emails lead to a man in Nashville. We've got a team on their way."

The president chewed at his lip. "This man in Nashville—what do we know about him?"

Nancy smoothed her pantsuit. "He's a sheikh."

The president rolled his eyes. "That's all I need. Half the people hate me because they think I'm a liberal pacifist, and the other half hate me because I haven't pulled all the troops out of Iraq and Afghanistan. Can't you turn this over to the FBI or DHS?"

Nancy snorted. "We'd like to prevent a nuclear incident, not start one."

Smith noticed the man's entire countenance change, sinking in upon himself, but before he could speak, Eric said, "Sir? We'll handle this."

The president turned to each of them, his eyes cautious but hopeful, then nodded. "No matter my reservations about the necessity of your existence, I have the *utmost* faith in you."

Smith stood and took the president's hand, giving the young man his firmest handshake. "It's an honor, Mr. President."

* * *

Smith kept his eye on Eric and Nancy as Robert drove them back to Reagan International Airport. They barely talked, but when they did, it was cordial. Smith listened, until finally asking Eric, "How was Mr. Frist?"

Eric craned his head around to face him. "The technology is *amazing*. He dropped into the desert, just one man, took out the hostiles, gathered the intel, and exfiltrated before anyone knew he was there."

"Yes," Nancy said. "Your pet Frankenstein is *amazing*."

"He's a valuable asset," Eric said, "and Frankenstein was the *doctor*. You're thinking of Frankenstein's monster. John is *no* monster. You've worked with him. Have you seen any sign that he's anything more than a loyal soldier?"

Smith turned to his daughter. He loved her fiercely. Hobert thought she was a borderline psychopath, that her experiences as a youth had killed any chance for empathy, but she *had* matured in the past two years. He wanted to believe she was growing, but he was afraid much of it was to impress Eric.

Perhaps she just wants to please me.

Whether real or imaginary, her newfound growth had only sharpened her instincts. He trusted her opinion. "Nancy? You have concerns?"

His daughter blinked slowly, then turned to stare out the window. "He's shown no signs of his previous behavior. He's performed above expectations. What more do you want to know?"

"Are we ready for the next stage?"

Eric cleared his throat and raised an eyebrow. "Next stage?"

"Not yet," Nancy said. "Too many unknowns."

"Excuse me," Eric said. "What next stage?"

Nancy turned to Eric. "Nothing you should concern yourself with."

Robert eased the Lincoln into the hangar reserved for the OTM and parked between Eric's Gulfstream and Smith's own.

Eric stared at Nancy, then turned to him. "Sir, if there's something I should know…"

Smith shook his head. "You will know when you *need* to know."

"I don't like being kept out of the loop," Eric said. "If I'm truly your successor, then I should know everything about the StrikeForce technology."

"You *are* my successor," Smith said, "but I'm not ready to divulge all my secrets *just* yet."

Eric bit his lip but nodded respectfully. "Yes, sir."

"Can you give me a few minutes with my father?" Nancy asked.

Eric nodded and got out, motioning for their driver to do the same. Eric boarded the plane while Robert went looking for coffee in the hangar office, leaving the two of them alone in the backseat of the Lincoln.

"Can I speak frankly?" Nancy asked.

"Of course."

"You don't seem yourself."

"I'm tired," he said sincerely. "I'm not a young man anymore. I feel it in my bones."

Nancy's gaze sharpened. "You've been repeating yourself. You've never done that before."

He patted her on the knee. "I'm usually the one worrying about you."

"There's something you're not telling me."

"Perhaps I'm worried about young Eric. How is he?"

Nancy turned to stare at the Gulfstream. Her hand dropped, and her fingertips lightly stroked against her leg. "He's everything you thought he would be. He's smart. Competent. Kind."

Hobert Barnwell provided the broad details of Eric and Nancy's working relationship, but he was glad to see it for himself. Eric was a good man, a man they trusted. Nancy would be in good hands. "I've studied your reports. You work well together."

Her eyes darted back to his. "I ... *like* him."

He snorted. "Of course you do. He's a good soldier, like his father."

Eric's father, William Wise, had been one of Smith's closest friends, as had Eric's grandfather, Joseph. After Truman had ordered the OTM's creation, Joseph had been his first recruit. He remembered the look on Joseph's face, his wide, honest grin, and his desire to serve his country. Together they had set up offices, gathered the analysts to plan and predict, and recruited the hard men to act on that intelligence. Together they had made history.

Before Joseph had retired.

When William had joined the Army, Joseph was reluctant to let him join the OTM. It had taken considerable persuasion, but finally William became the OTM's main operative. With Hobert and William's help, the OTM had stemmed the tide as best they could. When William finally retired, he'd stated in no uncertain terms that the Wise family had paid their debt to the country.

Smith had promised his still-young friend that no Wise would serve in the OTM. He'd watched Eric rise through the ranks, advancing quickly to the Rangers, before being selected for Delta Force. Eric was a phenomenal Operator. The OTM *needed* a man like him.

He held his promise until William died, and when he received the news, he pulled strings to get Eric's deployment canceled. The timing was fortuitous. Project StrikeForce was ready to implement, and they had already captured Frist. It took very little convincing to recruit Eric. The simple truth was, he needed Eric to run Project StrikeForce *and* the OTM.

I have so much to do before I slip away. I need Eric to protect the country, the OTM, and Nancy.

CHAPTER THREE

Chicago, Illinois

VALERIE SMILED MISCHIEVOUSLY. "That went well."

Deion sighed and leaned back against the couch. From the kitchen, he heard his father cleaning and putting dishes in the dishwasher. "Just how I *expected* them to act."

Truthfully, he had expected *worse*, but he still found his family's behavior appalling. They had pulled together after his mom died in '93, but Deion had been away at Harvard. The World Trade Center had just been bombed, killing six people. It was a wake-up call to the CIA, and one of his linguistics professors had approached and recruited him. Not long after, he was sent to The Farm, the secret CIA training facility at Camp Peary.

He remembered the glares from his family when he told them he had to return to school. Kelvin took it the hardest, but Jamal and Darrel also resented his leaving.

He didn't blame them. He couldn't explain why he had to leave so suddenly. They were worried about their father, who was devastated, and his brothers were always checking on him, with occasional help from his mom's sister, Sonya.

He called home as often as his schedule allowed, but it wasn't the same.

They just assumed I abandoned them.

"So," Valerie said, nodding at the kitchen. "Your father knows."

Deion considered that. "It appears he does."

Valerie moved closer, snuggling against him, the warmth of her body a pleasant sensation against his skin. "He's a good man. He probably figured you didn't want to worry him."

It was true. He *didn't* want to worry his father, not after his mom's death, but it turned out his father was hardier than everyone assumed. "I guess Pops knew all along. He's got a way of reading people."

Valerie squeezed his arm. "That must be where *you* get it from."

Deion jerked as his cell phone buzzed, sitting up suddenly, causing Valerie to fall into the spot he had just occupied. He pulled the cell phone from his pocket and saw the caller ID. "I have to take this."

Valerie shrugged, but her eyes were full of concern.

He darted down the hall to the bathroom and shut the door before answering. "Go for Freeman."

The familiar voice on the phone was apologetic. "Deion," Sergeant Todd Clark said. "Sorry, but something's come up. You need to get to the airport. Eric and Nancy will pick you up at fifteen hundred."

He shook his head, even though no one could see. "You've *got* to be kidding. I've still got a week."

Clark laughed. "You told me you'd rather go back to Afghanistan than spend time with your brothers."

"Point taken. What's the problem?"

There was a hesitation on the other end. "Possible Empty Quiver."

A cold pit settled in his stomach. "What do we know?"

"Eric will brief you himself. Oh, and make sure your girlfriend comes with you."

It was the *last* thing he'd expected. "Why?"

Clark's voice sobered. "No idea, I'm just relaying orders. Will you make it?"

Like I have a choice. "It's going to be pushing it."

"I'll email you directions to the hangar."

Clark hung up and left Deion to worry about a possible loose nuclear weapon and why Eric would request Valerie to accompany them.

* * *

O'Hare Airport Chicago, Illinois

Eric waited patiently with Nancy in the Gulfstream. It wasn't long before Greg Clayberg, their pilot, paged them. "They're here."

Eric keyed the mic. "When can we leave?"

"I've got priority clearance. Just give the word. They don't call me 'Hot Dog' for nothing."

"I want us wheels up in twenty." He climbed out of the soft leather seat and exited the Gulfstream with Nancy in tow.

The September sun was barely past its apex, but there was a slight chill in the air. He watched as Deion parked his black Toyota near the front of the hangar.

Deion got out, still dressed in a black T-shirt and jeans, opened the trunk and rummaged around before extracting his go-bag and slamming the trunk shut.

Valerie exited the vehicle and spoke quietly to Deion. The silver strands threaded through her short pixie bob only made her more attractive, and Eric understood why Deion was smitten.

They approached, and he greeted Deion, then turned to Valerie and stuck out his hand. "Glad to finally meet you."

Valerie turned to Deion, then back to Eric, returning the handshake. "You're Steeljaw. Or should I call you Eric?"

He laughed. "Eric will do. Deion's been talking about you nonstop since Afghanistan. I believe you already know Nancy?"

"Good to see you," Nancy said, hand outstretched, something approaching warmth on her face. "I'm glad your wounds in Afghanistan weren't serious."

Valerie had suffered minor wounds and a concussion on a mission two years before. If he hadn't managed to pull strings, get orders rescinded, and commandeer a CIA drone, Nancy, Valerie, and Deion would have died in Kandahar.

"Crazy times," Valerie said as she shook Nancy's hand. "If not for you, I would have been killed."

Eric saw Deion wince. Valerie's involvement in the operation had been at Deion's request, and Deion still blamed himself for putting her in danger. He nodded meaningfully at Deion. "We need to talk."

Nancy stepped forward. "Valerie, would you join me on the plane?"

Valerie nodded and followed Nancy onto the Gulfstream.

Deion stood with his arms crossed and jaw clenched, his go-bag laying on the tarmac. "You know I was on vacation, right?"

He didn't blame Deion for being boiling mad. "I wouldn't have called if it wasn't important," he said with a smile. " John's mission in Syria found valuable intel. Looks like they purchased the weapon from the North Koreans."

Deion's eyes widened. "Jesus."

"Karen decrypted the drives from Syria. We have emails from a man in Nashville. The rest of the team will meet us there."

Deion picked up his go-bag, tossed it over his shoulder, and shook his head. "Why interrupt *my* vacation?"

"We'd like you and Valerie to pose as a married couple."

Deion shook his head. "Nuh-uh. I don't like bringing Valerie into OTM business."

"She'll be fine. She's a CIA officer, remember?"

Deion scowled. "Are you recruiting her?"

Eric *had* been thinking of recruiting Valerie. Her experience—and her connection to Deion—would make her a valuable operative, but he could tell that Deion wasn't thrilled with the idea. "Technically, no. I pulled some strings. She will act as a liaison between us and the CIA. We'll tell her *just* enough."

Deion glanced away. "Bad enough she got hurt in Afghanistan because of me. I don't want to put her in danger."

"Trust me, she'll be fine."

"Why not just grab this guy? A little time with me and he'll sing like a canary."

"You know that gets poor intel. They'll say anything, or even lie, to make you stop. No, Karen's working on electronic surveillance. We'll watch him for a couple of days, *then* snatch him. *If* necessary."

"I don't like it," Deion said.

"I'm not *asking* you to like it," Eric said. "You have your orders."

"You pulling rank?"

"Testy, aren't you. Family reunion went badly?"

Deion shrugged. "Not as well as I'd hoped."

"Sorry to hear that." He liked Deion, not only as a coworker but as a friend. During John's training, they had spent time together, taking each other's measure, and the years since had only strengthened that bond. He had encouraged Deion to take vacations, to recharge his batteries. It had been his suggestion to introduce Valerie to Deion's family. "How was your father?"

Deion smiled. "Good. He was receptive. He *liked* her."

"Your brothers?"

"Jackasses."

Eric snorted. "I'm sure they'll warm up. I'm going to fill her in on the mission. Wait here."

Deion looked as if he wanted to speak, but he finally nodded and walked away, swinging his go-bag over his shoulder. Eric entered the Gulfstream and found Nancy and Valerie sitting at the table, discussing their shared experience in Afghanistan.

"Valerie," Eric said, "we would like you to work with us on a mission."

Valerie's eyes narrowed. "I don't even know who *you* are."

Nancy started to speak, but Eric interrupted. "You know Deion's still officially with the CIA, but no matter where you looked, you drew a blank. You've wondered about his purview, about what he does. He works for us. Let me tell you a little about who *we* are."

"You're going to tell me everything?" Valerie asked.

Nancy laughed and said, "Trust me, you *don't* want to know everything."

Eric took one of the leather seats next to Nancy. "We work for an organization that reports directly to the president. We're currently working on an issue related to domestic terrorism. We want you and Deion to pose as husband and wife and run surveillance. We have the target's name and address, but we need more."

"The CIA's not supposed to operate on domestic soil," Valerie said, her eyes wide. "Is that what Deion's been doing? Running operations in the US?"

Damn, she's quick. "We are not the CIA. We are tasked with doing what's necessary to protect the United States. Sometimes that means we have to skirt the law. You were an analyst at the CIA when 9/11 happened. If you could go back in time to prevent that, would you?"

Valerie bit her lip. "Of course I would, but that doesn't mean I would break the law."

It was Nancy's turn to lean forward. "We take the world as it is, *not* as we wish it to be. Sometimes you have to get your hands dirty."

"I'm not above getting my hands dirty…"

"I studied your record," Eric said. "You're a good CIA officer and a patriot. I know you like Deion. He's not happy looping you in on this, but it's not his choice. We *need* you."

It *was* true. Nancy could run operations, but had a tendency to overreact. No, Valerie's case records spoke volumes. She would make a valuable asset to the OTM, even if Deion didn't see it. Plus, with her help, perhaps he could finally get a handle on Nancy. They had shared an uneasy alliance in Afghanistan, and he hoped that relationship might help take pressure off Karen. However, it wasn't his intention to bring her into the OTM.

Not quite yet.

"When do you need your answer?" Valerie said.

"We're leaving in ten minutes."

Valerie swallowed hard, then nodded, her blue eyes shining. "I'm in."

Eric smiled. "I *knew* you would be."

* * *

Nashville, Tennessee

After speaking with Eric, Greg pushed the Gulfstream to its limit, making the flight from Chicago to Nashville's International Airport in record time. The C17 carrying Taylor Martin, Mark Kelly, and John, however, would have stood out among the passenger aircraft, so the C17 diverted to Arnold AFB.

Eric was eager to move, but the C17 also contained their vehicles and equipment. He bit back his frustration and ushered Valerie, Deion, and Nancy off the Gulfstream.

They were walking through the terminal when his cell phone went off. He grabbed it and punched the answer button. "Where are you?"

"Just pulling up to the entrance," Taylor Martin answered.

Eric hustled them to the front, where a pair of white unmarked Ford transit vans waited with their motors running. It was still muggy in Nashville, and sweat began to dampen the back of his shirt. He motioned for Deion and Valerie to join him and Taylor in the first van while Nancy climbed into the rear van with Mark and John.

"Took you long enough," Taylor grumbled.

"You know how it is," Eric said, fumbling with the air conditioning. "Always waiting on Deion."

Taylor raised an eyebrow, then turned and winked at Deion and Valerie. "Sorry 'bout your vacation. You know Wise, if he ain't having fun, *nobody's* having fun."

"Don't you know smart-asses get double duty?" Eric asked. "Drive."

Taylor smiled, displaying a mouthful of pearly white teeth. "I'm driving, Miss Daisy."

They exited the airport and headed north. After a few minutes of navigating the heavy traffic, Taylor pulled into a parking lot next to an abandoned manufacturing plant, the jobs long since moved out of state or out of country. Mark pulled the rear van next to theirs, and they all got out and Eric introduced Valerie to the team.

She gave them each a nod, then asked, "You *all* work with Deion?"

"*We* do the heavy lifting while Steeljaw and Deion kick it in the rear," Taylor said.

I do miss this. "Mark?" Eric asked. "Did you get their covers?"

Mark handed Valerie and Deion manila envelopes. "These contain driver's licenses, Social Security cards, and the other things you'll need to secure the apartment. There's also walking around money."

Deion took the envelopes, inspected his, then passed the other envelope to Valerie. "What's our cover?"

"You're Deion Smith. You work as a fry cook at Captain D's," Martin said. "Valerie Smith works at a preschool."

Deion nodded. "Nice."

"We've done a quick drive-by," Mark said. "The complex is several blocks south of the mosque. Your apartment is the third from Sadir's."

"That's a lucky break," John said.

"Do you know anything about the other inhabitants?" Nancy asked.

"All civilians," Mark said. "The usual suspects. Poor, alcoholics, small-time drug users. Abduhl Sadir lives in apartment three. You'll be renting apartment one."

"How far from here?" Eric asked.

"A couple of blocks," Martin said.

"Good. Let's do a drive-by," Eric said, motioning for them to load into a single van.

Martin drove the short distance and Eric discreetly gave the complex the once-over. It was a long two-story brick-fronted complex, with a dozen units. The windows were dirty, and the parking lot had weeds sprouting through deep cracks.

It's seen better days. "Deion and Valerie?" Eric asked. "You're up. Mark, when do they meet the apartment manager?"

"Approximately twenty minutes."

"You were sure I was going to accept?" Valerie asked.

Eric grinned. "You couldn't withstand my charming personality."

Taylor, Mark, and John laughed. Valerie smiled, but she also shook her head. "I'm not ... comfortable with this."

"You'll do fine," Nancy said. "Meet the apartment manager, rent the apartment, and try to get the keys before he leaves."

"Isn't it going to look suspicious if we get out of this van?" Valerie asked.

"Don't worry," Mark said. "There's a car parked around the block and registered in your false names."

Valerie turned to Deion. "Your team thinks of everything."

Deion rolled his. "They have their days."

Taylor stopped the van, and Deion and Valerie exited and got into the rusty blue Honda Accord. They drove off while Taylor headed back to the deserted parking lot, where Mark and John waited with the second van.

Eric nodded at them, and they followed in the second van as Taylor drove back to the apartment complex and parked half a block down the street. It was only a few minutes before a beat-up red pickup truck pulled in. A fat man in a stained white undershirt got out and stood in front of the empty apartment, tapping his foot.

Deion and Valerie pulled into the apartment complex and parked next to the truck. They got out and shook hands with the apartment manager, who withdrew a master key ring, unlocked the door, and led them inside.

"Should we get audio?" Taylor asked.

"No reason," Eric said. "We're not here for *him*."

"At least let me get it set up and directed towards Sadir's apartment."

There was a crackling over the radio. "Do we know where Sadir is?" Mark asked.

"Let's see if Karen has anything," Eric said. He pulled out his laptop, plugged in his wireless card, and made the secured connection back to the OTM.

Karen appeared on the screen. "I can't find a cell phone for this guy," she said with a frown. "Nothing in any of the cell carrier's records. He doesn't even have the phone in his apartment turned on."

"A paranoid terrorist," Eric mused. "Great. You have his file?"

"Immigrated to the United States when he was a teenager. Hasn't done much of anything since. Quiet. Preaches at the mosque. No social media, no Internet postings, no sign that he's *anything* but legit."

"Does he have an Internet connection?"

"Records indicate yes. I'm trying to get a tap on his ISP. If I can infect his computers with malware, I can remotely enable his microphone. Then you wouldn't have to bother with this."

"You don't have a lot of respect for HUMINT," Eric said, "but it's a necessary part of intelligence."

"What if you spook him?"

"We *don't* want to spook him, but he *might* already know about the Syrian mission. He might already be spooked."

"I vote we snatch him now," Taylor said, giving Eric a hard look. "I promise you, we *would* make him talk."

Eric considered it. As an Operator, he was trained to act. But, as the head of Operation StrikeForce and Assistant Director of the OTM, he had to think bigger.

Those calls used to drive him crazy in the field, but he was beginning to understand their necessity. "What if he doesn't *know* anything?" he said. "What if the bomb is already in the United States? What if snatching him triggers his cell to detonate? No, we have to find out what he knows. The intelligence is our priority."

"Here comes Deion and Valerie," Taylor said.

Eric watched as they exited the apartment building, the fat man close behind, his eyes firmly fixated on Valerie's backside.

Deion made a show of withdrawing a stack of twenty-dollar bills from his wallet and passed them to the man.

The manager handed them the apartment keys, cast a lingering glance at Valerie's breasts, then got back in his truck and drove off.

"Looks like they got the apartment," Eric said. "No background check. No calling references."

Taylor raised an eyebrow. "Heh. It ain't that kind of neighborhood."

Deion and Valerie watched the apartment manager leave, then opened the trunk of their Honda and carried their suitcases into the newly rented apartment.

Not long after, Eric's com crackled to life. "We're here," Deion said. "How do you want to do this?"

"Point the microphones at the wall facing Sadir's apartment," Karen said. "We'll start recording as soon as we receive audio. Mark, point your gear to his window. I can use the laser to clean up the sound."

"Roger that," Mark said. They waited as he pointed his gear. "Laser online."

The laser bounced off the windowpane, and when it vibrated, the photo receiver picked up the vibration and amplified it. In conjunction with the audio from Deion and Valerie's gear, it allowed Karen to filter out unwanted noise and hear inside Sadir's apartment with crystal clarity.

"How long before you hack his Internet connection?" Nancy asked.

"I'm still tracking IPs registered to his ISP," Karen said. "I have to account for each computer connected to their network and registered to subnets in that area. I've gone through hundreds. As soon as I can find a computer that matches, I'll fire up the penetration software."

Eric sighed. "Okay, folks. Looks like we have a long afternoon ahead of us. Mark, I hope you packed coffee."

The radio crackled, and he heard Mark laughing. "There're two thermoses in each van," Mark said.

"That's why I love that man," Taylor said. "His attention to detail."

They waited for hours. Cars and trucks rolled by on the street outside, and the custom chillers in the vans worked overtime to quietly cool them. Soon, the computers and other equipment brought the temperature in the van to a low boil.

"Karen?" Eric finally asked. "Got anything on his computer?"

"Not yet. It *might* be turned off. I'll have to wait for him to power it up."

He shook his head. They continued to wait until a beat-up black Nissan pulled into the apartment parking lot and parked in front of Sadir's apartment. The man who got out was clearly of Arabic descent, dressed in black pants and a white dress shirt, with a thick shaggy beard and wire-rimmed glasses. He was bigger than Eric had expected, and he moved quickly, glancing around before pulling keys from his pocket, opening the door, and stepping inside.

"Has to be Sadir," Eric said. "Deion, carry some trash to the end of the complex. Make it look like you're moving in."

"Roger that, Steeljaw," Deion said. "The last tenants left some empty boxes. And a stink you can't *begin* to imagine."

Eric turned to Taylor, who was barely containing his laughter. "Better you than me, brother."

In a few moments, the door to their apartment opened and Deion stepped outside, carrying a stack of newspapers and a cardboard box. He walked the length of the building, threw the trash in the blue dumpster, then walked back. He entered the apartment and closed the door. The radio crackled again. "There's no sound coming from his apartment," Deion said. "You want me to put a tracer on his car?"

Eric looked out the window and squinted. "Still too much light."

Nancy shook her head. "Mark can follow him if he leaves. It's safer to tag his car after the sun sets."

Eric gave Nancy a sidelong glance. He would have preferred to have given the order, but technically he *was* only there to supervise. He didn't begrudge her stepping up. She was the senior commander of the operation.

He read the license plate number to Karen, who started searching. It was only seconds before she replied, "The car is registered to Abduhl Sadir. I'm still working on the computers."

"Are you getting any audio?" Deion asked.

"I'm *receiving* and filters are running. This would be a lot easier if he had a freaking cell phone I could remotely activate. HUMINT. It's like living in the stone age."

"Have you found anything *useful?*" Nancy asked.

"Wait for it. Yes, we have audio cleaned up. Sounds like he's just moving around the apartment."

It wasn't long before they heard Sadir speaking in Arabic. "It's hard to make out," Deion said, "but I think he's asking about an operation."

"It's a VOIP call," Karen said. "I just registered an outbound connection to Syria from an IP on his subnet."

"Can we hear the other party?" Eric asked.

"I'm boosting the gain, but I'm not a miracle worker."

"Can you decrypt the voice call?" Nancy asked.

"I don't have enough horsepower to decrypt it in real-time," Karen said. "I *can* break the encryption, but it's going to take me a couple of hours."

"That's better than nothing," Eric said. "Do the best you can."

"Wait," Deion said. "He just said something. Sounds like he's giving orders."

"Definitely our guy," Taylor said. "You sure we shouldn't just grab him?"

Eric shook his head. "No, we've got to find out who is on the other end of that call. Karen, are you recording the conversation?"

"Yes," Karen said.

They listened for several minutes. Occasionally Deion would interrupt, translating Sadir's end of the conversation. Most of it carried little meaning.

If only we could hear the other end.

Finally the man said something, and Deion translated. "He's asking about Syria."

"Karen?" Eric asked. "Have you tracked the other IP address?"

"It's an Internet café in Aleppo. I'm trying to install malware on that computer, too. If there's a camera, I can activate it and take a photo."

"He's winding down," Deion said.

"Karen? We need *something*."

"I've installed a backdoor," Karen said triumphantly. "There *is* a camera. Activating it now."

Eric's laptop displayed the screen capture. Halfway around the world, a small room was filled with young people, all typing away on computers. It was dark and the picture dim, but the Arabic man's olive skin was clearly visible, as well as the scar across his cheek.

"Good work," Eric said. "How long before we can ID him?"

"I'm cleaning up the image to give the software a better chance of a hit. We should know something in a few hours."

* * *

Honolulu, Hawaii

Liu Kong's face appeared on Huang Lei's computer. The short man was calm, his face passive.

"Yes, Kong."

"Preparations are underway."

Huang Lei nodded. "Do you expect complications?"

Liu Kong shook his head.

"Thank you, Kong." Huang Lei pressed the button to close the video call. He turned to stare out the window, his eyes watching the vast ocean, still fascinated by the breakers near the shore.

Kong would do anything for him, and he felt no small affection for the man.

Kong had been wild, almost feral, when Huang Lei had found him on the streets of Tianjin. He had taken the boy in, even though he was not much older, and raised Kong as his own. He'd fed Kong, clothed him, and educated him in the history of China. He had taken the boy to his first museum, introducing him to a world the boy had never imagined.

Huang Lei tried to be a father to the boy, because his own father's passing had struck close to home, a wound to his heart that time would never heal. He remembered everything his father had said about the Americans and Russians, and when the time was right, he'd taught Kong everything his father had taught him.

The circle of life. Karma. Justice.

CHAPTER FOUR

Nashville, Tennessee

KAREN'S VOICE SQUAWKED through coms. "We've got a hit."

Eric bolted upright. They had been waiting patiently for the search to complete, and the setting sun cast a dull red glow in the moist fall haze. He turned to Nancy and Taylor, both of them suddenly alert. "Who is he?"

"Reza Nazer," Karen said. "He's a low-level Al-Qaeda operative. I pulled everything useful from his computer, but it's a dead end. It's a rented desktop at an Internet café."

Eric shook his head. *Of course it couldn't be that simple.* "Why can't the bad guys play dumb?" he asked. "Just once?"

"I'm sending his file. Take a look. I'm not seeing *anything.*"

Eric paged through the document. Karen was right. There was nothing to indicate that Nazer was anything other than a low-level wannabe. "Have you started a backtrack?"

"On it, boss. It's going to take a few days before I can track down his cell phone, computer, and other electronic toys."

Nancy, who had been leaning over his shoulder, reading through the file, spoke up. "How the hell could a loser like this have purchased a nuclear weapon?"

"He can't possibly be in charge," Eric said. "Deion, we've identified the man that Sadir spoke to. He doesn't have the juice to organize this. You really think Sadir is giving the orders?"

"Sounded like it to me," Deion said.

Taylor raised an eyebrow. "*Now* can we snag and bag him?"

Eric considered it. If Sadir *was* in charge, capturing and interrogating him could stop any plans for the nuke. But, if Sadir *wasn't* in charge, they would tip their hand. It could drive the terrorist cell underground, and the OTM would lose their advantage.

Nancy watched him carefully. She leaned in close so that only he could hear. "It's hard when it's all on you, but you *have* to call it."

He smiled. "Let's take him."

* * *

John eased next to the door of Sadir's apartment. The plan was simple. Valerie would knock on the door, and when Sadir opened, John would burst in. He eyed the door critically. It was cheap metal, painted with thick coats of rippling white paint. The door frame was wood and painted a matching dirty white.

Valerie stood in front of the door and cast a quick glance his away. "Ready?" she whispered.

He nodded and his earpiece crackled. "Remember," Eric said from the van down the street, "we need him *alive*."

John grunted. He understood Eric had to make it look good, that Eric had to keep up the appearance of riding him, but surely Eric knew that he wouldn't deliberately kill Sadir.

Surely he knows.

The tech inside his body gave him a tremendous advantage. Sometimes he found himself striking harder than he intended, moving faster than he intended, hurting people more than he intended. It wasn't *his* fault. He was what the OTM had made him.

"Do it," Eric said.

Valerie rapped her knuckles lightly on the door. "Hello?" she asked. "Is there anyone there? I just moved in and was wondering if someone could help me with some boxes?"

There was movement from within. Finally, a man's voice in lightly accented English said, "Go away."

"Please?" Valerie pleaded, making sure to stand directly in front of the peephole. "I only need help with a few boxes."

John pressed himself against the exterior wall of Sadir's apartment. He felt the tension rise, his body's natural adrenaline spiking enough to give him a rush. It wasn't like the Implant, but he felt his heart thudding in his chest.

Valerie appeared to be a nonthreatening woman in her forties. He hoped that Sadir's beliefs weren't so strong that he would refuse to help a woman not of his family.

There was a rustling inside, and then the sound of the chain clanking against the metal door. "Fine," Sadir said. "I will help you if you *stop* knocking on my door."

John tensed. When Sadir opened the door, he struck it with his shoulder like an offensive linebacker. He slammed forward and heard a woof as the door knocked Sadir back into the apartment.

And, like that, John was inside. He had time to register the sand-colored couch against the left wall, the loaded bookshelf against the right, and a counter that separated the front living area from the kitchen.

Sadir was struggling to sit up on the dirty brown carpet, but John kicked with the heel of his foot, a solid blow that struck Sadir in the chest, slamming him back against the floor. As Sadir tried again to stand up, John dropped to his knees and grabbed the man's right arm, twisting the man's hand at the wrist, while pushing against his triceps.

Sadir howled in pain and tried to break the hold, but John used the leverage to ram Sadir facefirst against the carpet. Sadir's legs kicked uselessly as the rest of the team rushed into the apartment.

"Let me go," Sadir shouted between gasps. "You have no right."

Eric strolled leisurely into the room. "Abduhl Sadir," he said, standing over the man. "You've been a naughty boy. We have some questions. We want to know just *how* naughty you've been."

"I don't know what you say," Sadir moaned. "I have done nothing!"

John held Sadir tightly as the man squirmed beneath him. He relaxed the rotational pressure on Sadir's arm, allowing the man to suck in a deep breath of air. "You're going to answer the man's questions," John said, "or I'm going to twist your arm off your body. Do you understand?"

"I am a humble servant of God," Sadir said. "You are treating me this way because you are against Islam! I have done nothing, I tell you."

Sadir struggled to pull away from John's grasp, and he reapplied the rotational pressure against Sadir's arm, causing Sadir to yelp.

Taylor, Mark, Deion, and Nancy stood in a semicircle, watching as Eric questioned Sadir. Taylor and Mark held their M11s to their sides, but Nancy held hers in a tight grip, pointed steadily at the man on the floor.

Valerie watched in shock, and John thought she would speak out against their brutal takedown of Sadir, but she remained silent.

Eric squatted down to the floor and rocked back on the heels of his shoes. "I'm going to give you an opportunity. I don't feel like arguing for the rest of the afternoon, so let's skip the part where you pretend you don't know what I'm talking about. You've acquired a nuclear weapon from North Korea, and you were just discussing it with your flunky in Syria. Tell us everything we want to know about that weapon, where it is, and how you acquired it, or we're going to disappear you into a hole so deep you'll *never* be found."

The man still struggled against his grip. "I know nothing of the things you speak—"

"John," Eric interrupted. "Start breaking his fingers. Personally, I'd start with his pinky, but I'll leave it up to you."

John turned to Eric, but Eric wasn't smiling.

Surely he doesn't mean that.

Valerie stepped forward, but Eric turned his gaze upon her, and she froze in her tracks. "Valerie, you might want to step outside. This is going to get ... messy."

Deion put his hand on her shoulder, but she recoiled.

"You can't do this," she said.

Eric's laugh was more of a bark. "We're not the police. We can do anything we want. John?"

John shrugged but relaxed his grip enough to grab the man's pinky and started to bend it backward.

"No, no," the man screamed before John could break the bone. "I'll tell you. I'll tell you everything."

Eric nodded at him, and John released the man's finger, giving silent thanks that he hadn't been forced to follow through with Eric's threat.

He leaned close and whispered in the man's ear. "Good choice. You wouldn't like what he would've ordered me to do next."

* * *

Washington, D.C.

Smith stared at the monitor for several minutes before finally initiating the video conference.

There was a long pause before the call connected. The tired old man on the other end squinted into the camera. "Fulton?"

"Sorry for calling so late."

Hobert Barnwell fumbled at his keyboard, then wiped the sleep from his bleary eyes. "What time is it?"

"It's … late."

Hobert shook his head. "Has something happened?"

Smith wanted to tell him that of course something had happened. He wanted to scream at the monitor, to yell at his old friend, to tell him that his mind was finally slipping away and he was about to lose all memory, all sense of self. "I need to increase the medication. How much higher can I go?"

Hobert frowned. "You're already above the highest recommended dosage. You're well past unsafe levels."

"Unsafe? I need more time."

"There's nothing more I can do," Hobert said. "We are giving you massive doses of an experimental drug. Any higher and we could cause the exact problem we're trying to prevent. We just don't know enough about it."

"I'm the one taking the risk, Hob. It's *my* decision."

Hobert rocked back in his chair. "I'm sorry, but you knew this was coming. That's *why* we've worked so hard."

Smith wanted to reach through the video monitor and grab his old friend by the neck, but the anger quickly faded. "I'm aware. How goes the research?"

"We are pushing the boundaries of technology. Elliot and Oshensker have made incredible leaps, but they haven't been fully tested. Implementation will be hard. We can't test on prisoners the way we did before."

Smith sighed. Hobert was right, of course. The tech was already years ahead of what even the most hopeful scientists had imagined. The experiment that had turned John Frist into a formidable weapon was almost on the border of science fiction. For all that, it was still cumbersome. Clunky.

So many opportunities for improvement.

The next generation would be an order of magnitude beyond the existing platform. They just needed the right candidate. "And lots of luck," he murmured.

"What's that?" Hobert asked.

"Just talking to myself. I'm slipping. I'm not just repeating myself. There are other things. Smaller things."

"Have you told Nancy?"

"The timing isn't right. The current mission is too important, too dangerous."

"There's always some dangerous but important mission. You *have* to tell her."

"Just a few more months."

Hobert paused, and then his hands fumbled for something. When he raised the glass to his lips, Smith felt a stab of anger. He had promised Hobert's wife that he would keep watch on his old friend.

Hobert took a long swig of scotch, then glared at the monitor. "You know I've been drinking. I'm sure you even know how much and when."

The stress of their lives had taken a toll on both men, and nowhere was that clearer than when it came to Hobert's drinking. Years of sobriety, AA meetings, and even experimental medications hadn't been enough to make him stop.

"It's less than you drank ten years ago," Smith admitted. "You've kept a handle on it, but you're dancing close to the edge."

Hobert's face turned red. "Victoria's been spying, hasn't she?"

"She worries about you. She wants you to retire. *I* want you to retire. Don't end up like me."

That stopped his friend, who put the glass down. "What about Eric? Have you told him?"

"There's so much I *haven't* told him. If I just had more time—"

"We can increase your dose by forty milligrams," Hobert said. "That's as far as we go. Any more and you risk suffering a synaptic storm. If that happens, you would lose not only your memories, but possibly higher functions. The best-case scenario? You'd be a drooling idiot. The worst? Brain death."

"Thank you." He knew Hob wanted to protect him, but their work was too important. To the country. To Eric. To Nancy. To the office that had taken so much from him.

"What about Alexandra?"

"You know the risks. You know what's at stake."

"If you're really concerned about taking care of your affairs, you *will* do the right thing. You of all people have the means to reconnect them."

"If my plans come to fruition, young Eric will take my place. He will ensure that Nancy is cared for."

"You've got a lot riding on him."

"Eric is capable of much more. He has yet to realize his full potential."

Hobert shook his head, deep lines in his face that stood out in the glare of the monitor. "I just hope he doesn't walk away when he discovers the truth."

"He won't. He's better than us. That's why we picked him, remember?"

* * *

Nashville, Tennessee

Eric resisted the urge to smile. The mere threat of violence had been enough to break Sadir. He was glad John had played along. Of course, he *was* prepared to order John to break all the man's fingers if it came to that.

Deion frowned and leaned in close. "You want me to do this?"

Eric shook his head. "I got it." He turned to the terrorist. "Tell me about your plan. Who's in charge?"

"I am," Sadir said, a hint of pride in his voice. "It is *my* plan."

Nancy rolled her eyes. Eric agreed. Sadir didn't seem smart enough to devise the plan himself, but they would come back to that later. "What was your target?"

"New York City. We were to bomb the infidels in New York City."

He turned to Deion, who raised an eyebrow.

Why does every terrorist want to bomb New York City? He shrugged and turned back to the man. "Where's the bomb now?"

"I don't know," Sadir said.

"How can you *not* know?" Eric asked. "I thought this was your plan. I thought *you* were in charge."

"I *am* in charge, but I prepared for this. How could I give away the location if I didn't know myself?"

Eric thought about that. Perhaps Sadir *was* smarter than he appeared. "Who knows the location? Does your man, Nazer, know?"

He watched Sadir's face carefully. When he mentioned Nazer's name, Sadir frowned.

"Nazer? No, he does not know. No one knows."

"How can that be?" Nancy asked. She stepped forward and pointed her gun at Sadir's head. "How can *nobody* know?"

Sadir offered a weak smile. "I am a smart man. I planned carefully."

The muscles in Nancy's forearm twitch.

She's more dangerous than John. I wonder if Fulton understands that. "Nancy," he said quietly. She turned to him with empty eyes, then slowly lowered her weapon. He turned his attention back to Sadir. "What about Al-Hakim?"

The man froze. "It was not *his* plan. It was *my* plan."

Aha. Touchy subject. "Al-Hakim is the name I hear. He's a rising leader, isn't he?"

The man's face reddened. "He is not a true Muslim," Sadir sputtered. "If he is so smart, why was *I* trusted with the operation? He wanted to lead this martyrdom operation, but *I* was chosen."

There it is. Resentment. Jealousy. Anger. So predictable. "I've heard Al-Hakim's been planning all the major attacks. He's stepped in to fill bin Laden's absence."

"Not true," Sadir growled. "You are a liar. He might have access to funds, but that does not make him a leader in Jihad. I do not take orders from *him*."

That was all he needed to hear. Al-Hakim was the money man but had allowed Sadir to lead the mission. The emails were summaries, checking on his investment. "Taylor, cuff him. Let's take him home."

Taylor withdrew a thick plastic zip tie from a pouch on his belt, then zip-tied Sadir's hands behind his back. With John's help, they yanked the man to his feet.

"I must be read my rights," Sadir protested. "I know your laws. That is what you *must* do."

"I told you," Eric said patiently, "we're not the police." He tilted his head toward the door, and John and Mark led Sadir outside into the fall twilight.

Valerie turned to Nancy. "You've mellowed."

Deion's eyes narrowed, but Nancy offered her a wry smile. "I'm doing my best."

They stepped outside of the apartment and were following John and Mark to their van when Eric saw the spray from Sadir's head.

Time slowed to a crawl, and he tried to make sense of the scarlet mist. Sadir's body fell limply to the ground, and then time sped back up as his mind connected the dots.

"Shooter!" he screamed, dropping to his knee.

An echoing report from a rifle bounced between the apartment buildings, making it impossible to track. The rest of his team dropped to their knees, scanning the cars and apartments in the distance.

He hadn't seen a flash of light, but he hadn't been looking. He tried to guestimate the bullet's trajectory from the spray of blood from Sadir's head and figured the bullet had come from a low angle to the east.

Apartment doors opened as people poked their heads out, then quickly slammed the doors shut when they saw the body on the ground.

Eric pointed in the distance. "It came from that way, John. Karen, if you're listening, activate his Implant."

John came to his feet in a fluid motion and started pounding down the road, followed by Taylor and Mark.

"Activating," Karen whispered in his ear.

John staggered, then caught his footing and practically flew down the street, quickly outpacing the Delta Operators.

Eric turned back to Sadir. Deion knelt over him, checking for a pulse, then shook his head in disgust. "He's gone."

Nancy and Valerie stared at Sadir's dead body sprawled on the still-warm asphalt, blood pooling around his head in a crimson halo.

"The police will be here soon," Eric said. "Valerie, don't say a word. Don't answer any questions, not even your name or agency."

He gave Karen instructions as the wail of distant sirens approached. John returned with Taylor and Mark as the local police screeched up in squad cars.

"The shooter was gone," John said. "I couldn't even find his perch."

Behind him, Taylor and Mark nodded their agreement.

The police opened their car doors and trained their guns on them, yelling at them to put down their weapons.

"Don't worry," Eric said. "Just put your gun down and we'll have a conversation with these good officers."

* * *

John took a swig of cheap coffee while Eric and Deion argued with the room full of law enforcement professionals on the other side of the police station. "Think this will take much longer?" he asked.

The rest of the team sat around the table, watching the show through the glass window. Nancy shrugged. "We have authority. Nothing they can do about it."

Taylor sat close to Valerie but turned to glance at the conference room across the bullpen, then turned back and smiled. "When a body drops, every swinging dick with a badge wants a piece. Eric can handle it. This isn't his first rodeo."

John nodded and leaned back in his chair. He noticed the way the uniformed police kept a discreet watch on them. The Memphis FBI agent, John Waverly, was especially displeased with their operation. He had taken the local DHS team into the conference room with Eric, and the other high-ranking members of local enforcement agencies soon joined them.

"Why would someone kill Sadir?" Taylor asked. "Another cell member?"

John smiled at the tall man. "Perhaps it's a secret government agency dedicated to protecting the country?"

Mark laughed, but Nancy gave John an icy glare and snapped, "Drink your coffee."

The yelling in the conference room subsided, then the door opened and Eric stepped out, followed quickly by Waverly. Eric walked through the room with catlike grace, and the officers turned their heads, eager to avoid eye contact.

Deion followed close behind, shaking his head.

"Here comes trouble," Taylor murmured.

John agreed. While Eric appeared calm, Waverly's face had the pinched look of someone who had swallowed a lemon, his black hair layered in sweaty peels.

Eric stopped next to their table. "Okay, folks, shows over. Let's get moving."

"Not so fast," Waverly said, placing his hand on Eric's shoulder.

"We've discussed this," Eric said blandly. "Your concerns are duly noted. Now, take your hand off me."

John glanced at Mark, who shrugged, then caught Taylor's smirk. Apparently they were used to Eric's way of doing business. Waverly was a big man, taller than Eric and built like a pro wrestler, but John knew that Eric could take the FBI agent apart without breaking a sweat.

Nancy turned a hostile glare to Waverly. "You've reviewed our documents," she said. "That's the limit of your authority."

Waverly started to speak, then clenched his jaw. Finally, he said, "You're *not* DHS."

Valerie watched their exchange with concern but relaxed when Deion put his hand on her arm.

Eric gave Waverly a shrewd look. "What makes you say that?"

"Because Knoll didn't know you. In fact, I'm quite sure he's never heard of you. His attitude changed after he got off the phone with Washington. You're not DHS," he repeated. "I'm guessing military."

John almost smiled. Waverly *was* smarter than he looked.

"That kind of speculation can get you in trouble," Nancy said. "It might be a bad career choice."

Waverly's face turned red. "I've got a friend back at the Memphis office. I called him and told him what happened. He thinks you're Delta."

Deion stepped forward. "If that kinda thing *were* true, maybe you shouldn't spread it around."

"I have more friends," Waverly said. "I can find out who you *really* are."

Nancy started to speak but stopped when Eric shook his head. She looked down at the floor, then back up, her face blank.

"Nice meeting you, John," Eric said. "Stay in touch."

* * *

Deion was trying to speak quietly with Valerie, but it was almost impossible in the back of the van. They were on their way back to the airport, navigating the darkened streets of Nashville. Taylor drove, and Eric rode shotgun in the passenger seat. Nancy sat behind Eric, facing toward the rear, trying to give them some privacy.

"Sorry you got dragged into this," Deion said.

Valerie reached across and placed her hand on his knee. "This group you're in? It's crazy."

Deion tended to agree with her. Since his recruitment, they had stopped a bombing in New York City, intercepted a truck full of explosives in France, averted an airliner shootdown in London, not to mention tamping down a few more troublesome terrorist groups around the United States.

The terrorists had grown smart. It wasn't just a matter of killing Americans. Osama bin Laden had taught them they could bleed the enemy financially.

"Val, you see what we're up against. Our group? *We* keep America *safe.*"

He saw Nancy shaking her head from the corner of his eye. "I can't tell you *exactly* what we do," he continued, "but you've seen a glimpse. You understand."

"It's okay, Deion. I *do* understand, God knows I *do*, but the way you go about it is ... sketchy."

"It's for the greater good," he insisted. "It's necessary."

"Terrible things have been done for the greater good," Valerie said with a frown.

Taylor eased the van through traffic, safely depositing them at the terminal drop-off.

"Valerie, we'll drop you off in Chicago," Eric said. "Sorry, Deion. I'm cutting your vacation short. Taylor, join John and Mark. I'll see you back home."

Taylor nodded. "Maybe we can stop at the Ryman on our way back to Arnold."

Eric gave Taylor a sour look. "It's not even close to being on your way back."

Taylor winked. "I'll get the kids home, don't worry."

They piled out of the vehicle and Taylor drove off. Valerie turned to Eric. "It's been interesting."

Eric smiled. "Would you be willing to work with us in the future? We could use someone like you."

Nancy appeared startled. "Eric—"

"Valerie has her *own* career," Deion interrupted. "I'm sure she has a full plate."

Eric smiled pleasantly. "She's an excellent agent and could really make a difference. Let her think about it."

Valerie watched the exchange with a frown. "Am I being recruited?"

"Not necessarily. You *have* been involved in two of our operations. You handle yourself well. That kind of performance doesn't go unnoticed."

Deion wasn't sure of Eric's game. Was he trying to bring Val into the fold to protect her? He'd filled out the necessary paperwork, notifying Eric of their relationship. Eric hadn't voiced any objections, but the idea of an OTM agent romantically involved with a CIA case officer was far from ideal.

"She doesn't know enough to make an informed decision. Don't shanghai her."

"Ms. Simon can speak for herself," Nancy said.

Nancy sound reasonable, which was the last thing he expected. He didn't know which was worse, Eric recruiting Valerie or Nancy's psychopathic approval.

"I need some time to consider your offer," Valerie said.

Eric continued smiling. "There's no rush. Take a few days. Hell, take a few weeks." He shook her hand. "Know this. We do incredibly important work. Deion can vouch for that. Let's get going. Greg's waiting with the Gulfstream, and Deion, Nancy, and I have to get home."

"And where *is* home?" Valerie asked.

Eric winked at her. "That's only *if* you accept the job."

CHAPTER FIVE

Area 51

DAWN BROUGHT HIGHLIGHTS of orange and pink across the desert floor of Groom Lake. Greg landed the Gulfstream and Deion followed Nancy and Eric off the plane, through the dry morning air, and into a Humvee. He couldn't stop thinking about Eric's offer since dropping Valerie off in Chicago. "Are you really trying to recruit my girlfriend?"

They roared over the dusty road. As they approached the entrance to the underground base, Eric checked the LCD screen in the Humvee's dash for satellite overflies. Satisfied they were in the clear, he pushed a green button on the LCD screen and the desert floor in front of them rumbled open. Eric's attention flickered from the tunnel's glassy walls to Nancy in the driver seat and then to Deion in the rear. "We need to scoop up good talent when we find it."

They approached the steel door to the base. Eric braked hard, then spun the Humvee around and pointed it back to the surface. They got out and showed their identification to the guard at the door, who waved them through.

As they climbed into a small electric cart, Nancy spoke up. "It *was* a little unexpected."

Eric guided their cart down the long stone tunnel until they reached the second checkpoint. He turned to Deion and raised an eyebrow. "It would make your relationship easier. She's smart. She'd do well here. What's really bothering you?"

"She lacks a certain ... moral flexibility," Deion said.

"I've read her file," Eric said with a knowing grin. "Her *real* file. I'm not sure you're giving your lady enough credit."

He's right. During their time together in Afghanistan, some of Valerie's operations had approached the edge of legality. "I would have appreciated your speaking to me first about it."

They reached the underground base proper and navigated the final checkpoint. "I'd *love* to listen to you continue questioning my judgment," Eric said with an impish smile, "but we've got work to do. Get cleaned up and meet me back in the War Room in thirty."

* * *

When Eric entered the War Room, he noticed the subdued click-clacking of the analysts' keyboards. Then he saw Karen waiting for him and noticed how her eyes lit up when he smiled at her.

"Clark has your team assembled," she said before he could speak.

"Good." He gave her a small nod, then strolled through the room, stopping by several analysts to check other threats the OTM monitored while he waited for Deion and Nancy.

Karen followed him, keeping a respectful distance, but not so close that it would cause gossip. Satisfied the OTM was running smoothly, he turned to her and asked, "Have you found any intelligence on the North Koreans?"

"For a country that's been economically devastated, they have a *fantastic* ability to hide." She leaned close. "How was the mission?"

She smelled faintly of lilacs. *Perfume, perhaps, or maybe shampoo.* "Mrs. Kryzowski, how forward of you," he said softly.

She smiled, and his heart thumped in his chest. For a moment he imagined them in bed together, then shook his head, trying to ditch the mental image.

At that moment, Deion and Nancy entered the War Room, refreshed, having changed their clothes. They returned Clark's salute and nodded at Eric.

He quickly made his way to the conference room and followed them in. They took seats around the table as Karen ran down the information on their Nashville mission.

"I was able to pull a log of phone calls and video conferences," Karen said, "all connected to that same coffee shop in Syria. There was nothing else of interest on Sadir's laptop."

"Did the FBI find anything on the Nashville shooter?" Eric asked.

"Nothing," Clark said. "It was a professional hit. They identified an empty apartment three blocks away with traces of GPR. No witnesses. Forensics came up clean."

"Just doesn't sound right," Deion said, shaking his head. "A shot from that distance? Sounds like somebody with serious training, not Al-Qaeda."

It troubled Eric as well. "Karen, start working on the video surveillance from traffic cams. There's bound to be video of the shooter."

"I've already pulled the records. Analyses of street cam videos in the vicinity have come back blank. Widening the scope to the rest of the video cameras in Nashville is going to take a lot of horsepower."

"I will authorize it," Eric said. "This situation stinks."

"I agree," Deion said. "There's something funny going on. What are our options?"

"What do we know about Reza Nazer?" Nancy asked.

"Nazer is a low-level flunky," Clark said. "If you want more info, we're going to need HUMINT. I contacted your friend, Mr. Burton, and his team is ready to insert into Syria. They're on the Iraq border, awaiting your orders."

Eric smiled. Bill "Redman" Burton was one of his oldest friends in Delta Force. They had been on countless missions together, and he had seriously considered recruiting the squat little Georgian into the OTM. "Deion, I'd like you to work with Redman. Nancy, a woman in this kind of situation might make things worse."

"I agree," Nancy said. "However, I might better monitor the situation from Turkey."

The surprised look on Karen's face mirrored his own. Nancy *had* changed. She was still violent and unpredictable, but more open to new ideas. She listened to other points of view, reviewed her actions and modified her behavior. He'd seen glimpses since the operation in New York City. It made her more effective. In fact, he was impressed, and apparently he wasn't the only one.

Clark raised an eyebrow and said, "I can get you a temporary office in Incirlik."

"Fantastic," Eric said. "I want you wheels up in sixty. Take Taylor, Mark, and John. Make sure John has the Battlesuit. Send the order to Redman that he has permission to insert into Syria. I want surveillance on Nazer as soon as possible. What about Al-Hakim?"

Karen typed furiously on her keyboard. The photo of a young man with sandy blond hair and dark blue eyes in his early twenties appeared on the monitor. "Gary Hite, born in Fresno. Left for Somalia in 2006 and joined an Al-Qaeda affiliate. He was quickly named Al-Hakim, the American, and began making recruitment videos. The CIA has been looking for him ever since. They think he's hiding out in England or possibly Europe. We suspect he's planned and helped carry out multiple operations."

Deion rapped his knuckles on the table. "I've looked through the CIA's case file on Hite. Typical spoiled punk with a liberal upbringing. He converted to Islam when he was seventeen. His father was a defense contractor at Lockheed Martin, his mother a nurse. They went on CNN calling for him to return home, but Hite disowned them both in a video shortly after he joined Al-Qaeda. He's declared war against them, and against the United States."

Clark cleared his throat. "This guy purchased a nuke?"

Eric agreed. "Sadir claimed Hite was the money man, but I can't see Sadir planning this. If we get eyes on Nazer, we might have a better idea of what's really going on. Above all, we *have* to *find that nuke.*"

"I'll have the team in the air within the hour," Deion said. "It's a long flight. We won't be there until tomorrow."

"Redman will pick up the slack," Eric said. "Good hunting."

Deion and Clark exited the conference room with Karen close behind. She turned and cast a long glance at Eric and before slowly closing the door.

"Was there something else?" Eric asked.

"I'm surprised you're not going," Nancy said. "Isn't this the kind of mission you love?"

It was true. He *wanted* to insert into Syria. He wanted to be at the heart of the action, but the director of the OTM had more responsibilities than any single mission.

There was still the problem with the Iranian centrifuges. The Russians were moving arms into Venezuela. Osama bin Laden was still on the loose, believed to be somewhere in Afghanistan. AQ was active in Iraq and Afghanistan, with dozens of plans to strike Europe and the United States, and that wasn't counting the splinter groups. The OTM had dozens of other high-value, high-target operations currently in flight, but there were only so many resources.

He hated to admit it, but his place was back home, leading the OTM. "I'm not a field agent anymore. Isn't that what you're always reminding me?"

Nancy smiled, showing the barest hint of teeth between her lips, and fine lines appeared around the corner of her eyes. "It's hard sitting back and letting others do the dirty work. As much as I disagree with my father sometimes, he was right about one thing. You are capable of *so* much more."

She stood and headed for the door. The muscles in her legs were clearly visible under her tight skirt, and he couldn't help but admire the firmness of them and how smoothly she walked. Her body was like a coiled spring, full of energy, but with a bounce that stirred something in him.

She put countless hours in at the gym, running on the treadmill, lifting weights, and practicing martial arts. She was at peak fitness, and for the second time in an hour, a vision of a naked woman came unbidden—an image of them, together, sprawled naked on the sheets.

She stepped through the door, and her eyes lingered on him for a moment. She caught him watching, and the briefest of smiles played across her face.

That woman is going to be the death of me.

* * *

John made his way to the coffee shop. It was one of the base's smaller rooms, eight meters square, with six round faux-wood tables on slender stainless steel bases. The shop was one of two in the underground base, staffed by soldiers who volunteered during their spare time for the privilege of running the coffee machines and wiping down the tables.

Kara Tulli waited, and her face flushed when he took the seat next to her. It was slow in the shop, and half the tables were empty. Kara held two large white paper cups and handed one to him. "Black, just the way you like it."

He took it gratefully. "Thanks."

"How was your mission?"

"You probably know more about it than I do. Elliot and Oshensker reviewed the metrics while I was in the field, and I sent them my after-action write-up while still in the air."

"True, but I wasn't asking about that. How are *you?*"

"I didn't find the shooter."

She took a sip of coffee. "That's not what I meant, either."

He had to tread carefully. Kara used to despise him. He didn't want to give her any reason to go back to that, or any reason for her to suspect he remembered his past. "I think if Sadir hadn't talked, Eric wanted me to break his fingers." He hesitated, then said, "That's not something I want to do."

She leaned back in surprise. "Sadir was a bad guy?"

"That doesn't mean I wanted to torture him."

Her face flushed. "Eric wouldn't give you an order if he didn't have a good reason."

He took a drink of his coffee and enjoyed the complex and bitter flavor as it rolled over his tongue. "I don't want to hurt someone when I don't have to."

Her eyes narrowed. "But you *would* hurt someone? If you had to?"

"*If* Eric ordered," he said slowly. "*If* it meant saving lives. I wouldn't want to. I'd tell myself it was for the greater good. I'd tell myself it would all be worth it."

She shook her head. "You don't believe that. You think that would make you a bad person."

"Wouldn't it?" He reached across the table, took her hand in his and squeezed softly.

His cell phone vibrated, and he removed it from his pocket, glanced at the message from Deion, then sighed. "No rest for the wicked, I guess." He held up the phone so she could see the message. "Kara, I have to do bad things. Kill people. I know it saves lives, and I know it's necessary. That doesn't make me a monster. As long as I feel empathy? As long as it hurts inside? That means I'm *not* a monster."

Kara glanced around the room, then quickly leaned in and kissed him before anyone noticed. "You're *not* a monster."

He squeezed her hand tightly and smiled.

I wish I believed her.

* * *

Karen stared at her monitor. It didn't make any sense. She pored through the video footage again. There were video cams mounted to streetlights on every corner in Nashville, but the more she combed through the video footage from the area around Sadir's apartment, the more gaping holes she found.

It was as if the cameras had been instructed to turn off.

That's impossible!

She ran through it again. The cameras fed their data to servers in the Nashville Department of Transportation, and then copies of the traffic were sent to the NSA. At the NSA data center, the packets were duplicated and sent on to the OTM's data warehouse. The OTM servers were safe, but she began to wonder if the Nashville servers were compromised. She scanned the servers in the Nashville DOT headquarters with a series of hacking tools for several hours before finally giving up.

The servers were hardened and firewalled. Direct attacks were impossible. No, the servers were fine. The only logical conclusion was that it had to be in the cameras themselves.

The hot coffee burned the back of her throat as she took a deep gulp. For the thousandth time, she wondered if Eric would approve her requisition for a coffeemaker at her desk.

Just thinking of Eric warmed her to her core, and she longed to be with him. Her husband, Brad, was a good man but was always on deployment. Her arrangement with Brad was simple—sex with others was acceptable, as long as there were no emotions or ties.

Unfortunately, she had taken a liking to Eric and part of her worried she might actually be cheating—emotionally, at least—on her husband. She shook her head. She would continue with Eric and try harder not to become emotionally entangled.

Eric needed the release. The stress of the office was crushing him. The last thing he needed was emotional baggage.

No, sex with Eric was stupid good, and she wouldn't jeopardize that.

He needs me.

She glanced around, but the other analysts were busy working on the Syria mission. She grabbed her near-empty cup of coffee, nodded to Sergeant Clark, and navigated the mantrap. It was a long walk down several hallways before she took the three flights of stairs to the deepest part of the underground base.

Dewey's office door was dark blue steel, most of it obscured by a vintage *Xena* poster. She rolled her eyes and jiggled the handle, but the knob refused to open. She banged on the door.

"Dewey," she yelled, over the sound of a cranked-up television, "I *really* need to talk to you."

There was a shout from inside, the television volume dropped, and the door opened. Dewey greeted her with a big smile plastered across his face. He was one of her oldest friends. They had worked together at the NSA before she was recruited by the OTM. In fact, she was the one who had suggested Dewey for the OTM.

Dewey's shock of brown hair stood in all directions, giving him the appearance of a scarecrow. "What are you doing here?" he asked. "I thought you were working on that thing in Nashville."

Frustrated, she punched him in the shoulder. "Damn it, Dewey, quit hacking my terminal. I thought *you* were working on that Iran centrifuge problem."

His smile widened, and he motioned for her to step into his office. "Already done. I shipped off the code last week."

Dewey's office was a large concrete box, twenty meters on a side. Tables were filled with monitors, making the room one giant clutter of computer gear. A door in the far corner led to his personal quarters. Dewey was the only member of the OTM who had personal quarters attached to his office. Karen shuddered at the thought of him living with the rest of the base personnel.

As she navigated through tables of gear, she felt her nipples stiffen under her shirt. The room was freezing cold. She wondered if the little creep kept it that way just for that effect. "You solved the Iran thing? What have you been working on for the past week?"

He pointed to a giant monitor on his main desk. "I've been playing an MMORPG. I thought there was something funny going on with the in-game economy, so I've been working with a friend in London to try and see if players were manipulating the market."

She shook her head. With all the work on the OTM's plate, their smartest analyst was playing video games. "You better not let anyone find out what you're doing."

"Hey," he protested. "I've also been watching all the episodes of *Airwolf*." He pointed to a smaller screen at the edge of his desk. A black helicopter was flying through a desert, piloted by an actor who she couldn't place. "I *love* that show."

"Dewey, you love crap."

He turned back to her. "I heard that. It's important to *me*, even if it's not important to anyone else."

She sighed. Dewey was right. He focused on things no one cared about but which were deeply meaningful to him. Messing with that messed with his process, which was partially why the OTM gave him such a large office hidden away from everyone else. "I need your help."

His eyes widened, and his grin grew larger. "I'd do anything for you, Karen. You know that. Tell me what you need."

"I'm trying to find someone from traffic cameras in Nashville, but it seems like data is missing. Can you take a look?"

Dewey leaned back in his chair. "A second set of eyes? Sure!" He started typing. The MMORPG disappeared, replaced by a copy of her desktop. He clicked through her folders until he came to the one with the video feeds. "Is this it?"

She bit her tongue, then said, "I *told* you to stop hacking my workstation."

He turned to her in shock. "You were serious about that?"

"*Yes*," she said, tapping her foot against the floor. "I told you before. You need to respect boundaries."

"Sorry. Won't happen again."

Sure it won't. "Just take a look and see if you see anything ... hinky."

"Hinky. Got it." He turned back to the monitor, his jaw dropping slightly as he practically flew through the folders, looking at time and date stamps. He pulled up multiple camera angles and fast-forwarded through the video footage. He would stop, rewind, then slowly move his mouse, paging through the video frame by frame. "You're sure none of the video feeds were compromised in the DOT server farm?"

"I don't think so." Her stomach sank. It couldn't be what she suspected.

Could it?

"This is pretty weird," Dewey said, rocking back and forth in his chair. "If you're correct about the server farm's integrity, the only logical explanation is the cameras have been compromised. You know how hard that is?"

"How can we be certain?"

He squinted at her. "Leave it to me. It'll take a few days, but I'll figure it out. Hey, do you want to stay and watch *Airwolf* with me?"

"Sorry, Dewey, I've got to get back to the War Room." She turned to leave, then stopped. "How are things with Nancy?"

He turned to her, puzzled. "Why do you ask?"

"You're my friend, Dewey. I care about you."

"It's a good relationship. I mean, it's a good *sexual* relationship." He scratched at his unruly brown hair.

"Is that all it is?"

"Yes. She doesn't *like* me. She just uses me for sex."

"How do you know she doesn't like you?"

"I've spent my entire life noticing how people don't like me. I can tell. She … just wants sex."

"Is that what you want?"

"You know how hard it is for me," he said. "Now I have a beautiful woman who uses me for sex. It's a *perfect* relationship."

"Don't you wish it was more? You're a good guy. You could meet someone else."

"Come on. Most women think strange." He rubbed his hand against his eyelids. "I'm lonely. Nobody wants to come down here, and you only visit when you need something."

She started to protest, but he raised his hand. "I don't mind. But if it weren't for you and Nancy, I wouldn't have *any* visitors. Well, and the Old Man, of course."

"The Old Man? Smith visits you?"

He scanned her face. "I thought I'd mentioned that before. It started after they caught me downloading all that porn. The Old Man came down and talked to me, said it was okay, not to do it again, that I wasn't in any trouble. He told me to focus on some special projects that Nancy would send my way. That's how I met her."

"You've been doing special projects for Fulton Smith and you never told me?"

His eyes widened. "Oh wait, I wasn't supposed to mention it. It's *highly confidential.*" His eyes darted around his office. "Promise you won't tell?"

"I won't."

"You're the best. I'll work on your camera problem." He turned back to his monitor and began pounding away at the keyboard.

"Thanks, Dewey." Dewey didn't acknowledge her, or even notice as she left, closing the steel door gently behind her.

Dewey was a genius, but when he became involved in a problem, the rest of the world faded away. His attention would wander while trying to do the most mundane tasks, but when he was fully engaged, there was very little he couldn't learn or accomplish. She knew he would resolve the issue of the missing video footage, but she also wondered what "special projects" the Old Man had him working on.

* * *

Atlantic Ocean

The Gulfstream raced over the northern Atlantic. As they approached Ramstein Air Force Base to refuel, Deion noticed John looking out the window at the newly rebuilt entrance to the Landstuhl Regional Medical Center.

It seemed a lifetime ago that the OTM had raced to stop terrorists from blowing up the hospital with an improvised truck bomb. Repairs had returned the facility to its former pristine state in the ensuing two years, but John was staring off as if he still saw the devastation, the dead and dying, and the bodies buried under dusty chunks of concrete.

Deion searched John's face for any sign that his mental state had changed. He liked John, but liking him was a far cry from trusting him.

I just wish Wise would put a tighter leash on him.

After refueling, Greg turned the Gulfstream southeast toward Turkey. They landed in darkness at Incirlik Air Base, the lingering heat finally giving way to a cool breeze that was almost pleasant as they packed their gear into a pair of Toyota Hilux trucks. Deion had worked out the logistics with Eric before they left, and they crossed the Syrian border early in the morning, the border guards requiring only a small bribe before waving them through.

They entered the city of Aleppo just before dawn. John kept glancing out the window.

"What?" Deion asked, driving through the narrow streets, Taylor and Mark following close behind in the second Toyota.

John pointed to the dark semicircular shadows on the buildings around them "What are those?"

Deion looked up at the rooftops. "Satellite dishes."

The sun was just peeking over the horizon when they came to a stop in front of a dusty warehouse. Deion honked the horn three times in rapid succession, the wooden door rumbled open, and a man with a ball cap and sunglasses waved them in.

They pulled the trucks through the small opening and the man shut the door behind them, plunging the warehouse into darkness. They waited patiently until the man with the bushy brown beard and scraggly hair knocked on the window. "Clear."

They got out, and the man shook his hand. "I'm Morse."

Deion squinted in the darkness. Sean "Flipper" Morse was plainly built, dressed in local street garb, but Deion knew that Morse was Redman's second-in-command and another of Eric's friends.

Taylor and Mark joined them, slapping Morse on the back. "Been a long time, Flipper."

Morse grinned. "Gentlemen, the pleasure is yours. Can't believe you're working for Steeljaw."

Deion waited patiently while the men spent several minutes catching up. As their conversation and good-natured ribbing came to an end, he said, "What's the sitrep?"

Morse shrugged. "Redman has eyes on your target. It's almost a mile from here."

There was a crackling from his earpiece. "Took your sweet time getting there," Nancy said, loud and clear from Turkey.

Deion agreed. It was time to move. "How soon can we get there?" he asked Morse.

"Grab your gear. I'll drive."

As they loaded their gear into a Mercedes van, Deion asked, "Where'd you get this?"

"Borrowed it from a CIA facility."

"You *do* know I'm CIA?"

"Relax," Morse said. "I didn't *steal* it, just *borrowed*. Besides, the CIA ought to be more careful with their equipment."

Taylor, Mark, and John all smiled, but he frowned. "Seriously, you better return it when this is over."

Morse laughed, and it echoed in the warehouse. "Don't get your panties in a bunch. Things are little more fluid here. You have to roll with the punches. Now, you better get in the back."

Deion climbed in the back of the Mercedes. The service panel separating the cabin from the rear discouraged bystanders from noticing his team as Morse navigated the streets of Aleppo. It also inhibited the cabin's AC from reaching the back. By the time they arrived, they were sweating profusely in the morning heat.

The streets of Syria were a uniform tan-and-white stone, with brightly colored awnings differentiating individual apartments. Morse parked the van in a narrow alley, then got out and a few moments later knocked against the van's rear door, signaling the coast was clear for them to step out.

The van was parked behind another, blocking the view from the street. Morse ushered them through an alleyway door, up two flights of stairs, and down a dark hallway, where he knocked on a door, a quick pattern that elicited a soft voice from within.

"Clear," the voice said.

Morse opened the door and hustled them inside. The only occupant, a sturdily built man with shaggy black hair and a thick beard, glanced up from his laptop to greet them, pausing to spit a thick squirt of tobacco juice into a paper cup. "Freeman," Burton acknowledged. "Glad you could join the party."

Deion smiled. "I guess Steeljaw doesn't need *me* here. He's got Redman on the job."

Bill "Redman" Burton smiled lazily. "And lookee lookee, you brought the idiot squad with you."

Taylor, Mark, and John took turns shaking Redman's hand.

"Been a while," Taylor said.

Redman grinned, exposing yellowed teeth stained from chew. "Aw, Martin, you know you missed me. Kelly, you *still* look like shit. Frist, keep an eye on these two. You go to sleep one night, and when you wake up, they're playing grab-ass."

Kelly shook his head, and a smile finally reached his sad puppy-dog eyes. "He was *trying* to keep that sand spider away from me."

Redman winked at Deion. "I'm sure that's what they tell each other to make themselves feel better."

Deion liked the man, and it wasn't just because Redman had saved their lives in Afghanistan. Redman was tough, a skilled warrior and a highly trained killer, but with a fierce intelligence that shone through his eyes. He understood why Eric and Redman were such good friends.

"What have you got?" Deion asked.

Redman pointed to the laptop. "Nazer lives in the apartment across the street. I've got regular and infrared cameras pointed at his place, and a laser microphone pointed at his window. Stratello and Young are watching each end of the street. Nazer hasn't left the apartment since we got here."

"What's he been doing?"

"Eating, sleeping, watching television."

"That's it?"

"Seems like a mellow dude," Redman said. "We could breach the apartment and do a snatch and grab, have him out of the country in no time."

"Any other organization have eyes on him?"

"No. Al-Asad's been cracking down, but there's no sign they're keeping tabs on Nazer. *That* info cost me fifty bucks and a case of cigarettes."

"We'll reimburse you."

"You better, hoss."

"Let's get settled in. I want to see your recordings, but first I have to make a call." He stepped away from the others and spoke quietly into his earpiece mic. "We made it."

"What have you got?" Nancy asked.

"Nothing yet. I'll have Redman upload the data."

"What about Al-Hakim?"

"That's a negative. Nazer hasn't left his apartment, and no sign of Al-Hakim. Redman wants to do an extraction."

There was silence on the phone. Then, "Eric says hold. Too many risks during the daylight. If it comes to that, I've arranged a place for the interrogation."

"Copy that. Anything else?"

"Karen is working on something from Nashville, but she has nothing on the location of the bomb."

Damn. We're going to have to grab this guy. "Just give us the signal for the extraction."

"Will do. Watch yourself. We still don't know why they killed Sadir. If Al-Qaeda decides to kill Nazer, you don't want to get caught in the crossfire."

He snorted. "Going soft on me? That's not like you."

"You've grown on me. I would hate to carry you home in a body bag."

"Touching," he said, then ended the call.

Redman was watching him. "That the girl from Afghanistan? Simon?"

He guffawed. "No. The other one. Nancy."

Redman's eyes narrowed. "A real ballbuster, that one. Spooky." He tapped his index finger against his temple. "No one at home, if you catch my drift."

"You don't know the half of it."

* * *

Aleppo, Syria

The day passed slowly. Deion and Redman took turns monitoring the camera while Taylor, Mark, John, and Morse played poker with an ancient set of Bicycle cards Morse carried in his pocket. Deion tried to follow the rules of the game but found the men kept switching it, making for an ever increasingly complex game whose rules were understood only by them.

They stopped late in the afternoon to eat cold MREs, filling their water bottles with gritty powdered sports drink packets. The window air conditioner did little to lessen the afternoon heat, but Deion couldn't complain. He had endured far worse in Kandahar and Bagram, not to mention the moist hellhole of Guantánamo.

The sun was setting when his earpiece crackled to life. "Extraction is a go," Nancy said.

"Roger that. When?"

"Midnight. Once you have him, I want everyone out. Redman's team follows you."

"We'll be there before dawn."

Redman raised an eyebrow. "We gonna blow this popsicle stand?"

The others stopped their card game. The tension in the room was thick, the men's boredom finally giving way to excitement. He knew sitting all day with nothing to do was torture for them. As he looked into each of their faces, he saw the eagerness, the resolve, the desire to act.

Except for John. His face was oddly blank. It wasn't the first time he had noticed John's hesitation, his lack of engagement. The StrikeForce technology might have turned John into a fierce warrior, but John lacked something. The killer instinct.

It was a conundrum. How could John, a man who had bombed the Red Cross and killed hundreds of innocent civilians, be so reluctant to fight? He'd tried to broach the subject with Eric, but Eric always brushed aside his concerns.

"The extraction will be at midnight," Deion said. "John, you're in first, followed by Flipper and Mark. Taylor, find a hide. Redman, your men will drive the vans. Once we have Nazer, we head for Turkey. I want to make the border by zero two hundred."

Redman grinned again, exposing his stained teeth. "I like your thinking."

"We've got time," Deion said. "We go through it. And when we're done, we go through it again."

They talked over the operation, each man verifying his job, and then the other men's jobs. It was important they understood every man's position. The last thing they needed was an accident.

It was almost eleven when Deion glanced out the window. Even with the light from the nearby apartment windows, the sky was an inky black. The men and women of Aleppo had briefly enjoyed the evening, taking the opportunity to eat and talk before turning in, and now the streets below were deserted, the sound of traffic a muted rumble in the distance.

He watched as Stratello and Young moved from their positions at each end of the street. From a distance, both men appeared to be locals. He was impressed. With their dark tans and beards, he would never have guessed they were Delta Operators.

Taylor had disappeared shortly before, carrying a long canvas bag. Now Deion's earpiece crackled. "I'm in position. You have overlook."

Deion nodded. Taylor's sniper rifle would provide them protection if needed. He turned to John, who was putting on the last of the Battlesuit. The transformation was terrifying. The black liquid armor panels gave John a sleek, almost space-age look, the impression only reinforced when John closed the VISOR's clamshell.

Deion had asked Doctor Elliot why the VISOR's face was smooth, and Elliot had replied that it provided more protection, but then admitted that a faceless, featureless black carbon-fiber helmet scared the daylights out of enemy combatants.

John holstered his M11s, then picked up his HK. It was a cut-down version of his usual HK417, chambered for a 7.62mm round, and had excellent stopping power. John inserted a magazine and cycled the bolt, then turned to Deion and bowed his head.

Deion gave him the thumbs-up. "Flipper, everything you see is classified. It never happened, you dig?"

Morse stared at John's suit, open-mouthed. "Holy shit. I … I've heard rumors, I just never *believed* them."

Deion scowled, then turned to Redman.

Redman stared at the ceiling. "He didn't hear it from me, brother."

They had worked with numerous Operators and SEALs over the past two years. It was crazy to assume that no one would talk about the mysterious young man in the fancy combat gear.

"I want you ready to go," Deion said. "In the meantime, we need to pack this gear and be prepared to haul ass."

Redman nodded. They packed up and carried the gear to the vans.

When they got back, John was waiting. "I saw something. A man entered Nazer's apartment building."

Damn. They had just stowed their gear. "We saw others enter the building," Deion reminded him.

"I know," John said, "but this man had *blond* hair."

"How could you tell? It's dark."

John tapped his hand against the VISOR. "Multiple overlays. Blond hair shows up differently."

The VISOR's computer could extract more information and process it visually, something Deion kept forgetting. "You think it's Al-Hakim?"

"How many blond-haired young men would be meeting someone in the *one* building in Syria that has a *known* AQ member, who is in *contact* with a terrorist cell, that *might* have bought a nuke?"

"Dang," Redman said with a big smile pasted across his face. "He's got you, brother. He sounds kinda like Wise, don't he?"

Deion sighed and activated his mic. "Nancy, we have a complication. We think Al-Hakim is here."

Moments later, Eric joined the call. "You've got a visual on Al-Hakim?"

"We believe so." He relayed John's description.

"We can't pass this up," Eric said. "You can take both of them?"

"Yes. We're T minus forty from our extraction."

"Speed it up. I want them both in Turkey. Nancy, you're in charge of the interrogation. All means necessary. I *want* the location of that nuke."

CHAPTER SIX

JOHN CREPT THROUGH the apartment building. His VISOR showed the darkened hallway in vivid detail. It also picked up the faint sound of televisions. The few people left awake would soon turn in for the night, and he wanted to grab the two men and be on their way before they roused the building.

He turned to look back at Morse, who wore NVGs and clutched his MP5SD. Mark was at the end of the hallway, watching their exit. He pointed to Nazer's door and signaled for Morse to move to the right of it and hug the wall.

"I'm in position," he whispered.

"Do you need activation?" Deion asked.

He considered it. The Implant was amazing, but not always necessary. While the drugs boosted his strength and attention, the Implant carried a finite amount. Refilling it required Doctor Elliot to guide needles through his abdomen using a CT machine, replenishing the chambers of the Implant. It didn't hurt, but he didn't enjoy it, either.

"I'm good."

"Your call," Deion said. "On *your* mark."

"Got it." He took several deep breaths, then stepped back and kicked the door, the shock running up his good leg. The strength training paid off as the door splintered around the lock and swung open.

He surged forward, his HK tracking from left to right, looking for movement.

The two men sitting at the table looked up. He registered surprise on their faces. Nazer, with his dark hair and slight beard, gawked, but the young man with blond hair jumped from the table and was reaching for a short-stocked AK-47.

Unlike in the movies and television shows, the suppressor on his HK didn't eliminate the sound of the gun firing. But, with the low-grain ammo, it quieted the report. He was taking a calculated risk. The sound might wake the neighbors, but he had to stop Al-Hakim without killing him.

Time slowed, and he fired once, near Al-Hakim's AK. The young man jerked back, then rushed toward him.

So much for doing the smart thing. Nazer was rooted in his chair, and John knew that Morse had him covered. Al-Hakim was another story. As he approached, John snapped the butt of his rifle against the man's head. The effect was instant as Al-Hakim dropped to the floor. John took the opportunity to jam his prosthetic foot against the man's chest, pinning the struggling man in place.

Nazer took it all in, then slowly raised his hands. The fight was over before it began.

John nodded toward Morse, then spoke. "We got them."

It was the last thing he said before there was a crash through the window and an explosion of sound and light knocked him unconscious.

* * *

Deion had a fraction of a second to process the sound of the RPG firing before the room across the street exploded.

He dropped under the windowsill as debris blew across the street and slammed into the wall of the apartment building where they hid. The roar of the explosion was deafening in the small space. He shook his head, trying to clear the ringing from his ears.

There was shouting in his earpiece, and he realized it was Taylor Martin.

"I'm taking fire," Taylor shouted.

"What's the sitrep?" Eric demanded.

Next to him, Redman was scrambling to stand, pointing across the street. He staggered up and peered through the windowsill. The glass had been blown away, and only razor-sharp shards poking from the top and bottom remained.

The wall of Nazer's apartment was gone. There was thick smoke inside, and small fires cast shadows through the haze.

"An RPG just took out Nazer," Deion said. "TM, what do you see?"

"I'm pinned down," Taylor said. "I can't see anything. One shooter, I think. Probably the guy with the RPG, to my east."

The operation has gone to shit.

They had only minutes before the Syrians arrived. If they were caught on Syrian soil, their chance of survival was close to that of a snowball in hell. "Mark, what do you see?"

"Christ, it's a mess. I'm inside. John isn't moving." There was a pause. "Flipper is dead. Nazer and Al-Hakim, too."

"Nancy," Deion said, "how much time do we have?"

There was a pause. "Four minutes. Maybe five."

Above, the gunfire trailed away. "The shooter is leaving," Taylor said.

Before Deion could order Taylor to pursue, Eric preempted him. "Do *not* engage. Get the bodies and any evidence and get out."

Deion gritted his teeth. He wanted to lead a full-scale assault on the man or men who had just killed one of theirs, but Eric was right. They couldn't be taken by the Syrians. "Mark, start gathering evidence. Stratello and Young, grab body bags and get your asses up there. TM, watch for police. Redman and I will help load the bodies."

Redman's face flushed but he nodded. "Make it happen, people, before we wind up in a Syrian jail."

Deion led Redman through the hallway. A few heads poked out, but the now-wakened locals quickly slammed their doors shut when they saw the grim-faced men running through their building.

They exited the building and entered Nazer's, and the same opening and slamming of doors repeated itself. "Locals are stirred up," Deion said into his mic.

"Don't worry about them," Nancy said. "Get the bodies out of there."

They entered the remains of Nazer's apartment. The apartment was trashed. Nazer's few possessions were strewn across the floor. Stratello and Young loaded Nazer and Al-Hakim into green body bags while Mark stuffed notebooks in a canvas bag.

John stirred, then sat up and frantically ram his hands over the body armor. "What happened?"

"RPG," Deion said. "You hurt?"

John turned his head from side to side. "VISOR says my vitals are elevated, but I feel fine, except for the pain in my arm."

John raised his arm and Deion saw the armor gaping open, a long bloody gash across his forearm. He noticed John's right hip holster was missing, and saw another deep cut across his thigh. "What about your leg?"

John struggled to stand, then collapsed to the floor. "Oh, hell!"

"You've got three minutes," Nancy said.

Deion knelt and took John's emergency medical kit from his belt, removed the clotting agent, tore open the paper pouch, and dumped the contents into John's leg and arm wounds. He saw John's M11, still in its hip holster a few feet away. It had been blown off the webbing. He grabbed the gun and hauled John to his feet, then bent down and slung the young man over his shoulder, picking him up in a fireman's carry.

Redman had Morse's body slung over his shoulder, and Stratello and Young both carried a dead terrorist. Mark led them down to the vans, his own HK held in front, the bag full of evidence hanging from his neck.

Deion helped John into the back of the lead van. The street was a mishmash of lit windows, and men and women watched fearfully from the relative safety of their apartments.

He grabbed a pair of smoke grenades, pulled the pins, and tossed them in each direction. "TM, fall back to your pickup position."

The grenades whumped and began filling the street with billowing clouds of smoke. The smoke would provide them with visual cover, but also contained metals to confound any IR and thermal imaging. They tore off in the vans, screeching to a halt at the end of the block, where Taylor jumped in. Deion took the opportunity to fling another pair of grenades down the street as Redman floored it.

They turned north on a side street as sirens filled the air and were soon heading east again, following a route Redman and his team had mapped the day before.

It was a tense twenty minutes before the sound of wailing sirens receded in the background.

Nancy's voice crackled through his earpiece. "I've diverted a Predator and we're tracking your movement. You need to get across the border as soon as possible."

"Understood."

"How is John?" Eric asked.

He glanced back through the partition and saw John swaying as the van bounced over rough streets. "John?"

John popped the VISOR and the front clamshell opened. His face was pale. "I'll live. What happened?"

"You already asked that."

"I did?"

Redman gave him a sidelong glance. "The boy done had his bell rung."

"Just sit back and try not to bleed to death," Deion ordered.

John slumped against the van's wall. "I'll work on that."

* * *

Area 51

Karen pounded on Dewey's office door. There was a rattling, and then the door opened and Dewey appeared. He was disheveled, and his clothes hung loosely on his lanky frame.

She wrinkled her nose. "When was the last time you showered?"

He smiled, but his eyes were unfocused. "Sorry, got busy. It was a bear putting all the pieces together."

He ushered her into his office and directed her to one of the empty desks covered by an electrostatic mat. He pointed to a disassembled camera. "That is a standard PanDigitech CCTV camera. Same model as the ones used in Nashville. Weatherproof, decent resolution, networked back to the DOT's server farm. Nothing suspicious, right?"

"It *looks* like a regular CCTV camera."

"Right," he agreed, then carefully picked up the circuit board by his fingertips. "*This* is where things get interesting. The board appears clean. The code is clean. But when I sniffed the traffic, I found a keep-alive packet being sent to an IP in China. It was phoning home."

Her stomach sank. "It's in the hardware, isn't it?"

"Bingo. The IC chip for the wireless network adapter has the code embedded in the hardware." He tossed the circuit board up in the air and caught it. "This is some cool shit. Someone knows what they're doing. I did the same thing back in 2003. Great minds think alike, eh? I pulled some of the same ICs from a few other devices. They *all* have the *same* malware."

"This can't be the work of a terror group."

Dewey clucked his tongue. "It's not some Al-Qaeda offshoot, I can tell you that." He dropped the card on the mat. "I tracked the IC manufacturer to South Korea. It's a conglomerate. They make ICs for literally *everybody*. Those ICs are used by *everything*. Pretty scary. I've written up a briefing. It's going to take years to track down all the equipment that uses that chip and get it replaced."

A new thought occurred to her. "What about other chips from that manufacturer?"

"A random sampling shows hardware-embedded malware in most of them."

"We've got to run this up to the Old Man."

"The research is in your inbox. Knock yourself out. *I'm* going to sleep."

He turned and began to shuffle away, but she caught his arm. "You'll get credit for this, Dewey. This is a big find with big implications."

"I don't need credit," he said with a yawn. "Besides, I have *other* stuff to work on."

He staggered to his bedroom and slammed the door behind him. She shook her head. All Dewey wanted was a steady supply of interesting problems. Fortunately for him, the OTM had a never-ending series of problems.

* * *

Washington, D.C.

He woke from his dream, thrashing about wildly before finding the thin blanket and clutching it tightly to his chest. He blinked several times to clear his eyes. The bedroom was dimly lit, and he could barely see the brown age spots on his hand. For a moment, he thought they belonged to a stranger. They were the weathered and broken hands of an old man. He tried to *think*, to reconnect to the world, to remember who—and where—he was.

The only thing he remembered was the dream. It was a jumble of images, dark rooms and hallways, maps of the world hanging from walls of steel huts, an unbearable heat as men moved pins around a map. He remembered basic training and a drill instructor named Joseph Wise. He remembered meeting someone important, a short, balding man who cursed in a gravelly voice.

Slowly but surely, Smith's memories returned. He was in his apartment bedroom in D.C., a place that hardly felt familiar. His bladder was full, and he tried to remember the location of the bathroom. He staggered up and made it in time to void in the toilet. The stream came in starts and stops, a sensation that felt more familiar.

The longer he stood in front of the toilet, the more he remembered. The apartment contained his bed, changes of clothes, and a bare minimum of bottled water and soup cans in the kitchen.

He returned to the bedroom and found his briefcase, a shiny metal box, on top of the dresser. Inside was a secure cell phone, a weathered Colt M1911, and a folder. He removed the folder and climbed back into bed, switching on the nightstand lamp. He opened the folder and thumbed through the papers until he found the series of mathematical puzzles that Hobert had given him. He ran through them, trying to clear his mind.

His memory was slipping, and there was nothing he could do about it. Hobert was dosing him well above maximum, but it was a race against time.

I'm going to have to tell her. Soon.

His thoughts turned to the man Nancy had killed after John Frist had stopped Abdullah the Bomber. She had to know he would be alerted when Jim Rumple was found dead in his apartment from a bullet to the head. True, Rumple had almost cost Nancy her life, not to mention valuable HUMINT.

He had planned on assigning Rumple an unpleasant detail in Eastern Europe and then forcing his retirement, but Nancy had disrupted those plans. It had taken considerable time and effort on his part to clean it up, and even more to ensure Eric knew nothing of it.

His daughter's temperament had improved considerably since her assassination of Rumple, but he wondered if his only child was capable of handling the world without him.

She has so much anger, so much hate.

Nancy didn't care about rules or proprieties. She was cunning and ruthless. Those traits had served her well in the field but caused him considerable concern.

Will she survive without me?

He needed more time. He opened the folder and replaced the puzzles with another page. It was his last hope. He had tasked the boy in the basement—the strange, smart one—with the research. He didn't want Hob finding out until the device was ready.

It must *work.*

He would finally have to bring Hobert and Elliot together and loop them in. The operation would have to happen soon, before it was too late.

CHAPTER SEVEN

Turkey

THEY BYPASSED SEVERAL roadblocks and impromptu checkpoints with Nancy's help, doubling back three times before they reached the Turkish border. The guards, who had previously waved them through for a small bribe, demanded an exorbitant amount of money but finally agreed to let them pass for two thousand dollars in US currency.

Three miles past the border, they slowed and were met by a convoy of Rangers. Deion spoke to the soldier driving the first Humvee, and they were soon barreling through the mountain passes. They arrived at Incirlik Air Base, outside of Adana, well after the sun was high in the sky and baking the dry brown earth.

The drive had given Deion time to think. Someone had known Nazer's location. Someone had known that Al-Hakim would join him. Maybe it was the same group who had executed Sadir. He shook his head. It was like fighting a nebulous cloud, just out of sight and always one step ahead of them.

They entered the base and made their way to the hangar, where Nancy waited with a team of doctors, technicians, and airmen. The airmen unloaded the bodies of Al-Hakim and Nazer and placed them on plywood tables where the forensic technicians could do their work.

Redman helped Stratello and Young unload the body of Sean Morse and placed it on a gurney. The men milled about, joined by Taylor and Mark, and they paid their last respects with a moment of bowed heads and softly uttered prayers.

Deion helped John to another table, where the nurses and doctors removed his body armor and went to work cleaning and stitching his wounds.

Nancy joined them. Her eyes sparkled with anger, but when she saw Frist, naked except for a bloodstained white sheet across his pelvis, her expression softened. "John?"

John gave her a thumbs-up with his good arm. "Sorry for almost dying, ma'am."

Nancy shook her head. "You don't have to call me ma'am. We're going to find out who did this, I promise." She turned to the doctors. "How bad is it?"

The first doctor, a young man with short red hair, regarded her coolly. "I'm cautiously optimistic. His wounds are deep, but not life-threatening. He's not in shock. Luckily, the clotting agent stopped most of the blood loss." The doctor looked at the disassembled Battlesuit resting on the concrete floor. "I don't know *what* kind of body armor that is, but it saved his life. If he hadn't been wearing it, the shrapnel would've shredded him and we'd be having a very different conversation."

John looked up, eyes unfocused. "I had *that* going for me."

"Do whatever it takes," Nancy said to the doctor. "When you're finished, update his medical records and give them to me." She turned to John and said, "Just relax."

John glanced around. "Gotcha, Nance."

Deion choked back a laugh at the expression on Nancy's face.

"Nance?" she asked.

The red-haired doctor pressed John firmly back to the table.

"It's the drugs," John said with a wink, tapping his finger against his temple. "They make me strange in the head."

A nurse plunged a needle into John's arm and his eyes snapped wide, then he relaxed against the table and his eyes closed.

"Sorry," the nurse said, "but it's better if he quits moving."

"Carry on," Nancy said. She spun on her heels and headed for the table where the forensic technicians worked. "Coming with me?"

Deion followed, and they found the technicians working on the dead bodies. The smell of blood and bowel was thick in the air, and Deion gagged, then saw Nancy watching out of the corner of her eye. He bit back the bitter taste of bile and shook his head.

Nancy noticed the look on his face and rolled her eyes. "What have you found?" she asked the lead technician.

The man pointed at a cell phone lying on the corner of the table. "We found that. We'll have the SIM card removed and analyzed as soon as possible."

Nancy glanced down at the phone, then back to the technician. "I want it double time, understand?"

The technician gulped. "We'll have our best people on it."

Nancy turned and grabbed Deion by his arm. "Get Redman and your team. Meet me in my office."

"You got it." He tracked down Redman and the others watching a pair of young airmen loading Morse's body into a truck. "Boss lady wants to speak to us."

They followed him to the far side of the hangar, where the airmen had built a temporary office from two-by-fours and plywood sheets. Inside, they took seats at the wooden table with Nancy at the head. A large laptop rested on a shelf behind her, and when they were seated, she clicked on the button and initiated the video call.

A small room appeared. Eric was sitting next to Clark in the conference room at Area 51. "I'm sorry, Bill. Sean was a good man. A good Operator."

Redman stared off into the distance, then turned back to the monitor. "Yes, he was."

"He had a wife, didn't he?" Eric asked. "Rita?"

Redman shook his head. "They divorced last year. She was riding his ass about spending so much time away from home. He has a son. Griff. He's seven. Lives with his mom."

"We'll look after them. My organization takes care of its own."

Redman's eyes focused on the monitor. "He wanted to go out a warrior. Doing something important. I think a loose nuke qualifies. It's all a man can ask for."

Taylor and Mark nodded their assent.

On the screen, Eric bowed his head. "It is, brother."

Redman looked around the table. "You have a problem. Who fired that RPG?"

"That's what we need to find out. Let's do the hot wash. Maybe the techs will have something by the time we're done."

* * *

Around the table, the faces were grim. Nancy's hands balled into fists as she spoke. Redman's comments were terse, interjected between Nancy and Eric's questioning. Mark and Taylor recounted their actions in precise detail.

Deion struggled to remain calm. The hot wash was thorough but did nothing to illustrate their mistakes. They had performed well, given the mission's parameters. Flipper's death was the result of a third-party combatant, an enemy they couldn't identify.

That's twice. We've lost three suspects and a good Operator. We don't even know who we're fighting!

There was a soft knock on the plywood door, and the lead technician entered the room. "We've analyzed the SIM card and uploaded the data. You can track Al-Hakim's movements and calls."

Eric's face disappeared as the laptop display changed to a world map, then homed in on Somalia. "This is the port of Eyl," the technician said. "It's the base of operations for pirates attacking ships in the Gulf of Aden."

The map shrank and Eric's face reappeared. "A SEAL team worked there just a couple months ago. How solid is this data?"

"We've tracked every cell tower that Al-Hakim's phone pinged," the technician said. "Over the last three days, he traveled from Somalia to Yemen, on to Saudi Arabia, then passed through Iraq and into Syria."

There was a long pause. "Just about the time Sadir was executed," Deion said. "He hightailed it to Syria to speak with Nazer, then got wasted by our unknown friends."

"Sounds right," Eric said. "We know that Al-Qaeda has cells in Somalia and Yemen. I'm putting Karen on this. If anyone can find something, it's her."

* * *

They were still discussing the implications of Al-Hakim's location when Karen appeared on the screen. Deion was shocked by the intensity on her face.

She really needs to lay off the coffee.

"I've backtracked Al-Hakim's location to within a couple hundred yards in Eyl," Karen said. The location appeared on the map, highlighted in red. "We're talking a mile inland of the Gulf." The map zoomed in to the southeast. "This is the port where the pirates moor their mother ships. After they hijack a ship, they take the prisoners inland while anchoring the vessels offshore or in coves farther north. There are currently twelve ships still being held by pirates, and over fifty different men being held for ransom."

"Does JSOC have intel on this?" Deion asked.

Eric reappeared on screen. "Of course. The negotiations are delicate. Somalia has a collection of warlords instead of a functioning government. JSOC vetted numerous plans to invade and wipe out the pirates, but Mogadishu spooked the international community. Plus, millions are starving. The aid groups are hard-pressed to feed them, and the CDC is monitoring outbreaks of dozens of diseases. A full-blown invasion gone wrong would cause an international backlash."

Everyone at the table shook their heads in disgust. Deion knew that most of the pirates were local fisherman who were furious that large shipping vessels dumped pollutants into the Gulf of Aden, causing massive fish kills. They had first organized as a makeshift coastguard, trying to bring attention to their plight, but soon found that ransoms paid more than fishing. A cartel of warlords and kingpins ran the pirating as a lucrative business, farming out the work to the poor and desperate young men of Somalia, many of them stoned out of their gourd on khat.

The pirates blocked shipments of food and medicines the rest of the country desperately needed. It was a vicious circle. Starving Somalis emboldened the pirates, but the more ships hijacked, the fewer supplies made it to the people, leading to more piracy.

Eric vanished, and the map reappeared, this time zooming out to the Gulf. "Here's where it gets interesting," Karen said. A blob of red appeared. "This is a South Korean cargo vessel, the MV *Rising Star*. Watch."

The red blob approached the eastern edge of Somalia.

"I don't understand," Deion said.

"It appears it was hijacked, but it was too far out for the speedboats from Eyl. The only way it could have been hijacked was if the speedboats were launched from a mother ship, and there was no mother ship nearby."

"So, it wasn't hijacked?"

"It would appear not. This was the day before John's mission in Syria."

"Where's the *Rising Star* now?"

"It's nearing the southern tip of Somalia, but moving very slowly."

"I think it was carrying the nuke," Eric said.

"What do we know about the ship?" Taylor asked.

The screen split and both Eric and Karen appeared. "It's owned by a South Korean company called the Jade Group," Karen said, "only the Jade Group isn't real. It's a shell corp, and the deeper I dig, the more dummy paperwork I find. I've never seen *anything* like it."

Deion let that sink in. A shell corp that Karen, one of the smartest data analysts on the planet, could not track. "Am I alone in thinking this is way beyond Al-Qaeda?"

"What kind of player has that kind of resources?" Mark asked. "Staying with Islamic fanatics, it would have to be a state-backed group. Iran, maybe? If it's a private group, it would have to have deep pockets. A member of the Saudi royal family?"

Deion was impressed. Mark was a good Operator with a wry sense of humor, but he also possessed a keen mind.

"It gets worse," Karen said. "We have new information about Nashville. We've analyzed the traffic cameras, and Dewey found malware built into the integrated circuits. They phone home to an IP in China, an IP I've been unable to hack."

Dewey? The goofball with the TV fixation? "How hard is it to put malware into an IC?"

"We're talking either *serious* money or nation-state backing," Eric said. "It gives them a backdoor into so many devices that it boggles the mind. They assassinated Sadir, then used the backdoors to turn off the video surveillance in Nashville. The same enemy probably killed Nazer and Al-Hakim. We've got no idea who it is, what kind of resources they have, or what their motivation is." He scowled. "We have to face facts. We are at *war.*"

CHAPTER EIGHT

Honolulu, Hawaii

KONG GREETED HIM with, "There were complications. The Americans."

"Not unexpected. We have planned for such an event."

"Yes. Everything is in place."

Their operation was reaching the tipping point. "Good. I have faith in you. Proceed."

Kong bowed his head and terminated the video call.

Huang Lei stood and approached the thick glass window. Below, the city stretched to the water's edge. He peered down, watching people in their early-morning commute, no more than specks as they bustled among the streets, off to their jobs in the dawning light.

How could it come to this?

The Americans. Always the Americans. They wielded their outsized influence without thought or discretion. They lumbered from crisis to crisis, spilling blood around the world, wrecking lives and destroying economies with dismal results.

That will soon end. Order will be restored. The world will emerge from madness and my people will finally flourish.

* * *

Turkey

The dream. Always the same dream. He stood on a roof a hundred yards from the Red Cross building in Fairfax, Virginia. It was a blustery Tuesday in January, and the wind knifed through his thin jacket. He pulled his hat low with one hand, readjusting his binoculars with the other, and watched in horror as the yellow school bus pulled into the parking lot. He wanted to scream, to get their attention and wave them off. He wanted to save them but knew he couldn't.

Because that's not how it happened.

The children piled out of the school bus, and even from his distant vantage point, he heard their shrieks, their banter, the playful sounds of youth. They were happy to be on a field trip, visiting one of their fathers, who worked there. None of them paid any attention to the white Ryder truck only thirty feet from the entrance.

He felt rising panic, a black void of dread that threatened to swallow him. He couldn't stop what was about to happen, no matter how much he wished and no matter how hard he tried.

A part of him whispered in the back of his head.

This is desperation. This is insanity. You deserve this, monster.

His heart raced, thump-thumping so hard he thought it might burst. He tried to turn away, to shield himself from the carnage below.

It was too late.

It wasn't like in the movies. There wasn't a slow roll of fire that blossomed out, creating a yellow ball of flame that grew and grew until it struck the building.

It wasn't like that at all. It was sudden, so sudden.

The truck disintegrated in a cloud of smoke. The blast wave struck the bus and ripped it to pieces. Children were blown apart in a jumble of arms, and legs, and heads, and blood. It happened so fast he couldn't quite grasp the image, and then the building shook and the front erupted in a billowing cloud of concrete and debris. He saw the front of the building collapsing through the black-and-gray cloud, and then the shock wave slammed into him and knocked him to the rooftop. His body slid through the loose gravel as the roar of sound hit, hammering him senseless.

Then, the building was intact. The school bus was gone. Just his Ryder truck, full of ammonium nitrate and diesel fuel, parked in front. He tried to gasp for air.

I'm going to relive it. Again.

Always the same dream.

The school bus was rounding the corner and approaching the front of the Red Cross building when he felt something new. A pressure on his arm.

He jerked awake and saw Taylor Martin standing over him. It all came rushing back. He had been hit. An RPG.

He remembered the docs working on his arm and leg, cleaning and stitching the wound, then a shot to help him sleep.

He was on a gurney in the hangar, thirty feet from the Gulfstream, and he was naked, IVs in both arms, a thin white sheet covering him in the heat. A breeze blew through the hangar, rustling the corner of the sheet, and he shivered.

Taylor grinned. "Welcome back to the land of the living."

John groaned. "I was dreaming. I was dreaming I was in hell, then I woke up, saw your face, and realized it *wasn't* a dream."

"Come on," Taylor said with a smirk. "No rest for the wicked."

"How long was I out?"

"About four hours. How do you feel?"

John thought about it for a moment. "I'm sore."

Taylor pointed to an IV bag. "You can thank one of those."

He recognized the bag, a standard piece of kit, thanks to Doctors Elliot and Oshensker. They carried plastic cases full of them in the Gulfstream, along with the rest of their gear. It was the same sea snail–based painkiller that he carried in his Implant. It was a thousand times more powerful than morphine, but with none of the side effects.

He pulled the sheet back. Thin gel strips ran the length of the wound on his arm, another gift from the docs. He knew from previous experience the drugs in the gel acted as an antibiotic, keeping the wound clean, and other compounds in the gel would speed the healing process and minimize scar tissue. He pulled back the blanket even farther and saw the same gel strip on his leg.

The wounds were ugly shades of purple and yellow, but were days ahead in the healing process. He flexed his arm. It ached, but he almost had a full range of motion.

He squinted at Taylor. "What did the medics say?"

"They weren't thrilled about shooting you up with experimental drugs," Taylor said, "until Nancy threatened them. They backed off real quick."

He shivered again. Nancy had a command authority presence like none he'd ever seen, and her dead eyes turned that up a notch to completely terrifying. "How's the suit?"

"The VISOR is good, but the suit is damaged. Good thing we brought along your spare, because we're deploying soon."

"Deploying to where?"

"They think the package was delivered to a pirate village in Somalia. A place called Eyl."

He rolled his eyes. "A pirate village? Good lord, what next?"

"It gets better. They're afraid the ship that delivered it might have another. We're going in hot while a SEAL team hits the ship."

"But Eric hates big missions. Too much exposure."

"Yep, but the risk is too great. We'll be flying out soon. You think you can make it?"

He laughed before he could stop himself. "Do I have a choice?"

"Nope," Taylor said, then grabbed his good arm and helped him up.

A worried-looking medic approached. "He can't be moved yet."

Taylor stopped her with a stare. "This *soldier* has work to do."

The medic shook her head. "This is against protocol. I'm going to have to report this."

John caught her attention. "Please don't. It would be best if you just forgot we were here."

The medic frowned, hazel eyes full of concern, then she bit her lip and removed the IVs, covering the skin with gauze and tape where the blood welled up. She left, glancing over her shoulder on the way out.

Taylor opened one of the black cases next to the Gulfstream and handed him underwear. "Hey, Mark said that hottie nurse back home asked about you."

"Kara? She's just … doing her job."

"Sure. She's got no other motives, huh? Have you and her…?"

"Not yet." He struggled to pull his underwear up without disturbing the gel strip on his leg. Taylor handed him a skintight one-piece suit, made of a cotton-like material, a new creation of Elliot's. It wicked away moisture and kept him cool and dry, but also contained a fine wire mesh that provided electrical stimulation to trigger his body's healing response.

Taylor coughed. "Look, it ain't my business, but the job we have? Take your opportunities when you get them. We're the walking wounded, and every mission could be our last. Don't miss out. *Seize* the day."

He considered Taylor's advice. If only he could tell him that his memory was back, that he remembered doing terrible things, that Kara Tulli had *hated* him, that his life was complicated and death might be the *only* release from his memories. "TM?"

"Yeah?"

"Shut the fuck up."

Taylor laughed. "Suit up, cowboy. Time to get back in the saddle."

* * *

Washington, D.C.

Smith waited patiently for his breakfast companion in the Old World splendor of the private dining room under the Golden Oak Hotel. The oak tables were stained a deep mahogany, the chairs trimmed in burgundy leather. Only one of the five tables was set, but the plates were the finest china, the flatware genuine silver, the coffee cups the same ones he had sipped from since the fifties.

He buttered a perfectly toasted slice of whole wheat bread and covered it with an orange marmalade they kept on hand just for him.

In his head, he replayed the terse conversation with Eric. His young replacement was concerned. He gently reassured Eric that it wasn't the first time they'd found themselves under siege, that there were *always* enemies at the gates.

The massive oak door swung open, and a heavyset man stepped through. His balding head was deeply tanned, and his brown suit rumpled and twenty years out-of-date.

"Vasilii," Smith said, raising his slice of toast. "You're late."

Vasilii Melamid smiled, but it never made it to his eyes. "It's been months. I thought you had forgotten your old friend."

Vasilii was the head of Group 27, a Russian think tank that performed the same function as the OTM. "Remember when we used to eat white bread? Before they started pushing fiber?"

Vasilii grunted. "To hell with fiber. I miss good steak, charred on the outside, bloody red in middle." He took a seat and glanced across the table. "Growing old is not for the weak. Is *terrible* that youth is wasted on the young." He poured coffee from the glass carafe between them, then added cold cream. "What worries you, my friend?"

Smith picked at his toast, took a bite, then washed it down with coffee. "The North Koreans have sold a device to an Islamic group."

Vasilii's eyes narrowed, the wrinkles deepening around the corner of his eyes, and he placed his coffee cup back on the table. "Bah. North Koreans are imbeciles. What do they think would come of this?"

"They play each side against the other. The pressure against them is great, but somehow they always manage to convince someone to hand them a lifeline."

The old man shrugged. "You know how game is played. I make recommendations, but sometimes is *not* enough. We've done good job, you and I. Together we kept our countries from madness. Because of this, world still exists. The people? They go about their lives with no idea how close we came."

Smith took another bite of toast. "Some might say you've not held up *your* end."

Vasilii glared at him. "Who says this? The man I risked everything for? Because of you, my country was overrun by oligarchs, and our economy collapsed. We never recovered."

Smith calmly waited for Vasilii to stop, then said, "This bomb? It is the work of a powerful group or nation. Are you saying you're not involved?"

"Involved?" Vasilii sputtered. "After all I've done, why would I allow this?" He shook his head, face splotched red. "I promise you, we have nothing to do with it."

"You speak for everyone?"

That stopped Vasilii. "You think me old? Lost touch with my people? No," he spat out. "I would know. I am not feeble old man who lost his way."

"That's what this is about?"

Vasilii placed his coffee cup on the table, and the cup clinked as his hand trembled. "I am not one who crossed line. You *knew* better."

"You're never going to find her. Even *I* don't know where she is."

The old Russian eyed him shrewdly. "I will never stop looking. Is my duty."

"And what would you do if you found her? Torture her? Kill her? How can you claim to be my friend when you would kill the woman I love?"

"Love?" Vasilii scoffed. "For love, she committed treason?"

"Remember the old Russian proverb? My neighbor has a cow, and I have no cow. I hope my neighbor's cow dies."

Vasilii's eyes narrowed. "You believe me jealous? I warned Alexandra. I warned *you*. We are not meant to have relationships. To have children. Is understood."

"You know we didn't plan for it."

"So you claim. But, it *did* happen." Vasilii shook his head sadly. "I will never stop looking for her. I cannot."

Smith watched the old Russian carefully. "Can't you let it go?" he asked softly. "You already look the other way."

"The sins of the father and mother do not translate to child. I violated my oath and let your daughter live. Is understood within my organization that your daughter remains safe."

"We are old men. I would like to see my wife while there's still time."

"Is not to be. Is not enough that you have daughter?"

No, Smith wanted to scream, *it is* not *enough*. The absence of Nancy's mother had wounded her in a way he could not heal. "This is your final decision?"

Vasilii stared at the table between them. "Where is rest of breakfast? We should have eggs. Sausage. Good rye bread. Porridge."

"I cannot change your mind." He'd known Vasilii still resented Alexandra Batalova's betrayal, and how the woman the Russians had sent to spy on Smith would suddenly have an affair, get pregnant, and forsake her country to give birth to their baby girl.

Vasilii slowly shook his head. "What is your American expression? Is not in the cards."

Smith sighed. In the twenty-nine years since Nancy's birth, he had never been so forthright with the old Russian. His time was running out, and it didn't appear that his wife would ever see her daughter again. He thought about ordering Vasilii's execution, but it pained him to think of killing the old man, not to mention the plans Vasilii had in place if he met an untimely demise.

No, he couldn't just kill Vasilii. The OTM and the Russian organization had reached equilibrium after decades of covert operations.

There was a soft knock at the door. "I'm sorry to say that breakfast will be scrambled egg whites with turkey sausage."

"Turkey sausage?" Vasilii bemoaned. "What has world come to? Better we let world burn than forced to eat like this."

His driver, Robert, entered with a small cart and placed it next to their table, then left, carefully closing the door behind him.

Smith raised the elegant silver domes from the plates to reveal their breakfast. Vasilii frowned in disgust but took his plate and began eating.

"This device the North Koreans sold," Vasilii said between mouthfuls. "I will inquire. Perhaps I find something."

"I would be terribly grateful. I just wish I could change your mind on the *other* matter."

"Bah. You are never content. Always looking for more. Eat your breakfast, old friend, and let us be about our business before your country suffers an attack that undoes our hard work."

* * *

Saudi Arabia

The C130J Hercules refueled twenty thousand feet over Saudi Arabia, just south of Prince Sultan Air Base, before flying over Yemen and on to Somalia. John watched the others through his VISOR. The vibration from the ship's airframe had rattled his teeth for the entire trip, and he felt his jaw muscles clenching. A pounding in his head, behind his eyes, made it impossible for him to catch any sleep.

They hadn't begun prebreathing, but would have to start soon or risk suffering hypoxia. Deion was talking to Redman at the front of the cargo bay, while Stratello and Young sat with Taylor and Mark, checking their gear with practiced ease.

His VISOR's coms dinged. "John?" Eric asked. "How are you feeling?"

He checked the com signal and found it was a personal satellite call, directed just to him. "Not one hundred percent, but I'll push through."

"I don't have to tell you how important this mission is. You know what that device could do."

John knew. He could see it in his mind as the bomb detonated in New York City, turning downtown Manhattan into a cinder in the blink of an eye. He shuddered. "Don't worry about me."

"Remember, your mission is to recover that device. Nothing else matters. Not the Operators. Not Deion. You kill anyone that gets in your way, without hesitation, you understand? Above all, *recover that device.*"

"Jesus, Eric, I got it. After all I've done for the OTM, you think I can't handle it?"

There was a long pause, then Eric said, "I'm proud of you, John. You're a good man, better than most I've served with. The past is history. You can't forget it, but you can live for today. Do your job and save the world."

John bit his lip. "No pressure or anything."

Eric finally laughed. "Make me proud, John. Hey, I have something for you. Consider it a present. I'm transferring communications. You've got five minutes."

"John?" It was a woman's husky voice. "Are you okay?"

He checked the signal and found he was speaking directly to Kara. "Hey."

"We've reviewed the records from the doctors in Turkey. You responded well to treatment. How bad does it hurt?"

He absently stroked his arm, even though his wound was covered by the Battlesuit. It had been less than sixteen hours since his injury, but the drugs in the gel had done their job. "Feels a little sore."

"Doctor Elliot thinks you need at least forty-eight hours of downtime before redeployment."

"I'll be fine. We're dropping soon."

There was a long pause. "John? I *like* you. Take care of yourself."

For a moment, his heart soared. For all he had done, Kara had forgiven him. "Kara? I *like* you too."

* * *

Somalia

John's VISOR blazed with colored dots in constant flux as the many drones, planes, and helicopters screamed through the night on their way to Eyl. He marveled at Eric's ability to plan and implement the complex mission in such a short time frame. The logistics were daunting.

They were in the lead Hercules, and two more full of Delta Operators lined up behind them, ready to HALO drop on the north edge of the city.

Eric had managed to requisition F-22 Raptors from Al Dhafra Air Base to shadow them. CH-46 Sea Knights from the USS *Peleliu* were last in line, ready to extract the teams when their mission was complete. Above it all flew a pair of MQ-9 Reaper UAVs and an RQ-4 Global Hawk, all commandeered over the past twelve hours.

The VISOR beeped, and he saw his teammates switch their masks from the onboard oxygen prebreathing tanks to bottles strapped to their chests. He unhooked the line from his VISOR and inserted the quick-connect for his tank, and the smell changed from cool metallic to medicinal as his air transitioned to his own portable tank. The Loadmaster, a tech sergeant named Jackson, opened the top cargo door and lowered the bottom ramp, waving at them.

It's time.

Stratello jumped first, leaping from the plane and plummeting to earth, quickly followed by Young, Redman, Taylor, and Mark. Deion turned to him and nodded before jumping.

The Loadmaster gave him a thumbs-up, and it was his turn to hurl himself down the plane's deck, out the back, and into the night. The VISOR's display blazed to life, turning the night into a fluorescent wash of color.

He could make out the rest of the team, far below, in tight formation. Dots in the VISOR lit up as Operators from the following planes followed suit.

There was a moment of clarity as he plummeted to the ground, a moment in which he wasn't angry or afraid. He noted the position of their target, the placement of the dropping Operators, the position of the planes and helicopters and drones relative to him, and the mission unfolded in his mind's eye.

With clarity came sadness, a bone-tired exhaustion that tugged at him as surely as gravity, threatening to pull him under.

He heard Eric's voice through coms. "John? We're activating the Implant."

He blinked as time sped back up. Liquid fire rushed through his veins, his heart pounding like a jackhammer. The exhaustion fell away, and his mind refocused on the mission. The ground rushed to meet him as his body sang with strength. He was a giant among men, and even though he knew it was the drugs, he still felt invincible.

"Don't forget your mission," Eric said.

I couldn't forget. Even if I wanted to.

Below, chutes popped open as the Operators reached the correct altitude. Unlike the rest of the Operators, his deployed automatically, the grinding of servos transferred down the lines as the cables pulled and retracted, guiding him to the ground.

The city of Eyl stretched out to the south, a collection of houses and shacks built from stone, scrap wood, and corrugated metal. The city had a population of over twenty thousand, but it appeared poor and run-down in the VISOR's night vision. He was already too low to make out the Gulf of Aden, two miles beyond the edge of the city.

He was coming in hard and fast, and he felt a twinge of pain when he struck the ground. The impact sent an electric shock through the prosthetic, and he cursed to himself. The fresh wound on his right thigh started throbbing, even with the painkillers from the Implant.

There was a click and a pop as his parachute disconnected from his backpack. He swung his HK into place and scanned his surroundings. The VISOR indicated he was three hundred yards from their target, a squat stone building that glowed ghostly green in his night vision.

Satellite surveillance had shown a dhow, a small fishing ship, rendezvous with the MV *Rising Star* twenty miles from the coast. The dhow had returned to the beach, where a large wooden crate had been unloaded and carted to the northeastern part of the city. A drone overfly had detected unusually high traces of radiation.

Occam's razor suggested the nuclear warhead was in *that* building.

He increased the magnification and activated the thermal overlay. Dozens of heat signatures bloomed to life.

He sighed. Satellite surveillance had detected radiation in the building, but it hadn't shown all the men guarding it. "We have hostiles."

"Roger that. We're picking up the VISOR's feed. The others will be with you shortly."

He turned and watched the last of the Operators land in the desert. The rest were busy collapsing their chutes and rallying near Redman, a hundred yards to his east.

The last man unhooked his parachute, and the Operators approached with their guns raised. Counting his team, there were now over thirty Operators on the ground and ready to engage the enemy. He waved them over, and they quickly surrounded him.

Redman and Deion watched the building through their own NVGs. "You have confirmation?" Deion asked.

He pointed. "Radiation is centered there." The building was nothing more than a stone box, fifteen feet high and thirty feet square. "Four heat signatures up top. They're not moving. Another ten signatures inside." He scanned the horizon. "No other signatures and no movement. They don't know we're here."

Redman snorted. "Once we hit that building, the *whole* town is gonna know we're here."

Deion turned to the rest of the men and spoke softly. "Assume everyone in the building is Al-Qaeda. Once we attack, the Somalis will join the fight. We don't expect *them* to put up much resistance. They're fishermen, not terrorists."

There was a crackling in their earpieces and John heard Eric's voice. "Once more unto the breach."

An Operator, a short black man John didn't recognize, spoke up in a gravelly voice. "Shit, is that Steeljaw?"

"Roger that, Ironman. Secure that package and watch your six."

There was a snicker over coms, and then Ironman said, "Don't worry, Steeljaw, we're used to doing your dirty work."

John noticed several of the Operators glancing at him, trying to figure out who he was. He ignored them and lifted his HK. "I'll be moving in five. Snipers take your positions."

Eight of the Operators—four snipers and their spotters— peeled off from the group and took cover, preparing for their shots and working their targeting computers. The rest broke into smaller groups and followed him as he approached the building.

When he was within fifty yards, he motioned for them to crouch down. "Snipers, are you ready?"

The four snipers answered with affirmatives.

In his VISOR, he saw the C130 quickly approaching the inbound CH-46 Sea Knights. Soon the plane would bypass them, just in time to acquire the package, followed closely by the F-22s.

"John," Eric said. The com channel was opened just to him. "You'll have three minutes before pickup."

He calmed himself. "I'm in position."

He knew Eric had everything timed down to the second. They only had one chance.

"Wait for it," Eric said.

He took a deep breath, held it, then exhaled calmly. "On your mark."

A counter displayed on his VISOR, decrementing from ten. "Good luck, John."

He nodded to himself as he watched the counter ticking down, then the counter hit zero and Eric spoke. "Mark."

It was the moment he'd been waiting for. All the excitement and tension and the full effect of the Implant took hold. He raced across the hardscrabble rock, faster than a Olympic sprinter. He approached the stone building, his feet practically floating over the loose rock. The other Operators followed as best they could, but his training and chemically enhanced musculature allowed him to easily outpace them.

He was almost at the door when Eric said, "Snipers. Send it."

He saw the four men on the roof collapse in the overhead drone feed, and he hit the door just as the reports from the sniper rifles echoed from the rocks. He slowed long enough to kick the door with his boot, and with his forward momentum, the door blasted inward.

He had time to register the men, some sleeping on mats, some still awake in chairs, as they jerked awake from his sudden intrusion. He pulled the trigger on the AG36 grenade launcher mounted under the barrel of his HK, but instead of grenades, he launched two screamers, each the size of a tennis ball. The screamers hit the far wall and began their intense shrieking, the LEDs flashing like strobe lights. The VISOR was barely able to dampen the noise and filter out the glare. He could only imagine what it was like for the scraggly men.

Stunned, they struggled to move, but he unleashed the HK, cutting down three men sitting on low wooden stools. He didn't even have time to notice their faces before he swung his rifle across and let loose on the four men still lying on sleeping mats.

The men jerked and flopped like fish out of water, but he was already on to the remaining men. The smallest one, barely out of his teens, was desperately trying to grab his AK-47, but John's HK unloaded and bullets struck the boy's face, tearing holes in his cheek, snapping the boy's head back. The boy fell to the floor, motionless.

Two men remained. They had finally found their AK-47s, and they fumbled to get them into firing position, but the light and the sound from the screamers blinded and deafened them. They finally managed to fire on full automatic, spraying gunfire blindly, trying to kill him.

Bullets were whizzing around, and he finally noticed the wooden crate in the center of the room. It was as tall as a man, and as big around as a small refrigerator.

"Don't let them hit the bomb," Eric shouted.

Probably a good idea. He dove to the floor, dropped the magazine from his HK, and inserted a new one, all in a matter of seconds, then got busy putting some holes in each man.

They dropped where they stood, their guns going silent. He hit the trigger on the AG36 and the screamers stopped their wailing.

In the sudden quiet, he heard a noise behind him, the crunch of boots on rock.

He turned to find Deion taking in the carnage with a look of awe.

"Christ, that was amazing," Deion breathed.

John nodded, then turned back to the room. The dead and dying littered the floor, along with dirty plates from their evening meal. A few ragged blankets lay next to the men who had been sleeping, now absorbing the blood from their wounds like a sponge. In the quiet, he heard choking breaths slow and stop as the living joined the dead.

He tried not to look at their faces. Most were no older than him. The youngest appeared to stare at him with wide, glassy eyes.

It wasn't the first time the dead had stared accusingly at him, but it still sickened him. He glanced at the crate in the center of the room and consoled himself that *he* wasn't the reason they were dead.

He heard gunfire outside, amplified by the VISOR. He switched to an overhead view and saw villagers approaching from the south, firing wildly. The Operators returned fire, and he saw one of the approaching villagers fall.

Half a dozen Operators rushed inside the building, and Deion pointed to the crate. "Lift!"

John joined them, and they lifted as one, picking the crate up and carrying it out the door. The sounds of battle were everywhere.

"Fast movers inbound," Eric said, right before a massive pair of explosions rocked the ground. John shook his head as he saw the giant plumes of light in his VISOR. The bombs detonated at the edge of a dusty street not far south of them, and the resulting wave of dust and debris temporarily blocked them from the rest of Eyl.

He tried not to think of how many innocents might have died in that blast, wives and children who knew nothing of the terrorists using Eyl as a waypoint.

He had a mission. There was no time to dally.

They carried the crate dozens of yards to the north. A pair of Operators had spread a nylon net on the ground, and they placed the crate in the center of it. He watched as the Operator to his right cinched up the rope, then took a metal canister the size of a beach ball from a duffel bag and attached a hose. The Operator's partner unloaded another duffel bag and quickly did the same. Together, they attached the hoses to a third bag, and when they flipped the valves on the tanks, the bag burst at the seams and quickly inflated into a giant balloon.

John knew about the Fulton Recovery System, but it was the first time he had seen it in use. There was a bright blinking from the bottom of the balloon, a laser strobe that—combined with a GPS signal—would guide the Hercules for pickup.

He watched the radar signature as the Hercules closed in. It had been in a holding pattern over the Gulf of Aden, and as soon as they dropped, it had started its approach. It was moving slowly, right above its stall speed, and he turned to the east and saw the ghostly outline of the plane hugging the horizon.

"Preparing for pickup," the Hercules pilot said over coms.

"The helicopters are almost there," Eric said.

"Roger that," Deion said, then raised his arms and pointed to the north. The Operators ran, heading for their exfiltration point. Sporadic gunfire echoed from the south, but the villagers offered no serious threat as Deion led them to the LZ.

John turned back to the south as the Hercules flew overhead, so low he thought he could reach out and touch it, and then there was a whoosh as the hooks on the front of the plane caught the cable and snatched the wooden crate from the ground.

A whump-whump began to thrum through his chest as the pair of CH-46 Sea Knights came rumbling through the sky. It was only moments after the Hercules scooped up the bomb before the helicopters' wake turned the LZ into a dirty hurricane of dust. They quickly scrambled aboard, filling both Sea Knights.

The pilots had the Sea Knights in the air just seconds after the last Operators climbed in. They headed east, then banked and headed back over the Gulf toward the USS *Peleliu*.

John leaned back in his seat and felt a tremor in his arm. No matter how fantastic the drugs in the Implant, they couldn't overcome basic human anatomy. He needed downtime to rest and let his wounded arm and leg heal. More importantly, and something he would never admit to Deion or Eric, he needed time to mentally process the battle, both in Eyl *and* in Aleppo.

"Good work, gentlemen," Eric said. "We have the package."

John sighed. Not a single Operator had been lost, and they had recovered a nuclear bomb. The crew members in the Hercules would be winching the crate onboard, heading northeast to Yemen and then back to Prince Sultan Air Base.

There was a collective whoop as the Operators finally let out their pent-up emotions. He watched as Deion high-fived Redman. Redman broke into a big grin and turned to slap Stratello and Young on the back.

John felt a hand on his shoulder.

"Hell of a job," Taylor yelled over the sound of the rotors.

He allowed himself a rare smile. "Thanks, TM."

Mark reached over and lightly slapped him on the back of the VISOR. "What he said."

He took a deep breath. *It's over.*

It was his last thought before the VISOR's display went crazy. They lost power, and the back of the helicopter plunged into darkness.

CHAPTER NINE

THE SEA KNIGHT plummeted toward the Gulf of Aden. John heard Operators yelling, telling each other to prepare for impact, and his stomach lurched into his throat. An emergency light flickered to life as the Sea Knight's engines went silent, but there was still a whoosh-whoosh as the blades continued to spin.

The VISOR's display came alive in a flash of color. To their northeast, there was a giant ball of red. The coms channel shrieked with static and feedback before going silent.

A voice he had heard once before—the VISOR's emergency protocol AI—spoke up. "EMP detected. John, are you okay?"

"Yeah," John said, "but I'm about to crash into the ocean!"

"Your vital signs are elevated. Please remain calm. You are about to crash into the ocean?"

He wanted to smack Doc Elliot. The AI had barely saved him in New York City, and now it was once again going through its protocol, trying to figure out how to save his life. "Yes!"

"Okay, you are about to crash into the ocean. John, the VISOR has three minutes of air. Once you enter the water, you will have time to ensure your survival. Can you swim?"

"Stop talking!"

Deion was staring at him from the other side of the helicopter. "What the hell is going on?"

He had the same question, but an EMP could only mean one thing.

The bomb detonated.

He pointed to the package stowed at the front of the cabin. "Grab the life raft!"

Deion gave him a thumbs-up and started barking orders to the men. John lurched to his feet and ran the length of the helicopter until reaching the cockpit. The pilot and copilot were screaming at each other, and he grabbed the pilot's shoulder.

"What's our altitude?"

"Six hundred feet and descending fast," the pilot said through clenched teeth. "Right before we hit, I'll flare, and the nose will lift. When that happens, tell the men to egress!"

"Copy that!" He ran back through the helicopter. The battery-powered emergency lighting barely illuminated the cabin. Redman and his men were handing out life vests, and Taylor and Mark had the life raft ready to go.

"Drop your gear," Deion shouted.

As one, the Operators began shucking their packs and equipment. John pulled his M-11s and threw them in the corner, along with his HK. The only thing left was his emergency medical pack, but it was integrated into a hard pouch on his waist. He grabbed the door handle, braced himself for the blast of air, then pried it open.

He turned to Taylor and Mark. "When the nose pitches up, be prepared to jump."

The men nodded. The Sea Knight was dropping fast, but suddenly it shook violently, then the nose pitched up. "That's it!"

There was a brief hesitation when the helicopter's descent stalled, and then it dropped like a stone. When it hit the water, he felt the stinging impact all the way up his feet, running through his thighs and back, and knocking his teeth together. Taylor and Mark jumped through the hatch, hauling the life raft with them. Operators quickly followed as the water rushed in.

The Operators bailed out as fast as they could until only Deion was left. "Come on, John."

The water was filling the cabin, swirling around their feet and rising to their knees. "The pilots!"

"We can't wait! It's going under!"

"Don't worry," he said and pushed Deion through the door. He spun around and ran back to the cockpit, where the pilot was frantically trying to unbuckle the copilot's harness.

The pilot turned to him, his face ghostly white in the VISOR's night vision. "He's unconscious," the pilot said, grunting with effort as he strained against the harness.

"Go," John ordered. "I'll bring him."

The pilot stared at him for a moment, ready to argue, then turned and ran toward the back. John grabbed the copilot's harness and yanked, but even with his enhanced strength, he was unable to rip the harness free. He pulled his KA-BAR knife from his ankle sheath and sliced through the nylon, but by the time he was finished, the water was up to his hips. He pulled the copilot up, and the man's foot caught in the controls. He yanked harder, trying to pull the man free, but the water was rising fast.

He finally managed to free the man's feet from the controls. As he did, the helicopter listed to the side. He tried to hold the copilot's head above the rising water, but he lost his grip and the man went under.

He dove, glad of the air supply. The VISOR displayed everything in a ghostly yellow and white.

"John, are you okay?" the AI prompted.

"Not now!" He was pulling the man against the current, trying to reach the back door, but the water pulled the man from his grip. He struggled to orient himself, grabbing for the copilot's arms and legs, anything to pull him to the door.

The water was now to the top of the cabin and his countdown air timer ticked away the seconds. "Damn it!"

"Are you injured?" the AI asked.

He gritted his teeth. The helicopter had slipped beneath the waves. He had seconds to get himself out before it was too deep to make it to the surface.

He squinted, his eyes burning. The copilot wasn't going to make it. The man probably had a wife and kids, maybe even parents.

If he left, the copilot would die but he would live.

He gave one last glance at the man's slack face, spinning in the water, then pulled himself along the cabin and exited the helicopter. The VISOR's thermal vision showed red heat blooms from the men floating above.

The countdown timer on his air supply was down to ninety seconds as he inflated his life vest and kicked his legs. Without the VISOR, he would have been lost, unsure of which way was up in the darkness of the ocean, but with its help, he made it to the surface, fighting the weight and drag of the Battlesuit.

He broke through, and the countdown timer climbed as the VISOR refilled its internal air supply. For a moment he thought of diving to rescue the copilot, but even with the VISOR, he could no longer make out the Sea Knight as it sank to the bottom.

The men were climbing one by one into the life raft. He kicked his legs, struggling to stay afloat. The life vest helped, but the Battlesuit felt like it was made of lead.

Deion clung to the life raft with his left hand, helping the men aboard with his right. When he realized it was just the two of them still in the water, he glanced down.

John leaned in and said, "He didn't make it."

"Get in."

"You first."

Deion started to argue, then hauled himself aboard. John waited until Deion was in the life raft, then grabbed the nylon straps and pulled himself aboard.

Finally safe, he stared at the giant fireball still visible on the horizon. He guessed it to be about twenty miles from their current location. He deactivated the VISOR, popped the clamshell, and took it off, slumping next to Taylor and Mark.

Deion turned from the fireball to John. "Nothing from Eric?"

John shook his head. "EMP messed up communications. The VISOR is hardened. It came back online, but I guess the atmospheric disturbances have to settle down before we regain contact."

Deion's head snapped around, searching the water. "What about the other helicopter?"

A sickening realization hit—he had forgotten about the other Sea Knight. He slammed the VISOR back onto his head and activated the electronics. There was a whirr as the air filtration started. He stood on the soft bottom of the life raft and scanned around, trying to pick up any signs of life, any heat signatures indicating the other Operators had escaped.

There was nothing.

He increased magnification and made a complete three-sixty. The pilot stared up at him. "Where's McHugh?"

John didn't know what to say, but he didn't have to say anything as the pilot sank back against the life raft. He grabbed the pilot by his vest and shook him. "How far away was the other helicopter?"

The pilot stared at him dumbly. "What?"

"The other helicopter. How far away?"

"Two hundred yards before the blast. I've never seen anything like it. It was like one of those old Army training films…"

John scanned again, maxing out the VISOR's range, but there was nothing.

The grim look on Deion's face indicated he had reached the same conclusion. There were fifteen men on the other Sea Knight, plus a pilot, a copilot, and one crew member. Unless they had life vests and were bobbing in the water—their temperature so close the VISOR couldn't distinguish them from seawater—the men were gone.

His coms crackled, and a voice came through. It was Eric, cutting in and out, but John could make out the gist. "John? Are you there? We're getting telemetry, so I know you're alive."

"We made it," he said softly. "The other Sea Knight didn't."

"Don't worry," Eric said after a pause, "the *Peleliu* will send out rescue helicopters as soon as they can. They took a hit from the EMP, but they're getting their systems back online. Just hold tight."

John laughed at the absurdity. "Yeah, we'll hold tight."

Deion slapped him on the shoulder. "Tell Steeljaw we're not getting paid enough for this shit."

* * *

Area 51

Eric glanced around the War Room, overwhelmed by the silence. The analysts stared at the row of monitors on the far wall, stunned, and Eric didn't blame them. It was the first above-ground detonation of a nuclear device in years and the first by a terrorist group. John had survived—as well as the other OTM members—but the military had lost a Sea Knight and eighteen men, including a list of Operators that he knew directly or by reputation.

He wanted to hang his head, to seek out comfort from Karen, but he had a job to do. He was the base commander and the assistant director of the OTM. Doubts and fears could come later, in private. He stood and nodded to Clark.

"Commander on deck," Clark barked.

The analysts turned to him, and he could tell by their faces that they were confused, even panicked. He cleared his throat. "Clearly this is an upsetting event." He searched their faces until he found Karen's. "Kryzowski, I want a working theory on what happened in the next thirty minutes."

Karen smiled and saluted, and he knew she was happy to be his steady port in an unsteady storm.

"Sergeant Clark," he continued, "coordinate the rescue with the USS *Peleliu*." Clark saluted. Eric searched the room until he found the face of Jack Rollings, their lead Middle East analyst. "Rollings, contact JSOC and inform them of the failure. They'll have questions. Don't answer them. Information flows from them to us, not the other way around."

Rollings saluted and turned back to his workstation.

Eric addressed the rest. "We still have an active mission, people. Let's get back to work and get it done."

"You heard the man," Clark snapped. "Make it happen!"

Having rallied the War Room, he turned to go but caught Karen's eye. He gave her a small smile and a barely perceptible nod, which she returned before turning her attention back to her monitor. He made his way to the empty conference room and shut the door, then called Nancy in Turkey.

She appeared on the wall monitor, hair tucked behind her ears, her face wooden.

"I'm assuming you heard all that?" he asked.

"Yes. I was still plugged in. Focusing them on their work was a good call."

"It's normal human emotion. A physiological response to external stimuli. It's *how* they react to those emotions that counts."

"Dealing with emotions? That's what you learned in Delta?"

"Are we talking about you or me?"

Her eyes narrowed. "Something I've realized about myself— I've had the training, but I'm no soldier. You said it yourself. I recognize that as a weakness. Perhaps I need better control of my emotions."

It struck him, then, that Nancy was confiding in him. She was admitting that her emotions often boiled over. Perhaps Karen was wrong. Perhaps Nancy wasn't as close to psychopathic as they feared. He tried to view Nancy not as Fulton Smith's daughter, but as a valuable member of the OTM.

"It's okay to feel. One thing I did learn in Delta? If you recognize your emotions, accept them and move on, you can still accomplish your mission. Feelings don't make you weak."

She regarded him thoughtfully. "I'm trying, Eric. I realize my behavior hasn't always been ... appropriate. I realize being the Old Man's daughter provided certain allowances. I don't want my position because of nepotism. I want my position because I've *earned* it."

"I have faith in you. Since you want to earn your position, perhaps you should be the one to contact your father and explain what happened."

Her eyes widened, and her face flushed. "This is what I get for trying to be a better person?"

He laughed before he could stop himself. "You'll be fine. Besides, I still have an ongoing operation."

"How close is the USS *Orlando*?"

He thumbed a button on the remote control and the display split into two, Nancy's conference call on the left, the mission feed on the right. "They're in position. They'll board the MV *Rising Star* in fifteen. We need to find out who killed the men in Aleppo, and what triggered that bomb."

* * *

Gulf of Aden

Petty Officer Terrence Hurd waited with the rest of his team in the dry deck shelter attached to the hull of the USS Orlando. The shelter was cramped, and he performed the mental exercises he used to remain calm in tight spaces.

He inspected the faces of his fellow teammates, all members of DEVGRU, or as the public knew them, SEAL Team Six. Chief Petty Officer Rick Kropf was in a deep discussion with Dwayne Bowen from the CIA's Special Operations Group. Bowen was one of their own, a member of DEVGRU before being recruited by SOG. The man was practically a legend, mentally tough and ridiculously fit, with a razor-sharp mind.

Their mission was simple. They would exit the dry deck shelter, use the SEAL delivery vehicle to approach the MV Rising Star, and board the cargo ship. They would take control of the vessel before the crew could react and perform a deck-by-deck sweep, looking for radiological threats.

He tried to contain his excitement. They had trained for missions like this, but this was no training mission. Every SEAL dreamed of an operation that would change the world, and he had finally made it. Across from him, David Vrooman checked his HK416.

For this mission, they were inserting plastic plugs in the barrel to keep out the seawater. The ammunition was airtight. When they surfaced, all they had to do was shake out their guns and the first round would blow out the plug. After the mission, the HKs would receive a thorough cleaning and oiling. Still, they went through weapons faster than most SEAL teams.

He checked his face mask. It was his most complex piece of gear, combining his oxygen supply with NVGs. Once aboard, he would pull the front mask off, turn off the air supply, and be ready for action. It was a far cry from their usual tanks and gear, but in a mission like this, there wasn't time to stow their normal equipment.

Vrooman looked up and grinned in the dim light. "This is gonna be major. You know that, right? Leisner would give his left nut to be here."

Carter Leisner was their friend, one they'd first met during BUD/S training. Leisner had washed out but passed on his second go-around. They gave him a constant string of shit over it, because Leisner always overcompensated, constantly trying to outdo everyone on the team. It made Leisner a hell of a soldier, and Terrence missed the younger man. "Shame he couldn't be here."

Petty Officer Brian Cozak leaned over and shook his head. "You'll never let him hear the end of this. You two are gonna drive him crazy."

Terrence chuckled softly along with Vrooman, then said, "He asks for it, I swear."

The man next to Cozak, Thomas Stinson, grinned along with them. "You two are terrible."

The radio squawked and Bowen answered, then turned and gave them the thumbs-up. "Masks on! Prepare to flood the deck!"

Terrence nodded, his grin fading. He saw the same in his teammates' faces. The time for joking was over. Now was the time for their training to kick in, time to become the consummate professionals.

They strapped on their masks and plugged the lines into the air valves at the top of the deck, then signaled Bowen. There was a rushing of water as the deck flooded, filling the cabin with seawater. They waited impatiently as the end of the dry deck swung open, exposing the vast darkness that stretched beyond.

He followed the rest of his team as they unplugged from the air manifold in the dry deck. They were now operating on their MK25 rebreathers as they made their way to the SEAL delivery vehicle, a squat tube with a flat face, strapped to the top of the *Orlando*, twenty feet in front of the dry deck.

He waited his turn until he could enter the SDV, taking his position next to Vrooman, then plugged into the air supply on the SDV to conserve air.

Once the rest of the team was aboard, Jose Alesio and Garret Froman, the two SEALS in the rear, disconnected the latches on the SDV and helped Bowen guide it above the *Orlando*'s hull, then strapped themselves in as Bowen started the SDV's electric bow thrusters.

He felt the SDV surge ahead, surprisingly quick given its blunt and ungainly appearance. They traveled for over a mile until the SDV slowed. There was a shaking as Bowen, Alesio and Froman attached the SDV to the MV *Rising Star* by magnetic docking clamps. The MDCs would hold the SDV near and allow them a quick retreat, if necessary.

Bowen unstrapped the ladder from the side of the SDV and, with Alesio and Froman's help, slowly surfaced and attached the ladder to the ship's hull. The rest of the team unhooked their air lines from the SDV and removed their flippers, stowing them inside nylon mesh bags hanging from the SDV, before following Bowen to the surface.

They scrambled up the ladder, mindful of their surroundings. Terrence followed Vrooman over the top of the *Rising Star*'s lowest deck, Cozak right behind them. They caught up to Kropf, who was waiting next to the lowest hatch. When Froman and Alesio joined them, Bowen gave the signal to Kropf, and they split into teams of two.

Bowen and Kropf headed for the bridge while the other teams fanned out. Terrence motioned for Vrooman to follow him and took the first hatch leading to the engine room. The ship was deathly silent. They had expected to encounter *some* members of the crew, but they found none as they headed deeper into the bowels of the ship.

There was a squawk over coms, then Cozak's voice. "We got something in the hold."

"Nobody in quarters," Froman said over coms. "The galley is clear."

"Bridge is empty," Kropf said. "This *isn't* right."

Terrence nodded at Vrooman, who chimed in, "Engine room is clear."

"Chief," Cozak said, louder this time, "you *got* to see this. They're all dead, sir. You *really* need to see this."

Vrooman shot him a questioning look. Cozak was as tough as they came, but his voice was clipped, almost panicked. Vrooman leaned close. "Don't you think this is weird?"

Terrence had to agree. The engines were running, and the boat was apparently on autopilot. He shook his head. It didn't make sense. A vessel the size of the *Rising Star* normally had a crew of at least twenty, but they hadn't encountered a single crew member.

They threaded their way through the main part of the ship until they reached the cargo hold door. What they saw when they entered stopped them in their tracks.

The rest of the team had beaten them there and stood in a semicircle, guns hanging limply at their sides. The cargo room was one massive space, covered in thick plastic sheets. Huge lights hung from the ceiling, illuminating the cavernous hold. Walls of high-tech equipment lined the room, machines that looked like they belonged in a hospital or lab. Everything was white and clean and spotless.

Everything but the floor.

Dead bodies were piled in the corner, and blood covered the white floor in sticky pink streaks. He gagged at the smell of human waste in the air, trying not to puke. Two bodies lay in the middle of the room, submachine guns still clutched in their lifeless hands. He stepped closer. The body on the right was wearing a captain's uniform. "What the hell?"

"Chief?" Bowen said quietly. "The captain and his first mate killed them?"

Kropf turned to them, ashen-faced. "Looks like it. Then they wasted themselves. What's all this gear?"

It was a good question. He didn't recognize any of it—except for the refrigeration equipment and the racks of glass beakers—but he recognized the biological hazard symbol on the side. "I don't like this," he whispered.

Vrooman nodded in agreement.

Bowen pulled a camera and started snapping photos while the rest of the SEALS milled about. He had taken over a dozen when there was a whump-whump that rattled the ship.

Vrooman's eyes widened. "What the—"

There was a grinding noise above, and Terrence tilted his head, searching for the source. The hatch covers above were opening, leaving the hatchways covered by thick steel slats. He turned and stumbled as the floor lurched to the side. There was another thump, and a section of the hull below them exploded upward. He froze, gaping. He had never seen anything like it. A hole had opened straight down through the deck to the ocean below. Another whump and another hole opened, this time in front of him.

Water rushed up through the holes, gushing harder than he would have thought possible.

"Get out!" Kropf screamed.

He grabbed Vrooman by the shoulder and pushed him forward, willing him to move. They stumbled through the water, but it was geysering from below, swirling around the room, knocking the men around like corks in a bathtub.

The room quickly filled, but they still had on their masks and rebreathers. They dove to the bottom as the water finally reached the top of the room. Vrooman was in front, the rest of his team behind him, and Vrooman struggled to pull the hatch open. He grabbed on, desperate to help Vrooman open the hatch.

There was a groaning of metal, like a metallic whale song, and the ship began to shake.

A sickening realization dawned on him. The ship was being scuttled. He estimated how much water they had taken in only twenty or thirty seconds, did the math, and realized the ship was going to sink and take them with it. If they didn't hurry, they'd be so far below the ocean's surface the lack of oxygen wouldn't kill them—the compression from the hundreds of feet of water would.

The hatch handle quivered, and the water amplified the sound of the ship's death throes. The cargo room lights finally blinked out, and they were plunged into darkness. The green glow from the integrated NVGs allowed him to see as he struggled with the handle.

He looked up at the hatches. The steel slats covering them appeared too thick to easily break. He had a pouch of explosives, purposefully made for underwater demolition, but at the rate the ship was sinking, he wouldn't have time to use them.

He felt the hatch finally move, and he knew it meant the hall beyond the bulkhead had filled with water, equalizing the pressure. With Vrooman's help, he opened the door, and the rest of the team swam through.

They made their way to the stairs at the end of the hall, but as they navigated through the water, the wail and groan of metal became louder, and then he heard a sound that made his blood run cold, a sound akin to a tin can crumpling.

They had reached a depth, perhaps only a few hundred feet, where the pressure was collapsing parts of the ship that were still airtight.

Surely we can't be that deep. The hind part of his brain, the primitive part, was screaming that he was in danger.

The *Rising Star* was a cargo vessel, not a military vessel. It wasn't designed for *any* depth.

"We've got to move," Kropf said from above.

He looked up and saw Kropf opening the hatch to the deck, the same hatch they'd come down just minutes before. One by one, they entered the hatch and began swimming for the surface.

He exited last, checking his dive computer. He read the pressure of the water, blinked furiously, then estimated his depth at seven hundred feet.

Seven hundred feet. He had never been that deep, certainly not with an M25 rebreather. *Maybe if we had MK16s or MK17s with a mixed gas system, but not with the M25s.* The water pressing against his body was crushing, and he felt the air being driven from his lungs, making it impossible to take a deep breath. He tried to follow the dive computer, careful not to ascend too fast.

It was too late.

Terrence felt drunk, light-headed and disoriented, and he heard Cozak giggle, followed soon after by Vrooman, and then he joined in, giggling like a schoolboy. There was a shooting pain in his knees and shoulders, and he laughed even harder.

We're not even going to make our first decompression stop.

CHAPTER TEN

Area 51

ERIC TRIED TO understand what he was reading. *Something* had happened aboard the MV *Rising Star*, something that had scuttled the ship and killed eight good men.

How is this possible?

He had taken refuge in the conference room, alone, poring over the data on the video monitor, trying to make sense of the debacle. Outside, the hum of voices and keyboards had returned to the War Room as the analysts busied themselves, frantically attempting to make sense of the data from Somalia.

There was the beep of an incoming call. He answered it and found Nancy staring back. It was dark in Turkey, and he could barely discern the outlines of her makeshift office. She said nothing for a moment, just watched him, then finally broke the silence. "I'm sorry."

He started to speak, to question her sincerity, then stopped. She was showing a different emotion from her usual anger or disdain. "Thank you. We've taken two on the chin. We can't afford a third."

She nodded, absently brushing a strand of hair behind her ear. "What do you need from me?"

He thought about that. According to the display, his men were being picked up by the USS *Peleliu*. It was still night in the Gulf of Aden, and conditions weren't the best for a quick recovery, but he had no doubt they would soon be safely aboard.

Unfortunately, the Orlando had found no signs of survivors from the MV *Rising Star*. It had simply gone down too fast. The SEAL team hadn't escaped.

"There's nothing you can do there," he finally said. "I could use your help *here*. How fast can you get back?"

She sat up straight. "I can be stateside within sixteen hours."

"Good. Can you stop in Washington and brief your father?"

"He'll have the reports by then, but if you think it will help—"

"It would be one less headache for me. I have to write up reports for those men's families. I'll tell them they died as heroes, that it was vital to the nation's defense—"

"I understand."

"Thanks. By the time you get here, maybe we'll have workable intelligence."

She started to close their video conference, then stopped. Her pale blue eyes lingered on his. "Eric? I'll *always* do what I can to help you. No matter how important or how trivial. I want you to succeed."

The look in her eyes wasn't the look of someone eager to help—it was the look of a shark before it took a bite out of someone. "Good to know," he said. "I'm holding you to that."

She closed the connection, and he sat back in his chair. His hand was trembling, and he realized he had been operating on pure adrenaline for the past twenty-four hours.

I need sleep and food, but not necessarily in that order.

There was a knock on the conference room door and Karen poked her head in. "I've worked up a possible scenario with the bomb."

He motioned for her to take a seat. "I appreciate it."

"What?" she asked, eyebrows raised. "Me doing my job?"

"You know what I mean. I take comfort in having you near. I know it sounds corny…"

She smiled, a hint of something smoldering in her dark eyes. "No worries, boss. You know I'm here for you."

He glanced out to the War Room, then reached over and quickly squeezed her hand. "You don't have to call me boss. Not when we're alone."

She smiled but gently pulled her hand away. "Eric, I know we've been intimate, but make no mistake. You *are* my boss. I like you, as a *boss* and as a *man*, but our relationship is just casual sex."

"Casual?" he asked. "Really?"

She grinned, but her eyes contained a hint of sadness. "Okay, maybe not *so* casual, but I'm your employee. What we do between the sheets is strictly physical release. I don't love you. I like you, and I really like you as a *boss*. The Office needs you. I'll do anything to help. Just tell me what you need."

His stomach churned as he realized she spoke the truth. She had been honest from the beginning, but he had developed feelings for her, even though she had told him from the start that she loved her husband.

"Brad is a lucky man," he finally said. "I *hope* he knows that."

Her grin widened. "Oh, he knows. Don't feel bad. You're one of the most honest men I've ever met. You've learned to be a killer, but you've kept a small part of yourself clean. Innocent. It's not a bad thing. It works wonders with John. You don't have to lose that piece of yourself."

"Innocent is not how I would describe myself."

"Really?" She reached for his hand and gave it a gentle squeeze. "That's *exactly* how I would describe you."

He held her hand for a moment, then released it. "What have you got for me?"

She sat back in her chair, glancing briefly at the door. "I wish I had more coffee. Hey, can you get me that coffeemaker for my desk?"

"Sorry. Can't make an exception. Everyone would want one."

She rolled her eyes. "Anyway, the nuclear detonation was not accidental. You know how permissive action links work?"

He had a high-level understanding, thanks to Delta's basic training on nuclear weapons. "It's a device attached to the warhead that prevents unauthorized use?"

"That's right. But it's not just unauthorized use. Depending on the type of PAL, it can also prevent accidental detonation. It's not necessary, but even North Korea and Pakistan implemented some type of PAL, thanks to Doctor Kahn. No, the detonation wasn't accidental. Remote activation is a possibility, but more likely it was GPS locked."

"GPS locked?"

"Yes," she said. "I believe they attached a GPS trigger to the arming device. As soon as the bomb moved outside of a narrowly defined set of coordinates, the device was armed and detonated."

"That's … pretty sophisticated. It just doesn't fit with Al-Qaeda." He shifted gears. "Have you found anything about the malware planted in the cameras?"

Karen leaned forward and typed on her tablet. The monitor on the wall displayed a dizzyingly complex amount of data. "It's shell company after shell company. It's turtles all the way down. I've never seen anything this sophisticated. The same goes for the registration of the MV *Rising Star*. The deeper I dig, the less I'm sure of *anything*."

"We have an unknown actor."

Karen scowled. "Our digital models are built for the things we don't know, but the things we don't know that we don't know? How can we plan for that? How can we fight back?"

She asked excellent questions, ones that had plagued him since he had accepted the position of assistant director. "What was on the MV *Rising Star*? Why scuttle it? Was there another bomb? Was there something that identified our unknown party?"

Karen started to speak, but her eyes narrowed, and he could almost see her mental gears turning. "The wreck is too deep for divers. Can we get a UUV to scan the ship?"

"Yes, but it's going to take some doing. The USS *Orlando* has a UUV, but it's for inspecting hulls. It's not rated for that depth."

She considered that, and then rocked back in her chair. "Maybe you should have captured some of the terrorists in Eyl."

He bit his lip. "An error on our part. We're going to have to go back in, see if we can get information. Find out exactly what went on when they brought that bomb ashore."

"How can I help?"

"I need a plan. Get Clark and get working on it."

She nodded and left to make it happen.

* * *

Washington, D.C.

Smith wasn't surprised when Nancy knocked on his office door. His office was sparse, much like his apartment, and located in one of the older concrete-and-steel buildings near the Capitol Building. It housed several government agencies, but his office occupied a corner of the building and had EM shielding, a secured Internet connection, and massive walls to separate it from his neighbors. All phone and video calls were routed over a VPN to a data center maintained by the OTM. Even the windows had been removed and the gaping holes covered with steel plates and concrete.

Nancy was one of the very few people on earth who knew the location of his office, let alone the means to access it. He glanced up from his computer but said nothing.

She bowed her head. "You already know."

"Of course." He had watched the feed from the OTM, as he often did, without Eric's knowledge. He was counting on the young man, and the feed allowed him to see not only how the team performed, but Eric's performance as well. "How are the men?"

Nancy took a seat in the chair across from his desk, wiping her palms on the hem of her short black skirt. "As well as can be expected," she said. "They've been picked up by the *Peleliu*. Freeman and the rest are upset. Frist seems to be taking it hard. He failed to save one of the pilots."

Smith nodded. Frist's compassion was ... unexpected given what the man had done. He reminded himself to ask Hobert about Frist's latest diagnostics. "And Eric?"

"Taking it just as hard," Nancy said. "I spoke to him on the way back from Turkey. He's got Kryzowski working on it. Her theory is that the bomb was tied to a GPS, and it detonated when moved from its preprogrammed path. She's also found evidence that many systems around the world have been compromised by malware."

"Yes, I read the report. The malware was actually discovered by Mr. Green, wasn't it?"

She caught his gaze and quickly glanced away. "Yes."

"Your relationship with Mr. Green? It's not an altogether poor choice."

"You want to talk about my sexual partners?"

He allowed himself a brief smile. "Child, I *care* about you. Dewey may be odd, but he *is* a genius. He's also *discreet*."

"He's useful," Nancy admitted. "Attentive. He does what he's told." She sighed. "I just don't see a long-term commitment. He understands that."

"I think the Mr. Green's peculiarities make him unable to process interpersonal communications." Nancy started to speak, but he raised his hand. "If you've found some semblance of happiness, I wouldn't hesitate to continue that relationship. Just keep in mind that Mr. Green is not like most men."

Her nostrils flared. "He's not Eric?"

"I did not bring Eric into the OTM for your benefit. He's a good man. If you find that appealing, I understand. I'm quite surprised by your friendship with Mrs. Kryzowski."

She glared at him, her face reddening. "Why? She's smart and dedicated."

"Given her situation with Eric—"

"You really do have your hand in everything, don't you?"

He allowed himself a self-satisfied smile. "You've had few friends."

"Why do I feel like this is more like an evaluation than a father asking about his daughter?"

Because you're quite smart. "Humor an old man."

"I'm not even sure what friendship is. I respect Karen. She irritates me less than others. I would be angry if something happened to her. I don't mind that she has a relationship with Eric. Does that make us friends?" She sighed. "You know I want Eric. You know that I would kill to have him. You probably have a risk assessment showing my likelihood of killing Karen just to be with him."

"I care about you," he repeated softly. "I want you to be well. I want you to have friends and find a man—or even a woman if that's your predilection."

"A woman?"

"I may be ancient, but I'm aware that societal attitudes have shifted on such things. *Try* not to look shocked. I never cared where people found sexual release."

Her face softened. "I'm trying to find my place. I'm trying to be a better person. It's *hard*."

"You've grown, as a woman *and* as an operative. "I couldn't be prouder."

"They're trying to find who infected the IC chips. We also need to know more about the MV *Rising Star*. Eric has a plan."

"I'll inform the president. The other Operators? The team from Syria? I've inspected their files. They would be a good fit, I believe."

"Redman? You want me to recruit him?"

"Mr. Burton is an ideal candidate. Offer him the job."

"What about the others?"

"I leave them to your discretion. Now, if you will excuse me, I have some matters that require attention. When I'm finished, I'll meet you at the Groom Lake facility."

She stood to leave, then turned back to him. "Is there something you're not telling me?"

"There are many things I'm not telling you. I'm your *father.*"

Her eyes narrowed, but when he didn't speak, she rolled her eyes and left, slamming the door behind her.

* * *

The president hunched over the desk in his underground bunker, his hands on his forehead. "I can't believe we detonated a nuclear bomb."

Smith sighed. "*We* did not do that, Mr. President. An unknown actor delivered the device to Somalia."

The president's eyes were dull, and puffy bags under his eyes added ten years to his age. "How many were lost?"

"Does it matter?" Smith asked gently. "Second-guessing will not bring them back."

The president shook his head. "No, we can't bring them back. Somewhere out there, mothers and fathers and wives and children have lost someone. Because of *us.*"

Smith understood how the president felt. It was easy to watch a president's actions from the outside, to criticize and complain. He had watched for decades as men took the oath with the best of intentions, only to find out just how far down the rabbit hole they would fall to keep the world safe. "I don't need to remind you that it *could* have been worse. The bomb could have detonated on US soil. It could have wiped out New York City. I would also remind you the men who lost their lives were *volunteers.* Each one of them knew the risks when they joined the service. They *believe* in the cause. It's who they are."

"Who they *were,*" the president mumbled.

"Mr. President, your predecessors felt the same. Each soldier's death is a tragedy, but we persevere, because if we don't..."

The president sat up straighter. "You are correct. You've done the nation a great service over the years. I trust you to resolve this. What are the next steps?"

It was good to see the young man stepping up, learning to lead. The public was not privy, but Smith saw how deeply the president cared for his country, just like the presidents before him.

"We need to know who we are dealing with," Smith said. "This is beyond a terrorist group."

"The Russians?"

"I don't believe so."

"North Korea?"

"Sir, all avenues are being explored. I promise you, we *will* find out who did this. We *must*."

"Of course. Tell me what I can do."

This was the part Smith dreaded. He looked into the president's brown eyes, worried about his reaction. "I need you to play dumb."

"You *must* be joking."

Smith shook his head. "When you give your briefing, say little. Deflect. Other world leaders will be releasing statements. Make yours as vague as possible."

"People already think I'm incompetent," the president said, placing his hands on the table. "This will only confirm their worst fears." He stood quickly, almost knocking over his chair, and began pacing the small room. "I don't *want* to play dumb. I want to act."

"You *will* be acting, just behind the scenes. Let us do our jobs so you can do yours."

The president stood, glaring, then finally said, "It doesn't mean I have to like it."

Smith watched a range of emotions play across the president's face. Sadness, anger, then determined resignation. "Mr. President? Many men have felt what you're feeling. Each of them wanted to take direct action but were forced to play their part."

And, like that, the president deflated. "You know the surprising thing about this job? How little I *actually* seem to accomplish."

"Believe me, Mr. President, I understand. Now, I had best be on my way." He stood, metal briefcase in hand, and walked toward the door. He removed his badge, waved it over the card reader, and waited for the heavy steel door to slowly rumble open. Before he left, he turned back to the president.

"Sir? Go upstairs. Spend time with your wife and daughters. Remain mum during your briefing. We *will* find who did this."

"Thank you, Mr. Smith."

Smith exited through the concrete tunnel system and made his way to his car. He got in, placing the briefcase on the seat next to him, then gave Robert his destination and sank back into the leather seat. Robert navigated south through the busy Washington traffic until pulling over on Constitution Avenue and parking close to the curb.

"I'll be back in an hour, Robert."

"You want me to stay?"

"No. Get something to eat. A cup of coffee, perhaps. Take your time."

Robert drove off while he strolled southwest, past the Vietnam Veterans Memorial. The September air was almost too warm for comfort, and he worked up a sweat that threatened to soak through his suit.

His mind wandered back to the time he had spent working with William Wise. Bill had been a boon to the OTM. With Bill and Hobert's help, they had managed to clear the CIA of its involvements in several misguided operations.

He chuckled bitterly. *Operations that were often more sordid than misguided.*

The OTM had whispered into the president's ear during the sixties, but so had other agencies, and no matter how many risk assessments he'd presented, the president had continued to allow the CIA to operate in the Asian theater. It had proven unwise. The CIA had done as much damage as the enemy.

He rounded the turnabout and headed east. The enemy he had fought so many years before waited at the edge of the reflecting pool, glaring at the tourists near the Lincoln Memorial.

When he was close, Vasilii greeted him with a small shrug. "I like this man, Lincoln. I read books about him. He fought hard to preserve your country, only to be shot by his countryman. He had Russian spirit, I think, but if he had been *more* Russian, perhaps he would have crushed rebellion sooner and lived."

Smith smiled and waited for Vasilii to fall in next to him. They walked leisurely next to the reflecting pool, passing families taking in the splendor of the National Mall.

He couldn't help but notice the dried grass and dirt. There were too many visitors. The grounds crew were unable to keep the Mall clean and maintained. It was symptomatic of the government itself, grown massive and slovenly, unable to repair the infrastructure.

He thanked his lucky stars that the budget didn't currently fall within his purview, but if conditions didn't improve, it would soon become a matter of national security.

Perhaps Eric will take up that challenge.

Vasilii broke his reverie. "This thing that happened. It gives me headache."

He turned to the old Russian. "Probably a sign of advancing age."

Vasilii grunted. "I may be old—"

"We're both old. Doesn't it worry you? Our work might be undone."

"Has nothing to do with *us*. I would *never* condone that."

"You speak for everyone?"

Vasilii turned and stared across the dirty brown water in the reflecting pool. "I poked angry bear and angry bear knows nothing. Was not us."

For all their rivalry over the years, their effort to eliminate the nuclear threat brokered the most common ground. They had risked everything, including their lives, to ensure a nuclear war never occurred.

"I'm at a loss," Smith said.

"Chatter is running high. Lots of theories. Very few facts. We will deny. Your president will talk tough. People will be afraid. Every action has reaction. This is setback. I cannot stop what will happen, but I will try"—the old man waggled his fingers—"to restrain them."

Smith understood. The Russians had their own terrorist threats. They would use the bomb as an excuse to go after them. They would also dust off their war plans, perhaps resetting the dial on nonproliferation.

The American politicians would see this and wonder if the Russians were indirectly responsible for the bomb. The president wouldn't be able to control Congress. Hard-liners would talk of missile shields, pushing for an expansion of NATO.

The Russians would balk, rejecting any calls for a missile shield, especially if it approached their borders. Already nervous at Western encroachment, they would feel claustrophobic, caught between the United States and NATO on one border and China on the other.

They walked quietly along the Mall, stopping when a harried mother brushed past them, calling after her child, a boy of three or four running down the Mall. They watched in silence as the mother caught the boy's shirt, dragging him to safety, yelling at him to stay close. The boy's father caught up and sternly told the boy to *never do that again.* The boy cried, sniffling and wheezing, and the father picked the boy up and gave him a reassuring hug. The family walked off and were soon lost among the crowd.

Vasilii watched all this, then turned to him. "Would be best if you found responsible party."

"I agree. It's the work of an irrational actor. They must be stopped."

Vasilii frowned, crease lines appearing among the liver spots on his forehead. "I will assist, if possible. I would hate to have done all that for nothing."

* * *

Honolulu, Hawaii

"There has been a setback."

Huang Lei browsed the report. "Was the primary package delivered?"

"Yes."

"No matter." He stood, nodding to himself, and strolled across the immaculate tile work of his penthouse office. He stopped to admire the painting on the wall—a painting that had cost a small fortune—by the artist Zhou Fang. It was a representation of the Great Emperor of Jade, dating back to the Tang Dynasty, and it provided him great comfort. He turned back to the monitor. "The plan continues."

Liu Kong said nothing, his face unreadable. Huang Lei could tell his young apprentice was troubled. He had noticed the signs as their work had progressed. "You have concerns?"

"I do not like the idea of killing so many innocents."

"As well you shouldn't," Huang Lei said. "We are not like the Americans. We do not *kill* for the spoils of war. We do not *kill* to establish a global hegemony. We only wish to restore China to its rightful position. If the American empire were to disappear, what chaos would ensue? There would be an upheaval like the world has never seen. They have provoked nation after nation with their imperialist meddling."

He paused, overcome with rare emotion, then continued, "I ask you, is it better to let the world continue down its current path? Is it the right thing—the noble thing—to sacrifice one *million* lives, precious though they may be, to save one *billion* lives?"

Kong could barely meet his gaze. "You are correct. I lack your wisdom."

"You are a loyal student." Huang Lei cared for the young man. The last thing he wanted was for Kong to feel guilty. "You credit me with more than I deserve. I, too, *detest* these measures. If there were another path, I would gladly follow it. No, we do what we must, no matter how distasteful. Our endeavor shall succeed and someday they will tell stories of our sacrifices."

* * *

USS *Peleliu*

John relaxed on the bunk, staring at the rack above his. Dawn had finally come, just as they'd boarded the *Peleliu*, and the men were grateful to be alive. The Operators huddled together in the ward room, writing down their after-action reports, and Deion was busy speaking with the captain.

That left John alone with nothing to do. The pain medication was wearing off, and his arm and leg throbbed in time with his heartbeat. The doctor onboard had checked him out and cleared him for duty, with a warning to mind his wounds for signs of infection.

He looked down at the fresh gauze and tape covering his arm. The doctors had been astounded to learn the wounds weren't even forty-eight hours old. Both his arm and leg itched maddeningly, like a thousand mosquito bites, and he scratched at the gauze. The more he scratched, the more it itched. It wasn't the first time he'd felt that way, and when he'd asked Doctor Elliot about it—after the disaster in New York City—Doctor Elliot had told him either put up with the itching and reduced pain or heal slowly.

He shrugged. It wasn't really a choice. They were going to feed him the drugs whether he wanted them or not. Knowing that, it still didn't stop the maddening itch.

He replayed the mission in his mind. Everything had gone as planned. They were in and out of Eyl before the villagers could mount a serious defense, and they had achieved their objective.

Until the bomb detonated.

He tried to put the copilot of the Sea Knight out of his mind. An entire Sea Knight had been lost, Operators who had fought with him in Eyl just minutes before, but it was the copilot's face that haunted him.

As soon as the doctor on the *Peleliu* had cleared him, he had pulled the man's jacket. Roger McHugh. Thirty-six years old. A wife and three kids back in McKinney, Texas. McHugh was lost, because of him. Gone because he hadn't acted fast enough to pull him from the sinking helicopter.

That's not true. It was an accident.

He had tried his best but ultimately had saved his own life over that of McHugh. It was the right decision. The OTM had billions invested in the StrikeForce technology.

No matter how hard he tried, he couldn't wish away the gut-wrenching sense of guilt. He tried again to wipe the image of McHugh out of his mind.

He closed his eyes, just for a moment. His body was heavy, so very heavy, and exhaustion finally crashed down on him. McHugh's face drifted away in a thick fog. He'd pushed himself hard, farther than his body could compensate.

His eyes were only closed for a moment, but in that moment he saw another face, a middle-aged Arabic man, glaring at him. He watched the man's eyes widen, the face going slack, and he looked down to see his KA-BAR knife sticking in the man's stomach. He yanked on the knife, and it came away with a terrible sucking noise. It took all his waning strength to pull it from the man's body, then plunge it in, again and again.

Abdullah the Bomber stared at him. The anger and hate were gone, replaced by a look of surprise, and then Abdullah spoke for the last time. "I miss my wife."

"*John.*"

The voice woke him from his slumber and his eyes snapped open. He jerked up, only to ram his head into the rack above his, then collapse back onto the bunk. "Sonofabitch!"

"Jesus," Taylor's voice came from his left. "What's wrong with you?"

John grabbed his head and rolled to the side. Taylor was standing next to his bunk, smirking.

"What happened?" John asked.

"I just came in to wake you. You were moaning and kicking. You okay?"

He nodded. The images from his dream faded, and he shivered, suddenly cold. "I feel like I just closed my eyes. What time is it?"

"You've been down about six hours."

"Six hours? It felt like a few minutes." He crawled out from under the bunk and stood on rubbery legs.

Taylor grabbed has arm and steadied him. "Relax. It's time for your briefing. You've got another mission."

He turned to Taylor in surprise. "Already?"

Taylor sighed. "I wish you had more downtime, but you're going back to Eyl."

CHAPTER ELEVEN

JOHN FOLLOWED TAYLOR from the berthing to the mess, and when he passed an open hatch, he noticed the setting sun and the vivid purple sky that stretched beyond the horizon. They had arrived at the *Peleliu* just after dawn, but by the time they had debriefed and stowed their gear, it had been late afternoon. "God," he said, "I just want to go back to sleep."

Taylor turned to him. "What?"

"Sorry," John mumbled. "Didn't realize I was talking out loud." He struggled to keep up with Taylor's long strides. He felt slow, like his movements were disjointed.

The mess was larger than he had expected. Mark and Redman were sitting at a table, and they nodded to him as he entered. He grabbed a tray and piled it with food, not paying attention to what he was placing on the tray, grabbed a cup of hot coffee, then made his way to join them.

"Feeling okay?" Mark asked.

He shook his head and took a bite of a roll he'd snagged from a basket on the table. It was hot and yeasty and surprisingly fluffy. "Tired," he sputtered around the crumbs, then took a sip of coffee. "Why does everything taste so good?"

Mark smiled. "The Navy does a good job of feeding their men. And you've been eating MREs for the past two days."

Mark was correct, he realized, then looked down at the remains of the roll. "Still, it tastes fantastic."

Redman nodded before spitting a gob of thick brown saliva into a paper cup he held in his left hand. "Could be that we almost died. Makes everything taste better."

A few of the sailors glared at them. John didn't hold it against them. By this time in their deployment, the sailors were both exhausted and bored, their blue camos covered in grease stains and a gray haze from deck paint. Three sailors sat at the table next to them, two of them listening to the third.

"I'm telling you," the third sailor said, shaking his fist for punctuation, "my friend slept with this chick in Thailand, but when the lights came on, it was a tranny. He *fucked* a *tranny!*"

The first sailor rolled his eyes. "Would you shut the fuck up so I can tell *my* tranny story?"

A new sailor joined them, fresh from duty, slamming his tray on the table. "All I do is paint. Gray. Fucking Gray. I *hate* gray. Any other color? No. Just gray."

The second sailor threw his fork at the new sailor. "Why are you being such a shitstain? Why are you talking about work? Why can't you talk about trannies like *everyone* else?"

Redman spat another wad of saliva into his cup and shook his head at the sailors' conversation. "These boys been out too long."

John nodded in agreement. "Where're the other men?"

Redman paused. "Sleeping. They've been through a lot in the last couple days."

"True," John said between mouthfuls of baked chicken. "So have you. You lost Morse."

Redman's eyes narrowed. "I did. And *you* lost McHugh."

"I didn't *know* McHugh. You *worked* with Morse. He wasn't just a soldier. Not to you."

Mark started to interject. "John—"

"It's all right," Redman said. He regarded John calmly. "Nothing can bring Sean back. It could be *me* next time. I know that. You know that. You tried with McHugh. Wasn't your fault. Let it go or bury it deep, but if you keep worrying it like a dog with a bone? Gonna drive you crazy, son."

John managed a tired smile. "I'm trying."

Redman leaned forward and nodded. "Me, too."

Taylor and Mark smiled, and John felt some of the weight lift from his shoulders.

"Finish up," Taylor said, tapping on the table. "We have to meet Deion in ten."

* * *

John entered the ward room and found Deion sitting at a table scanning through stacks of papers.

Deion brushed the papers aside. "Eric's waiting." He motioned for John to take a seat.

John sat and Deion pressed the button on the speakerphone sitting on the metal table. "John's here."

There was a burst of noise, then Eric's voice came through. "John. How are you?"

"Better than some on our team. Worse than others."

Deion eyeballed him, and he winced. He hadn't meant for it to sound *quite* so negative, but Eric spoke before he could apologize.

"I understand. I read the report. You did your best."

"My best wasn't good enough. How did the bomb detonate?"

"We think the bomb was GPS locked."

"Didn't we plan for that?"

"It was a mistake. We didn't think the enemy had that level of sophistication."

"It's not anybody's fault," Deion interjected. "We do our best. We can't be everywhere, all the time. Mistakes happen."

"Yeah," John agreed, "and this mistake killed good men. We lost an *entire* Sea Knight. That's not including the copilot of *our* Sea Knight. And don't forget the Hercules. How many were on board?"

There was a long pause before Eric spoke. "Seven. There were seven men on board the Hercules."

"How many mistakes like that are we going to make?"

"Enough," Deion said. "We all have a job to do. It's time for you to do yours."

John started to speak, but Eric's voice stopped him. "You're absolutely right. We made a mistake. But, imagine that bomb on US soil. Imagine the dead or dying from *that*. You feel bad for those men, and that's a good thing. It means you have compassion. But the mission isn't over yet. We need intel, and you're the man to get it. We're sending you back into the village. We want you to bring back Asad Hassan. He's the leader of the pirate band that controls Eyl."

"Why didn't we abduct one of the Al-Qaeda members?" John asked. "Maybe we shouldn't have killed them all."

"They could have triggered the bomb on the ground. It's a miracle more didn't die. Quit focusing on that. We need you to grab Hassan and bring him back."

"How am I supposed to get in? A nuke just went off. It's going to be guarded."

Before Eric could respond, Deion pulled the stack of printouts from the edge of the desk and shoved them at him. "They're mostly fishermen. Best estimate? There are less than two hundred active pirates in the city of Eyl. They're probably freaked the hell out that a bunch of Special Forces dropped in and stole their package. The *last* thing they expect is someone to come back."

"He's right," Eric said. "They won't be prepared."

It made sense, but he wasn't going to blindly follow along this time. "My HK is at the bottom of the ocean, and the Battlesuit is waterlogged. You think I can just stroll in and snatch this guy?" Deion's eyes flickered down and back up. John recognized it as one of Deion's nervous tics. "What aren't you telling me?"

"The bomb threw up a lot of dust and radiation," Eric said. "We're having trouble communicating. That's why we're on audio instead of video. The *Peleliu* is still rebooting systems and replacing fried parts. There won't be drones. You'll have the VISOR, but we won't be able to feed you telemetry, and we won't be able to track your progress."

I'll be completely alone. "Sounds like a suicide mission."

"You've trained for this," Eric said. "You're stronger than a normal man. Faster. With the Battlesuit and the VISOR, you can tear through that town, grab Hassan, and be back before they know you're there."

Deion arched an eyebrow. "It's all we've got, man. Helicopters are too loud."

John understood their position, but they didn't seem to understand—or care—about his. "Isn't there another way?"

There was another long pause before Eric's voice came through the speakerphone. "You'll do fine. I *believe* in you."

* * *

Somalia

They approached the shore, and when they were a mile away, the SEAL, Jenkins, a burly man with a perpetual scowl, cut the gasoline motor and flipped over to the electric trolling motor, carefully guiding the Zodiac silently toward the shore. The city of Eyl lay two miles to the north. John checked the thermal and night vision display of his VISOR but saw no lookouts.

He turned to his right. Taylor Martin was hunched over the side of the rubber craft, desperately clutching his HK. He leaned over and spoke softly to the tall black man. "I can't believe *you* get seasick."

Taylor turned to him, his face obscured by NVGs. "I can't believe you knew that and still requested I come along. You better hope I don't puke on you."

John smiled to himself. He *had* requested Taylor. They were going in quiet, just three men to the shore, and he wanted someone from his team waiting for him at the beach when he got back. "Hang in there. Only a few more minutes."

His preparations had consisted of making sure the Battlesuit had recovered from the dunking in the Gulf of Aden. The material had finally dried after spending the afternoon spread across the *Peleliu*'s steel deck. It had slowly stretched over his frame until the heat from his body had activated chemicals in the fabric, and it had relaxed, fitting like a glove.

Luckily, the Battlesuit's plates were still one hundred percent. He had spent the evening cleaning and oiling his spare M11 pistols. His waterproof backpack had protected his other gear, including the M11 suppressors, and the pistols now hung from his hips. He checked his HK416, on loan from the ship's armory, and cursed himself for not bringing a spare HK 417 from Area 51.

They reached the edge of the beach and jumped from the boat, landing in warm water up to their knees, then grabbed the nylon ropes and hauled the boat up the rocky beach. Taylor made a chopping motion with his hand up the beach, and John nodded.

Time to go.

He concentrated and activated the map overlay in the VISOR. It appeared on the split screen, above the output from the thermal and night vision. He headed north, up the beach, running in a slow jog, half-crouched.

He was tired. With the atmospheric disturbances still causing communication problems, he couldn't request Implant activation. The Implant had shut off sometime during his sleep, and the lack of pain relief was apparent when he woke.

His arm and leg still hurt from the wounds suffered in Syria, but it was his prosthetic that bothered him. Each step sent a mild electric shock of pain up the prosthetic and into his tibia.

He took a deep breath as he crested the hill and looked toward the village of Eyl. He was going to have to put the pain out of his mind.

Hard to focus when I feel like I'm moving in molasses.

The village—a small city, really, as rough estimates put the population over twenty thousand—was a collection of stone buildings, some no bigger than huts, and it stretched over several square miles.

He approached the village, trying to match the overhead map with the display in the VISOR. He tucked the HK behind his shoulder and pulled the M11 from his right hip holster. He couldn't risk the HK unless it was a full-out battle, because once he started firing, it would wake the town.

The M11 with subsonic ammo and suppressor had a much better chance of killing without raising the dead. And, if all else failed, he still had his KA-BAR knife.

Lights flickered in some of the houses. He stopped and pressed himself against the wall of a stone house with darkened windows.

It occurred to him, then, that without satellite contact, he was free. The OTM couldn't monitor him. Eric couldn't watch his data feed. For the first time since he'd been abducted after blowing up the Red Cross building, he could do as he pleased.

He hated himself for it, but he thought of running. He could remove the VISOR. Without it to act as a relay, the Implant would require a network connection or a satellite tower to give away his location. It would severely limit where he could go, but he could disappear into the Somali backcountry.

He suspected that they had a way to disable him—perhaps even kill him—as long as the VISOR could connect via satellite or cell tower. The OTM could reach him anywhere in the world.

Surely not in the center of Somalia?

Did they have taps on Somali's meager cell phone network? What if he crossed into Ethiopia or Kenya? Could he really escape the OTM? If he could find someone to operate, could the Implant be removed?

He shook his head. It was crazy. The Implant was connected to his aorta. Could he really trust a cut-rate doctor with minimal training to perform surgery in the bush?

Besides, he had another reason for staying. What he had done that cold January in Fairfax, Virginia, could not be forgiven. It couldn't be washed away.

I deserve this.

And, like that, he came back to his senses. The chronometer in the VISOR showed only five seconds had passed, five seconds where he had contemplated freedom.

The only freedom I can earn is death, and only after the OTM is done with me.

He peeked around the corner of the house and looked for heat signatures. A pair of men patrolled in the distance, but they were headed northwest, away from him. He stepped around the corner and headed up the dirt alley.

According to the intelligence, Asad Hassan lived near the center of the village, not down by the shore with most of the pirates. He believed himself to be an honest fisherman and leader of the local coast guard, committed to securing the shores and protecting the people of his village. Hijacking a cargo ship now and then and ransoming it back to wealthy foreigners was just another means to provide for his people. There were numerous reports of him giving speeches, protesting the world powers and their destruction of the fish habitats off the coast.

John continued through the village, ducking under the few lit windows. He was sweating, even though it was hours after sunset. He watched in the distance as a patrol rounded a corner and headed west down another alley.

According to the map displayed in the VISOR, he was close. The building in front was larger than the rest, but still barely half the size of a typical American house. Light in the front window was the only sign it was occupied.

He leaned into one of the house's darkened windows. The occupants blazed with heat in the VISOR's thermal vision. He flipped over to night vision and saw a woman, asleep on a cot against the wall. At least four children slept on the floor, their tiny bodies clutching bundles of rags for pillows.

It didn't surprise him. Hassan might be the local leader of the pirates, but pirating had become a business, like any other. Hassan paid fees and taxes to several warlords in Mogadishu, and rumors abounded of foreign investors bankrolling their activities. Hassan was wealthy by Somali standards.

He made a quick circuit around the house, peeking in all the darkened windows. Three men slept in another room, this time on a stone floor. He guessed they were guards, by the AK-47s leaning against the corner wall.

He crouched down at the front of the house and paused to remove a thin wire from his side pouch. It had a plastic ball on one end, the size of a pea. He made a ninety-degree bend in the wire and slowly eased the threadlike wire to the corner of the window.

The fiber-optic camera interfaced with the VISOR and provided him a fish-eyed view of the room. Two men were sitting at a table. The man he guessed was Hassan faced away from him, drinking from a bottle. Hassan was in his late fifties and was of normal weight, a rarity among the villagers. That, more than anything, tipped him off to Hassan's identity. The whip-thin man across from him stared at the table, slowly chewing.

Probably khat.

The thin man's eyes were glassy, the corner of his mouth drooping. Hassan would speak, and the thin man would slowly nod, then continue chewing.

John checked his chronometer. He needed to get Hassan back to the shore as soon as possible, but couldn't risk a firefight. The men patrolling the village would return, sooner or later. The Battlesuit offered him some camouflage, but he wasn't invisible.

He didn't have to wait long. Hassan barked an order, and the thin man stood, lazily picking up his AK-47, and staggered to the door.

John yanked the camera back and took cover around the corner, sticking the camera low around the stone wall and watching as the thin man headed northwest, following the same path as the patrolling men.

Without a drone feed, there was no telling how long it would take before the guards returned. He eased back around the corner and used the camera to look inside. Hassan was still in the same spot, drinking from the bottle.

He rolled the camera into a tight loop and placed it in his pouch, then headed for the door. He paused for a moment, then carefully opened it. Hassan didn't move.

He removed the syringe of sedatives from his pouch. As he stepped forward, the sound of his boots on the floor alerted Hassan, who, without turning, barked a question in Somali.

Hassan was still waiting for an answer when John wrapped his left hand around the man's mouth and jammed the syringe into his neck.

The man jerked as the auto-plunger injected the contents, and John wrestled him to the ground. The chair scraped against the stone floor, but John was already wrapping his legs around the Somali pirate, squeezing hard, pinning the man to the floor and waiting for the sedatives to take effect.

Hassan thrashed, desperately trying to cry out, but John's grip was like iron across the man's mouth. The pirate managed muffled grunts, his legs kicking uselessly. John prayed for the sedatives to hurry, hoping the man's panic would send blood rushing through his body, hastening their effect.

The man's thrashing slowed, his resistance fading, as the drugs finally did their job. It took another thirty seconds before the man went slack and sprawled on the floor in an unmoving heap. John stood, huffing for air, then bent to grab the man. What he saw stopped him in his tracks.

A small boy, no more than six or seven, stood in the doorway to the bedroom, watching him with wide eyes, the whites around the edges like brilliant marbles in the reflected light. The boy hadn't spoken. His head swiveled from Hassan to John in terror.

John froze.

A stream of options tumbled through his head, all of them ending in the boy's death. If he shot the boy, even with the suppressed M11, it would wake the others in the house. He had no other sedatives, and he couldn't take the boy with him.

Who am I kidding? I can't kill an innocent boy, even if he's the son of a pirate. Too many children are dead because of me. I won't add another.

He slowly raised his finger to his VISOR, approximately where his lips were. He stepped slowly towards the boy, praying not to spook him. The boy watched, rooted in place. When John was close, he grabbed the boy and wrapped his hand around the boy's mouth, his arm around the boy's neck. He squeezed hard, careful that the boy's throat was in the crook of his elbow, his bicep and forearm pressing against the boy's carotid arteries and jugular vein.

The boy quivered, and he tried to force John's arm from his neck, but it was in vain. The boy was too young to offer any real resistance and was soon passed out on the floor, barely breathing.

John relaxed his hold, praying that he hadn't inflicted any permanent damage and that the boy would stay unconscious long enough to allow him to get Hassan to shore. He squatted, grabbed Hassan, and threw him across his shoulder in a fireman's carry. He carried the pirate to the door, checked outside to see if the men on patrol had returned, then staggered south toward the beach.

Hassan weighed close to one hundred and fifty pounds, and John's legs quickly tired as he carried the pirate through the dirt streets. Without the Implant to help, his legs were burning, the pain in his prosthetic so great he could hardly think. He stopped two hundred yards from shore and shifted the man's weight, trying to catch his breath.

"TM, I'm *almost* there."

His coms crackled. "I've got eyes on you."

There was gunfire in the distance, coming from Eyl, and then gunfire from the pirate enclave to the east joined in.

Either the boy woke up, or the patrol found Hassan missing.

He staggered forward through sheer force of will until he saw Taylor standing near the ocean, his HK at the ready. He reached the boat and unceremoniously dumped the pirate into the rubber bottom.

Engines revved in the distance as the pirates started their trucks, ready to blast down the beach in search of their leader.

Jenkins glanced between them before giving them a thumbs-up and saying, "Time to get the hell out of Dodge."

They pushed the boat back into the sea until they were up to their hips in water and turned the boat around, then pulled themselves up over the edge and flopped inside. Jenkins started the gas motor—no time for stealth—and gunned it. The craft's front rose as they began pounding against the waves, heading back to the *Peleliu*.

Apparently, they had underestimated how badly the pirates wanted their leader back.

John turned and zoomed in with the VISOR. The pirates were launching boats into the surf, boats that were retrofitted to be fast and maneuverable. "They're coming after us," he shouted.

"Don't worry," Jenkins shouted back. "We've got this covered."

They pounded across the surf, well past the shore, and headed into deeper waters, the pirates in pursuit. He heard an occasional crack of gunfire, but the sound was nearly a mile behind them.

They headed back to the *Peleliu*, and he turned to watch as the pirates approached. Jenkins had the Zodiac moving at top speed, but two pirate ships were closing the gap, their boats rising well above the surf and slapping back down. Unlike Jenkins, the pirates didn't seem to care if they lost their ships. John looked over to Taylor, who watched the approaching pirates, then turned to Jenkins. "How far is the *Peleliu*?"

Jenkins gave a quick glance back to the pirates. "We've got this covered!"

"They're *gaining* on us!"

"I said, we've got this covered!"

He wanted to slap the man, but then he heard a dull roar and saw streams of tracer fire, like laser bolts from the heavens, streaking across the darkened sky.

He looked up and saw lights from the planes as they roared past, darts of flames blasting behind their engines as they roared past. Twenty-five-millimeter projectiles stitched across the boats following them, and the pirate's boats simply ceased to exist. They dissolved like cardboard, dropping men into the Gulf.

The chain guns screamed through the night, and he saw heat blooms in his VISOR as the fuel on board the remains of the boats ignited. Within moments, burning wreckage littered the ocean surface. The jets banked hard and headed back out to sea, the sound of their engines rumbling across the ocean.

Taylor watched the scene behind them with his mouth hanging open.

Jenkins had a triumphant smile plastered across his face. "Harriers, baby! We got this covered! Hooyah!"

John shook his head before collapsing, his weary body finally giving out. *Hooyah.*

CHAPTER TWELVE

Area 51

SMITH WAITED PATIENTLY with Dewey Green for Hobert and Nathan Elliot to join them. Dewey twitched nervously, his ungainly hands and arms moving in rhythm to an unseen orchestra, drumming his fingertips on the tabletop.

They were in the bottommost reaches of the complex. Dewey's office was a maze of desks, tables, and computers. Smith was amazed that Dewey could be productive in the whirlwind of clutter. Papers and USB thumb drives littered the desks around them, along with stacks of movies and science fiction novels.

Dewey's singular ability was becoming an expert in anything, given enough time. When assigned a task, he lost interest in the outside world, devoting himself to solving whatever problem consumed him. It was why Smith had assigned Dewey the very task they were about to discuss.

Dewey wiped the sweat dripping from his brow, even though the temperature in the office was frigid. It wasn't for comfort— Dewey had so many computers and servers that extra air conditioning was needed to keep the equipment running. The requisition form for the extra cooling had been the first thing to pique Smith's curiosity about the young man.

"Nervous?" he asked.

"A little. I don't like dealing with them. They *look* at me funny."

He smiled. Another of Dewey's idiosyncrasies—he said whatever popped into his head. "You will do well, Mr. Green."

Dewey's office door opened, and Barnwell and Elliot entered. Hobert made a sour face as he wormed his way through the piles of electronic gear until he reached the table. He glanced down at the metal chair. "Is it even *safe* to sit in that?"

"Yes, Hob. Try not to hold Mr. Green's ... habits ... against him."

"We'll see about that."

Elliot stood, his massive black hand on another chair, watching their interaction. He cleared his throat. "Mr. Smith. We're here. The question is why."

"Because I asked you, Nathan."

Elliot hesitated, then managed, "I know why *we're* here. I mean, why are we *here?*"

"Mr. Green has been working on a very special project. Mr. Green?"

Dewey watched their exchange with apprehension, then said, "I've done some work on your deep-brain stimulation hardware."

Elliot drew back and his eyes widened. "And how, exactly, do you know about *that?*"

"Be-because," Dewey stammered. "Uh—"

"Surely you didn't think your research here was secret," Smith said. "I've assigned Mr. Green many tasks over the years, including looking for work that I might find useful."

Elliot glanced over to Barnwell, who only shrugged, and said, "You had him sneaking around my work?"

Dewey started to speak, but Smith raised his hand. "Please, Nathan, he wasn't *sneaking* around. He was following *my* orders."

"What exactly is this deep-brain stimulation hardware?" Barnwell asked.

Before Elliot could explain, Dewey jumped in, "Doc Elliot discovered a way to thread microelectrodes into the brain and then use electrical stimulus to increase brain activity."

Hobert's expression changed from annoyance to dread. "You *can't* be serious."

"That's not an accurate description," Elliot interrupted. "It doesn't *increase* brain activity. It's been theorized that for treating epileptic seizures—"

Smith cut him off. "I understand the theories, but Mr. Green has devised a new use for your invention."

"No," Hobert said. "Absolutely not."

Elliot turned to Barnwell, confused. "What's going on?"

"Mr. Green, please continue."

"Uh, well, I did some computer modeling," Dewey said, "and I figured if someone were suffering from dementia or Alzheimer's, this device could provide electrical stimulation to the hippocampus. This would increase memory retrieval—"

"Hippocampus?" Elliot asked indignantly. "Do you even know what that word means? I'm sorry, I missed the part where you went to medical school." He glared at Dewey, who sat frozen, his face draining of color.

"You know Dewey's gift," Smith said. "He may not have the extensive training of a medical doctor—"

"Or *any* doctor," Elliot pointed out.

Smith continued, "But he *does* have a unique ability to absorb information and connect disparate ideas. I want you to examine his research."

"You're out of your damned mind," Barnwell said, "and I think it's time you told Nathan why you're grasping at straws."

All eyes turned to Smith. "You are correct, Hob. It *is* time. Gentlemen, I am suffering from Alzheimer's. Hob has been treating me with an experimental tau-protein inhibitor."

Elliot's eyes widened in recognition. "*He's* patient X?" he asked, angrily pointing his finger at Smith's chest. "Why didn't you tell me this before?"

Hobert ran his fingers through his gray hair. "It was need-to-know basis, and you didn't. I'm giving him well above the maximum dose, and he's barely holding on. He wants you to implant the deep-brain stimulator inside his head so that he can have a few more months to finish transitioning the directorship to Eric Wise." He spun around. "That's *all* it would give you, Fulton. A few months."

Nathan and Dewey appeared shocked, but Smith continued as if Barnwell hadn't spoken. "I'm sure you'll do your best, Nathan. I want your conclusions within the day."

Elliot shook his head. "I *can't* believe you've been taking the tau-protein inhibitor. It's still experimental."

"It's performed admirably. You should be proud. Now it is time for something else. Gentlemen, if you would excuse yourselves, I would like to have a word with Hobert."

Dewey craned his head, looking around the room. "Well, since this is my office, and I kind of *live* down here—"

Smith turned to Dewey and raised an eyebrow.

Dewey gulped. "I mean, hey, maybe I could go get coffee or see what Nancy is up to. Yeah, that's a good idea, I'll do that." He stood and made a beeline for the door, never looking back.

Elliot shook his head. "There is something *wrong* with that man." He stood, then paused, deep furrows upon his forehead. "I find this whole thing … inappropriate."

Smith said nothing. Elliot finally turned away and followed Dewey out the door, shutting it carefully behind him.

Hobert frowned. "I'm asking you … no … I'm *begging* you. Don't do this."

"Did you watch the president's address?"

"What? Yes, I did, actually. He appeared to be an incompetent boob."

"He did as instructed. He's not a bad man and certainly not the worst president I've dealt with."

"You still haven't gotten over Johnson, have you?"

"The man was an uncouth pig. I still detest him."

"For God's sake, he's been dead for almost forty years. For a man with a fading memory, you certainly do hold a grudge."

"How did Frist perform?"

"Quit changing the subject. We need to discuss this crazy idea you've cooked up."

"Hassan was captured without incident?"

"Damn it," Hobert said. He stood and paced around the desks in Dewey's office. "Yes, Hassan was captured. I wouldn't exactly say it was without incident, but Freeman is preparing to interrogate him aboard the *Peleliu. Now* can we talk about your plan?"

He slumped forward. "I'm sorry, Hob, but I need more time. I'm *committed.*"

"You *should* be committed. I won't approve this."

Smith looked up at his old friend. Hobert stood, hands on hips, red-faced. He knew the deep-brain stimulation had taken Hobert by surprise, but he wasn't prepared for such an emotional reaction. "It's *my* life, Hob," he said quietly. "I'm willing to take the risk. I need to know that Eric will continue our work. I need to know that Nancy will be safe."

Hobert exhaled deeply, then took his seat at the desk. "I'm sorry, Fulton. I'm sorry we grew old. I'm sorry that I recommended you bring her into the OTM."

Smith took Hobert's hand in his and squeezed. "It's worth the risk. It's all I have left. I *have* to make things right while I still can."

* * *

USS *Peleliu*

Deion took the seat across from Asad Hassan. They were in low-ceilinged gray steel room inside the *Peleliu*, a room the Marines had cleared out until there was nothing left but two steel chairs.

A black hood covered Hassan's head, and chains looped around the chair and fastened to his ankle restraints.

Deion smiled. Hassan was effectively hog-tied. The hood was a useful tool. Removing the subject's sight went a long way to removing any sense of power. The interrogation was going to be all about the balance of power.

Hassan has none, and the sooner he realizes that, the better.

He reached across and yanked the hood from Hassan, who shook his head and squinted in the sudden light. Normally Deion would begin questioning the subject before he could gather his bearings, but in this case, he let the man adjust to his situation.

Hassan let loose with a string of unintelligible profanity.

Deion let him wind down. When the man's anger had subsided, Deion shook his head and said, "You speak English?"

Hassan stared at him and said something in Somali.

Deion nodded. "So, you don't. That's fine." He spoke calmly and evenly, "I'm going to cut out your tongue and make you eat it."

The pirate's eyes widened, and his eyes darted toward the door.

"So you *do* speak English."

The man glared at him. "Yes, I speak English."

"I already *knew* you did. That was the first test. I don't have to hurt you. Yet." He paused, giving Hassan time to digest that. "Your name is Asad Hassan."

Hassan continued to glare at him. "You are American."

The old pirate was sharp and showed no sign of fear, even though Deion knew he was alarmed at his predicament. "Now that we know who we are," Deion said, "I have a few questions. Answer truthfully. Do you understand?"

Hassan's eyes narrowed. "I say *nothing*."

"I'm going to offer you a deal," Deion continued. "It's your one chance to get off this ship and back to your home. I'm not here because you've been pirating ships for the past eight years."

"I am *not* a *pirate*. I am the leader of the Coast Guard—"

"You *are* a pirate," Deion said calmly. "Don't pull that Coast Guard bullshit on me." He leaned forward and stared straight into the pirate's eyes. "I don't care about your fishing problems. I don't care about your pirating. I only care about one thing."

Hassan stared back, defiant, then his eyes slid to the floor, and he nodded. "You want to know about the bomb."

"I want to know about the bomb. Tell me about the bomb, and I let you go free. Do you understand? I don't *care* about what you've done. That's for someone else. I only care about the bomb. How did you get it?"

The pirate considered Deion's deal, then nodded and spoke. "It was an American. He came to us, offered us money. Paid for safe passage for his friends. Good Muslims. They paid us to take them to a boat. They unloaded the crate and we brought them back."

"When was this?"

Hassan squinted, considering. "Four days ago?"

If the pirate was telling the truth, and Deion had no reason to suspect otherwise, the bomb had arrived about the time they were in Nashville. "Did they say who they worked for? Who was their leader?"

Hassan shrugged. "The American?"

"Not the *men's* leader. The American. Who did *he* work for?"

"I don't know. The American. His name was Al-Hakim."

Deion sighed. "I *know* that. You need to give me something worthwhile if you want me to cut you loose. Something *valuable*. Tell me what else you remember about the bomb."

Hassan squirmed in his chair. "I know nothing. He paid us. I used the money to pay my men. I kept money for myself. That is what I did."

"You've got to give me something to work with. Tell me something I *don't* know."

"There *is* nothing else," Hassan said with a shrug. "The men came and helped unload the crate. One man left. The others stayed with the crate."

That was news to Deion. "A man?"

"He drove a motorbike."

"Where was he going?"

"They did not say."

"Tell me about the ship."

There was a flicker of something in the old pirate's eyes. "Yes, the ship. I saw it. It was a big ship. Many men. Some wore rubber suits. I saw things. You will let me go if I tell you?"

Deion nodded. He wasn't lying to Hassan—he honestly didn't care about his pirating. Others did, but the OTM wasn't interested in the old man's activities. "Tell me what you saw and I promise we will return you to your village. I can't promise that ships won't return if you keep hijacking vessels and taking hostages. I can only promise you that if you tell me what you saw, I will *personally* see to it that you're returned."

Hassan's mouth curled up in a smile. "I believe you, Mr. American. I will tell you because I am a *good* Muslim and I do not like that they used us. They put us at great danger, and we are *good* Muslims."

Sure you are. "Tell me."

"I saw something inside the ship. A symbol. Three circles centered on another circle. You know this symbol?"

Deion's heart sank. He *did* know that symbol. That symbol—combined with the men in rubber suits—could only mean one thing.

Biohazard.

* * *

Deion initiated the video call when the atmospheric disturbances finally subsided. Eric appeared on the screen, his face haggard, stubble on his chin, and his eyes dark and brooding. "You look like shit."

Eric managed a halfhearted smile. "I'm not the one who took a swim in the ocean. How are you?"

"Running on adrenaline."

"I just read John's hot wash. It sounds like he's performing above expectations, but how is he *really*?"

"He's the least of our worries. He's tired, yeah, and he needs downtime. His wounds need time to heal, and his prosthetic hurts more than he's letting on. Now that we got a connection, maybe you could activate the Implant. A little pain medication might take the edge off."

Eric's smile faded. "Worried about John's well-being? That's not like you."

Deion chose his words carefully. "He's growing on me. I still can't forgive what he did, and I still want to strangle him sometimes, but he tries, man. He's not the stupid little punk we interrogated in Guantánamo. He tried to rescue the copilot of that Sea Knight, and he was pretty broke up about it when he couldn't. Did you see his hot wash, about the boy in Eyl? He could have shot that kid. He didn't. That's a damned sight better than I expected."

"When you beat the hell out of him, you mean."

"I don't feel bad about it, either." Deion hesitated. "Doesn't mean he hasn't changed. A little."

"I'm not saying you should. It's hard to be objective when you're working directly with him."

Eric had a point. He had counseled Eric to never forget what John had done, to never forgive him for blowing up the Red Cross building in Fairfax. During John's training, he had kept an eye on him, prepared to put a bullet in the young man's head.

Just in case.

Now that he worked directly with John, he found he actually liked the young man. John was practically killing for the OTM. He was smart, focused, and courageous. Under different circumstances, they could even be friends.

But it's not different circumstances.

John had killed a lot of people. Men. Women. Kids. He remembered reading the interviews with John's unit in Iraq—the living members, anyway. John had always been something of an odd duck, and the IED in Iraq had pushed him over the edge.

No amount of drugs and memory replacement would change *who* John was, and he knew it would be a mistake to forget how dangerous the StrikeForce technology made him.

"He's useful," Deion said. "He's functioning. What more can I say?"

"What did you get from Hassan?"

"He saw something on the *Rising Star*. A biohazard sign. Men in rubber suits. There was something more than a bomb aboard that ship."

Eric's face paled. "*That's* why they scuttled the ship."

"Whatever was on that ship was worth killing everyone on board and putting it on the bottom of the ocean. And, it gets worse. There was a man with them, and he left on a motorbike. Hassan doesn't know where he went."

* * *

Area 51

Eric paced around the conference room table. Their enemy—their *unknown* enemy—had deep pockets, but it wasn't money that worried him. Their enemy was committed to action. That, more than anything, gave him pause.

A committed enemy can do a hell of a lot of damage.

The conference room door opened, and Fulton Smith entered, followed by Nancy. Smith took the seat at the head of the table while Nancy took the seat to his right. Smith nodded. "Begin."

"They sank the *Rising Star*," Eric said, "because they didn't want us finding out what else was on board." He took the seat across from Nancy. "There were men in rubber suits and there were biohazard labels. *That's* why they scuttled the ship."

"Perfectly reasonable conclusion," Smith said. "What do *you* think of this?"

He glanced between Smith and his daughter. When Smith questioned him, it always felt like a test. "I think that *someone* is determined to strike us. To hurt us. They have money, and they have technology, and they have the will to use it."

A smile spread across Smith's face, and his pale blue eyes lit up. "An excellent analysis. What else?"

Eric's mind struggled to wrap it all up. "Normally I would say it's a nation-state. Nukes and bioterror. That's the kind of thing I expect from Russia."

"But not in this case?"

"You've assured me the Russians aren't involved, and bioterror is not their style. I've read your files. They developed horrifying bugs during the Cold War. They *could* have used them *then*."

"They were not the only ones who developed such things." Smith leaned back for a moment, his eyes drifting around the room. "We had our own program, of course. Hobert theorized we had the means to kill most life on this planet with a modified version of the plague. I believe he was right. It was only by a gentleman's agreement with my Russian counterpart that we bottled up the research. We destroyed as much as we could without our governments' knowledge."

Nancy raised an eyebrow. "You both did?"

Smith's eyes focused on her. "We were *bad* men, but we did not want to be *evil* men. I've kept things from the Office and from the presidents I serve. I've done what I thought best to serve my country *and* to keep the world safe."

Eric gaped. Since being recruited, he had read many of the OTM's old case reports. He had known that they weren't complete—there were gaps that could not be explained. He'd suspected that Smith had sanitized the history, keeping things from being recorded.

"What things have you done, sir?"

The old man's eyes turned icy cold. "I've never pretended to be a saint. I *love* my country, but above all else, I am human being."

"How far off the reservation did you go to save the world?"

"I will always serve my country, to the best of my ability, but make no mistake—the world you see now exists because of actions I've taken, and I would take them again. Nuclear weapons? Biological warfare? I've done terrible things to make sure they never saw the light of day."

Smith paused again, lost in thought, then continued, "We developed a new plague, one that would kill eighty percent of those infected. It worked slowly, so the carriers would have enough time to spread the disease. But, during the testing, the virus mutated. It became even more deadly, and we worried that once unleashed it might kill us all." Smith's voice grew rough, and he shook his head sadly. "I halted the research and buried the program."

* * *

Eric stood to answer the knock on his door. Karen was waiting outside with a paper bag in one hand and a cup holder with two large coffees in the other.

"What's this?'

Karen smiled. "I figured you'd be locked in here, driving yourself crazy over the losses in Somalia." She held up the paper bag. "Brought you some cheeseburgers. You don't eat when you're upset."

He motioned for her to enter and she sat on his couch, in front of his wall screen, glancing down at the stack of papers and handgun parts on the coffee table. He grabbed them, clearing space for the paper bag and coffee cups. "Sorry, I wasn't expecting visitors."

She waved her hands around the room. "This is how it always looks, isn't it?"

He watched as she opened the bag and handed him a cheeseburger wrapped in wax paper. He opened it and sniffed, and his stomach growled at the smell of grilled beef and bacon. "I *am* hungry."

"Of course you are. You haven't eaten in almost twenty-four hours."

"I got caught up in the mission. Hey, are you stalking your boss?"

"Just looking out for you. Everyone else is afraid of you."

"Really?" He paused for a moment. Now that she mentioned it, people *did* seem to defer to him an awful lot. "What about Sergeant Clark?"

"Haven't you ever noticed the way he looks when you're near?"

"How's that?"

"When you enter the room, he gets the same look on his face as when the Old Man enters."

"People view me the way they do Smith?" It was news to him. Smith wasn't just his boss—Smith was a force of nature. The man had shaped the second half of the twentieth century.

"They do. You have to remember, people were watching you for years before you were recruited. The Old Man was *very* interested in you. Now, eat your cheeseburger."

He looked down at the sandwich in his hand, then took a bite and washed it down with coffee. Like everything the OTM did, the food at the base was top-notch. The coffee was black with a little cream, just the way he liked it. "Thanks for this."

Karen took a bite of her own sandwich and chugged half of her coffee. "Can I ask what Deion found?"

"It's not a secret. The pirate saw biohazard signs and men in rubber suits on the *Rising Star*." He quickly explained his theory about the ship and their unseen enemy.

Karen leaned back against the couch, staring off into space, and he knew her brain was working overtime to process the information, creating decision trees for investigations.

Her eyes finally focused on him. "I can't think of any nation that would do this. For all their bluster, North Korea seems fine with the status quo. The Chinese provide them just enough aid to keep their government from collapsing because the last thing *they* want is North Korea as a failed nation-state. They're terrified that hordes of refugees might pour over the border."

"Iran is playing the long game," Eric said. "They want to establish control over the Middle East that will last for centuries. Any attack on the US will push us to sanction the Israelis to finally bomb their enrichment facilities. Plus, based on our latest estimates, their knowledge of biological warfare is limited."

She took another swig of coffee. "We're sure the Russians aren't involved?"

"Smith says they aren't. He seems quite sure. No, someone went to the trouble to purchase a bomb and also had a biolab. They're determined."

"And smart. They concealed the owner of the *Rising Star*. They infected ICs with malware."

"They've got deep pockets. Al-Qaeda would love to have the intelligence and money to pull this off, but it's beyond them."

Karen shook her head. "It doesn't fit any terror group we've profiled." She slammed her coffee cup on the table and stood, pacing around the room. "This is exactly the thing we're supposed to find. The unknown unknowns. Not a single digital model I have is helping."

He understood her frustration. "It's bad enough we didn't find the bomb before it detonated. We're lucky it didn't happen here. We need to know what they were making on that ship and whether any of it made it off before it sank."

She stopped pacing. "When all else fails, nothing beats hard work. I'm going to keep searching for the owners of the ship. Nothing can stay hidden forever. If there's a paper trail somewhere, I'll find it."

CHAPTER THIRTEEN

Honolulu, Hawaii

HUANG LEI STOOD before his window, surveying the world below. Events were gaining speed, pushing his hand. He watched the ocean, the peaks and troughs of the waves as they crashed against the shore. The waves had battered at the island for thousands of years, but still the island resisted. It would ever be so until the island was finally swept into the sea.

He had dared to push back at the ocean of data, hoping to change the landscape, but there were forces threatening to wash over him as easily as the ocean over the island.

Unlike the island, however, *he* could fight back.

His computer dinged, and he took his seat. "You have the package?"

Liu Kong nodded. "I am at the facility. We will soon be ready for delivery."

"This is good news. We are nearing our goal. The world will be remade, and it will be a better place. A more civilized place."

"Thank you."

"No, Kong, thank *you*. You've done as I asked, without question, all these many years. I call you my friend."

Kong's eyes widened. "I am honored."

He smiled as his heart filled with love for the man he had plucked from the street. "I hope you succeed—"

"I knew the risk, and I would gladly bear it a thousand times," Kong said. "Great men do not ask to be great. They have it thrust upon them."

"Who said that?"

"You did, when you honored me by asking for my help." Kong smiled, bowed his head, and ended the video conference.

Huang Lei smiled. His net worth was staggering, but it wasn't money that made him rich. His father had told him that riches could only be determined by the love of good friends. If that was true, he was the richest man in the world.

* * *

Area 51

John absently rubbed at the quickly healing scar on his arm as Deion drove the Humvee from the runway to the underground base. They had been in the air for over twenty hours, and John was glad to be back on the ground. The return trip had seemed to take forever.

Deion barreled down the underground tunnel and navigated the checkpoints until they reached the inner bay, where Taylor and Mark helped unload the plastic cases full of Battlesuit gear.

"You didn't get the suit too wet, did you?" Doctor Elliot greeted them.

A pair of technicians grabbed the plastic cases and put them on electric carts and headed to the lab. John watched them go, then smiled wearily. "It wasn't my choice, Doc."

Elliot slapped him on the back with a meaty hand. "Don't worry. We'll take care of it."

"Sorry I lost the HK."

"We've got others. Let's get you to the lab and run some tests."

Taylor and Mark both grinned.

"Better you than me," Mark said. "I'm going to sack out for a week."

"No, you're not," Deion said. "You're *both* going with me. Steeljaw wants us in his office."

Taylor and Mark glanced at each other, smiles fading. "You sure *we're* not needed in the lab?" Taylor asked.

"Only John gets the deluxe treatment," Elliot said.

John followed Doctor Elliot through the halls and tunnels until they reached the lab where Kara was waiting for them, dressed in her blue scrubs.

Her face lit up when she saw him. "Good to see you made it back."

He nodded, but before he could say anything, Doctor Elliot pointed to the examining table and said, "Strip down and sit here."

John took special care to remove his prosthetic foot before stripping out of his fatigues and placing them on a metal table at the side of the room. Naked, except for his briefs, he hopped on his right foot until he reached the table and climbed up.

Kara took his hand and inspected the wound on his arm. The shades of purple and yellow were fading to a fresh pink.

Doctor Elliot put on a headband with magnifying glasses and inspected the wound. "It's healing nicely. I wish *I* could have stitched it up, but this will do. As it is, you'll have a lovely scar to add to your collection."

John sighed. His body was starting to look like a crazy patchwork of jagged white lines, from cuts and scrapes to a waxy circle the size of a dime on his left arm. "I'm gonna be more scars than anything else," he said.

Elliot pointed at his thigh. "How's the leg?"

He lifted his leg and let it fall back. "Hurts worse than the arm."

Elliot traced the diagonal scar across his thigh. "It was deep, but it looks like there's no sign of infection. I read your mission report. You haven't had enough time to properly heal. I'll talk to Eric and see if we can get you downtime."

When Elliot turned to take notes, Kara gave him a smile that warmed his heart.

Elliot took a vial of clear liquid from the cooler and handed it to Kara. "Give him this." He turned to John. "We're giving you a little kick start. Nothing major, just something to speed up the healing. Get something to eat and catch some sleep. Ten hours, at least. You'll need it." He nodded to Kara and left them alone in the lab.

* * *

After Elliot had left, Kara leaned in and kissed him. It wasn't their first kiss, but he certainly didn't *expect* it. His eyes widened, and he leaned in, tasting her lips. It was the nicest thing to happen to him in a long time, and he tried to savor it, but it was over too quickly. She pulled back, and he leaned forward, trying to kiss her again, but she stopped him with a raised finger.

"Uh-uh," she said. "You can't kiss me whenever *you* feel like it."

"What? You kissed *me*. I was just sitting here."

She turned and checked the door to the lab, locking it, then turned back and pulled her scrub top off and dropped it to the floor. She was wearing a simple white bra, which she unclasped in the front and removed.

"What's going on?" he asked. She knew about the Red Cross bombing. While they had dated, he never expected to consummate their relationship, given that she knew he was a monster.

Her naked breasts, full and firm, said otherwise.

She came to him and kissed him passionately. His body responded, even though he was self-conscious of his missing foot and scars. She was breathing harder, and soon she was naked, pulling his briefs down around his ankles.

Their lovemaking was short-lived. She was still kissing him as he struggled to speak. "Sorry. It's been a *long* time."

She giggled and rolled off him, then stood and began dressing. "Don't apologize. You don't *ever* have to apologize to me."

"Not that I'm complaining, but what was that about?"

She stared at him critically. "You don't know, do you? You've almost died numerous times in the field. It finally hit me when I read the medical reports from Turkey. You *could* die at any moment. I guess … I guess I never thought about it before. I realized I liked you."

"You like me? I *never* would have noticed."

"You know what I mean."

He wasn't actually sure *what* she meant. Somewhere along the line, after countless injuries and tests, her demeanor had changed. Maybe it was because she saw the man he had become, or maybe she saw how hard he tried to make up for what he had done.

"Do you believe in second chances?"

She stopped fastening her bra. "What do you mean?"

"I was just a grunt in Iraq. I wanted to make a difference. I wanted to make the US safe. Then my Humvee got hit. Everything fell apart after that. It felt like I failed. Then Eric and Deion recruited me. I was given a second chance."

A mix of emotions played across her face, from concern to suspicion, before finally settling on calm resignation. "You *have* been given a second chance, John. You *are* making a difference. It's what I love about you. Now put your underwear back on so I can give you that shot. Then we can eat and go back to your quarters."

Sounds good to me.

* * *

Dewey's IM popped on Karen's monitor.

HEY, GOT A SEC?

Just like Dewey to bother her when she was working. She gulped down the last of her coffee and answered.

BUSY, DEWEY.

I KNOW. I NEED TO TALK TO YOU.

I'M BUSY, CAN'T IT WAIT?

PLEASE.

She stared at the monitor. Dewey rarely said please.

WHAT?

NOT OVER IM. COME TO MY OFFICE.

She heard someone growling in frustration and realized it was her. She glanced around the War Room, but nobody had noticed. She stood and saluted Sergeant Clark, who acknowledged her with a tip of his head, then exited through the mantrap and took the nearest stairs through the bowels of the base until she found herself in front of Dewey's office.

She rapped her knuckles lightly against the door and counted to five before the door cracked open and Dewey peeked out. His pale skin was almost ghostly white, and sweaty strands of hair were plastered against his head.

"Come in," he said, ushering her through the clutter.

She noticed that much of the junk had been pushed to the corner and nine flat-screen monitors formed a grid behind his main desk. "What are you working on?"

"Not yet. I have to tell you something."

"What's wrong, Dewey? You look like crap."

He slumped into his chair and stared mournfully at her. "I think I made a *big* mistake."

"Start from the beginning. Just take a deep breath and tell me."

He nodded and took a gasping breath, then exhaled slowly. "I did some research for Fulton Smith."

"Okay. What kind of research."

"I hacked Doctor Elliot's files and found something he invented but never actually built."

Her jaw dropped. "You did what?"

"I broke—"

"No," she said. "I heard you. I just can't *believe* it." He started to speak, but she stopped him with a withering glare. "No, I *believe* you did it, but you *shouldn't* have."

"Will you let me finish?"

"Fine. What device?"

"It's a deep-brain stimulator. I don't think he had the time to finish it, but the Old Man asked me to research it, to see if it could help."

"Help *what?*"

Dewey took another deep breath. "The Old Man has Alzheimer's."

"*What?*"

He pulled his legs up, his heels resting on the edge of his seat, then wrapped his arms around his knees. "I guess he's getting worse. Doctor Barnwell has been treating him with an experimental drug, but it's not working anymore. They're going to implant the device in the Old Man's head."

Karen rocked back in her chair, staring at her friend. "That's crazy. Why did you ever think to *do* such a thing? How did you even know *how* to do such a thing?"

"It was the Old Man," Dewey said. "He asked me to break into Elliot's files. When I found it, the Old Man asked if it could help someone with Alzheimer's. I broke into a researcher's database at Harvard and … appropriated their work. The initial trials looked promising. With Elliot's device and some of the tech here, I figured out how to make it work."

"Appropriated?" Dewey was a dear friend, but he lacked boundaries. If Eric knew all the things Dewey had broken into and "appropriated" over the years, Dewey would probably be locked up in a box. And *that* box would be locked inside *another* box.

And they would lose the key. "Why didn't you tell me this sooner?"

"I didn't want to worry you. I knew you would say I shouldn't have done it."

"You *shouldn't* have done it."

"But the Old Man asked. I couldn't turn him down. He might get angry. Or Nancy. I don't want to make *her* angry. But now I think maybe she doesn't know about it."

"You can't base all your decisions off angering your girlfriend. You don't have to do things just to keep her happy."

He squinted at her. "Are you sure? That doesn't sound right."

"Damn it, Dewey! Will the device work?"

His eyes darted around his office before settling back on her. "I don't know. It should. The theories are sound."

"You don't have the background to judge that," she said. "I know you're smart, but you're not an expert. Did you tell Nathan about this?"

"He was mad. Real mad. Of course, he didn't say it *wouldn't* work, and he agreed to do the surgery..."

"I can't believe this. They're going to put this in Smith's head? When?"

"Soon," Dewey whispered. "You think Nancy will blame me if it doesn't work?"

Karen wanted to slap him. "If it doesn't work? What if it *kills* him?"

"I never thought about that. That would make Nancy pretty mad, wouldn't it?"

She wanted to scream. "If that happens, we'd have to get you out of here. There's no telling what she might do."

"That's not very comforting."

"You ought to be terrified, Dewey. You always do things like this. You always get yourself into trouble."

He hugged himself tighter, and they sat in silence while her mind raced. If the device worked, the Old Man would be grateful, but if it failed, his memory would continue to slip. She knew about Eric's mother and her sudden-onset Alzheimer's. If the same happened to the Old Man, it would be a disaster. He was the foundation of the OTM.

Maybe if she told Nancy, the procedure could be put on hold. "Here's what you're going to do," she said. "You're going to tell Nancy everything. Eric too. You've got to get ahead of this."

"That sounds like it might get me in *more* trouble."

"You'll be in a hell of a lot more trouble if he dies!"

"Oh. Okay. Thanks, Karen. You're a good friend."

"I'm your *only* friend, Dewey."

"You *are* my only friend," he conceded. "That's why I can tell you about this other thing."

"Other thing?"

He pointed at the wall of monitors. "I got bored, so I checked your work."

"You checked my work? I told you to stop hacking into my workstation."

"I know, I know," Dewey said. "I'm sorry. I just wanted to help."

"You are simply unbelievable. You've got to quit doing things like this. Aren't you in *enough* trouble?"

He nodded rapidly. "I'm sorry, Karen. I know you told me not to, but I just couldn't help myself. I found something."

Her anger started to fade. As oblivious as Dewey could be about personal space and privacy, he was also a genius. "What did you find?"

"You know the Chinese hackers? Unit 61398?"

She knew. The whole OTM knew. The People's Liberation Army had recruited an entire city of young hackers who had spent the last two years engaged in a shadowy game of cyberwarfare aimed at US companies. It no longer made sense for China to develop their own computers or weapons platforms, not when they could steal the data from companies in the US.

Everything from banking portals to medical devices to stealth technology was suddenly open season for the PLA's hacking division. Lockheed Martin had suffered a massive invasion that allowed the hackers to gather schematics and research for a number of classified drone programs, as well as the algorithms behind a myriad of stealth technologies.

The stolen data was provided to Chinese companies, giving them a competitive edge. It went beyond espionage. China was engaged in worldwide economic warfare.

She knew all this because they had an inside man in Unit 61398. "What have you found?"

He pointed to the monitor. "One of the other projects the Old Man had me working on. The network taps at all ISPs in the

United States have been capturing and forwarding a copy of every packet bound for Unit 61398."

She gasped. "Why didn't *I* know about this? I've been running point on the Unit 61398 case."

"I don't know. The Old Man likes to be thorough? Two sets of eyes, maybe?"

"How did you manage this?"

"I used the same network taps we have at the data centers. I just redirected a copy of every packet bound for IPs that we've registered to Unit 61398 to our data warehouse."

"I don't believe this. Any other bombshells you'd like to drop on me?"

"Uh, no? Well, just the last thing. I searched the exfiltrated data from the US companies for bioterror and bombs and found something interesting. How much do you know about Red Team?"

* * *

Eric shook his head. "Red Team? I've taken part in one." He knew that Red Teams were groups created to challenge an organization's effectiveness. Delta routinely participated in Red Teams. In 2004, he'd helped set up the Army's Directed Studies Office. They ran thought exercises about military strategy and possible threats to American military power, usually focusing on emerging threats. "What does Red Team have to do with anything?"

Nancy sat next to him in the conference room. Deion was to his left, and Karen sat at the head of the table, gulping down the remains of her coffee before answering. "The CIA has been running Red Teams for years, but after 9/11, they *really* stepped it up. They brought together scientists, science fiction authors, and business people, put them in a compound in Colorado and told them to go nuts."

"I'd heard about that," Nancy said. "The results were ... intriguing."

"I heard about that from Val," Deion joined in. "The eggheads came up with some wild shit."

"That's one way to describe it," Karen said. "Dewey ran searches against the copies of the stolen data that Unit 61398 pilfered from US companies. Have you heard of the EOS Corp?"

Eric had. EOS was a giant conglomerate that had its fingers in a million different high-tech and biomedical research pies. "Dean Palmer, right?"

"I *heard* about him," Deion said. "Real brainiac. Lives like he's broke. Puts all his money into R&D?"

"That's him," Karen said. "He took part in the CIA's Red Team from 2003 until 2006. The Red Team's mandate was to plan for a multipronged attack. Apparently Mr. Palmer kept thinking about it, and after the exercise was over, he wrote a detailed plan for detonating a nuclear weapon in New York City while also striking the United States with a genetically engineered virus."

Eric sat up so suddenly his chair squeaked. "You've *got* to be kidding."

"EOS was one of the corps that got hacked by Unit 61398," Nancy said grimly.

"Shit," Deion said, slapping his hands on the table. "Palmer practically *gave* it to them."

"Dewey was collecting a database of Unit 61398's stolen information. When he ran a search for bioterror and nuclear weapons, he found Palmer's report."

Eric's mind raced, but something bothered him. "How did Dewey gather this data?"

Karen swallowed hard. "The Old Man tasked Dewey with side jobs over the past several years."

"Side jobs?" Nancy asked. "*What* side jobs?"

"Jobs like examining the Chinese hacking threat and evaluating the stolen data," Karen said. "Palmer developed a plan using bioterror and a nuke. It's safe to assume the PLA has it."

Eric nodded. "Is there any chance that Palmer is compromised?"

"Unlikely," Karen said. "He's the most upright person you'd ever meet. He donates most of his money to charities, and he's competing with Bill Gates to give away his fortune before he dies."

Nancy cleared her throat. "We need to put an electronic leash on Palmer, just to be sure."

"Already done," Karen said. "What about the Chinese?"

"It just doesn't make sense," Eric said. "It's not like them. Stealing secrets are one thing, but implementing a plan to nuke America?" He shook his head. "Why attack now?"

Deion grunted. "They're pissed about Taiwan. Maybe that's the straw that broke the camel's back?"

"No," Eric said. "They've been claiming Taiwan for years. Nothing has changed."

"Instability in East Asia," Nancy said. "Think about it. We've attacked Iraq and Afghanistan. The fluctuations in global oil prices threaten their economic growth."

"That *does* sound more likely. We've got to contact our asset in Unit 61398 and find out what he knows."

Karen smiled. "On it, boss. I've drafted a mission for your review." Her smile faltered. "I've got something else. Well, Dewey has something else."

Eric clenched his jaw. He was going to have a long talk with Dewey Green, the man who suddenly had his fingers in every one of the OTM's pies. "What now?"

"He's been working on *another* project for the Old Man," Karen said. She turned to Nancy. "Your father has Alzheimer's."

Nancy leaned forward in her chair, her face pale, knuckles turning white as her hands gripped the arms of her chair. "What?"

Karen spoke quickly, the words pouring out. "He asked Dewey to research a treatment. It's called a deep-brain stimulator—"

Nancy didn't let her finish. She stood so suddenly her chair slid back and slammed against the wall of the conference room. She was turning to leave when Eric stood. "Nancy," he barked. "Stand down."

She wheeled around and glared at him. "Focus on the mission. I'm going to speak to my father."

He watched as she stormed out of the conference room. "I better go with her."

Deion whistled softly. "Better you than me, man."

* * *

183

Eric caught up to Nancy in a narrow tunnel. "What are you going to do?" he asked. He thought about grabbing her hand, but one look at the expression on her face and he quickly changed his mind.

Nancy continued her rapid walk through the tunnels and halls of the base. "I want to know if it's true."

Soldiers and technicians swerved around them as Nancy stomped through the base. "Slow down. He might have a good reason for not telling you."

She turned to stare at him but didn't slow her pace. "He keeps secrets, and nobody ever calls him on it. I'm his *daughter*. Why wouldn't he tell me?"

They reached Smith's office, and Nancy didn't bother to knock. She flung open the door so hard it slammed against the inside wall.

The Old Man was sitting at his desk, speaking calmly to Doctor Barnwell. Barnwell turned, startled, but Smith just smiled. "An unexpected pleasure," Smith said. "Please, come in."

Nancy started to speak, her jaw working, but Eric jumped in before she could say anything. "We just got disturbing news, sir."

Smith turned to Barnwell. "Did you?"

Barnwell shook his head. "*I* didn't say anything."

"Is it true?" Nancy demanded. "Do you have Alzheimer's?"

"I'm afraid it's true." Smith placed his weathered hands on the top of the ancient wooden desk. "I'm sorry I didn't tell you myself—"

"Are you?"

"My dear, I am sorry for *many* things. I didn't want to worry you. You've been through so much already—"

"You didn't think I could handle it? You wanted to protect me?"

"I've *tried* to protect you your entire life," Smith said. "What would you have me do? Shout from the rooftops? I had work to complete. Hobert has been treating me, but the treatments are no longer working."

Nancy turned her withering glare on Barnwell. "Why didn't *he* tell me?"

"Nancy, calm down," Eric said. "I'm sure they had good reasons."

She turned her stony gaze upon him. "This doesn't concern you."

"It *does* concern Eric," Smith said. "I must complete an orderly transition of the Office to Eric's hands."

The pieces finally clicked into place for Eric. "How long have you known?"

"You already know the answer."

It all made sense. Smith's rush to recruit him for Project StrikeForce, the push to promote him, even naming him assistant director of the OTM. "I guess I do."

Nancy froze. "I..."

Smith stood and stepped around his desk. Eric noticed how slowly the man walked, how carefully he approached his daughter.

"I'm an old man," Smith said, taking his daughter's hand in his own. "You've known this was coming. Deep in your heart, you've known. I'm sorry I kept you in the dark. It wasn't to hurt you."

For the first time, Eric saw the vulnerability on Nancy's face. She seemed to deflate, her anger disappearing only to be replaced by uncertainty. "How bad is it?"

Smith gripped Nancy's hand tighter. "I'm in stage two. Without Hobert's help, I would be in stage five."

Eric knew the staging system from his experience with his mother. Stage five would be bad for a man as powerful as Smith. "What about this thing Dewey worked on?"

"It will give me months," Smith acknowledged. "Perhaps it will be enough time to ensure you have the Office well in hand."

"I hate to be the bearer of bad news," Barnwell said, "but we have no idea if this will work. You're asking Nathan to implant metal probes into your *brain*. It's ludicrous." He turned to Nancy. "Can't you talk some sense into him?"

Nancy's eyes darted from Barnwell to her father. "*Dewey* created this? They're going to put something in your *brain*?"

Smith's smile faltered. "Dewey didn't create it. Nathan did. Mr. Green repurposed it." He released Nancy's hand and slowly lowered himself back into his seat.

"I'm sorry. Each of you deserves better. Hob, you've been a trusted friend. Nancy, you've deserved more than I've been able to provide. You, young Eric," he said, pointing. "It is *your* legacy to be my replacement. If the operation is successful, I will have little time to complete my transition. And if it fails, well, then my time has come to an end. There's nothing to be done about it." He nodded at them. "My decision has been made."

CHAPTER FOURTEEN

ERIC SAT WITH Nancy and Barnwell, watching the doctors through the thick glass. He hadn't been in the observation room in two years, not since they'd used nanobots to sheath John's skeleton in carbon graphene mesh. Smith lay in the center of the room, strapped to a table, while Doctor Elliot and Doctor Oshensker hovered nearby.

The observation room reeked of carpet cleaner and antiseptic, a stench Eric remembered well. He turned up his nose and cleared his throat, trying to shake the smell. "You sure you don't want to take one last stab at changing his mind?"

"It wouldn't do any good," Nancy said. "He's stubborn, and once he's made up his mind…"

Barnwell watched their exchange before finally speaking. "How can you be okay with this?"

"He's never cared for my opinion. What makes you think he would suddenly listen to me?"

"She's right," Eric said. "He's the Old Man. It's part of who he is."

Barnwell snorted. "He's an old fool. This is an unnecessary risk."

Eric agreed, but also saw the Old Man's point. He'd watched his mother lose her memory after his father's death. When he'd placed her in the assisted living facility, she hadn't known his name or acknowledged his presence.

He thought of Smith slowly losing his memory, with changes to his personality and cognitive ability. It terrified him. Smith had access to deep resources, not the least of which was the base at Area 51, but also including agents around the world. If Smith started making bad decisions, it could cost people their lives.

Lots of people.

Doctor Elliot checked the monitor. "The subject is under. We are ready to begin the procedure."

Smith lay upside down, his head surrounded by a halo of steel rods and tubes. The base of his spine was shaved bare of what little snow-white hair remained. Eric watched as a computer-controlled probe touched the bare skin.

"We're going to begin by making an incision," Doctor Elliot said. "We'll use a small core drill to drill into the bottom of the skull. Once we have our entry, the computer will insert the probes into the brain. Then, we will connect the wires to the controller and place the controller under the skin."

Nancy cringed, and he could only imagine what was going through her head. *Then again, she's not like most women. She might not feel concern. It could just be rage.*

She finally spoke. "Continue, Doctor."

"I want it recorded that I'm doing this under protest."

"Duly noted. You may proceed."

Eric shuddered as the computer activated the probes. The surgery began and the minutes slowly ticked by.

* * *

The probes finally completed their job, and Doctor Elliot delicately stitched up the small incision at the back of the Old Man's neck. Elliot stopped and turned to Doctor Oshensker. "Time to bring him up."

Oshensker nodded and punched the keyboard of his computer.

Eric watched the monitors as Smith's vitals began to climb. He also watched Nancy out of the corner of his eye, but she remained motionless, eyes fixated on her father.

"He's coming to," Elliot said. He patted Smith on the arm. "Don't move. Just relax. The procedure was a success. We will unclamp your head and remove your oxygen tube as soon as possible."

He nodded again to Oshensker, who keyed a series of commands, and the metal rods holding Smith's head retracted, leaving Smith's face pressed against the oval face rest. Elliot reached underneath and pulled the tube from Smith's mouth. It came out long and slimy, and Elliot placed it on a metal tray next to the table.

"Can you speak?"

Smith raised his head and asked in a rough whisper, "Was the surgery successful?"

"We placed the implant," Elliot said. "Since you're not a drooling idiot, I assume we didn't cause any brain damage. We'll get you cleaned up and in the recovery room. Then we'll start with the diagnostic questions to make sure there's no cognitive decline."

Smith cleared his throat. "How long ... before ... you can activate it?"

"Not for several days. We need to take it slow"

"S—slow?"

"Yes. We need to baseline your cognitive functioning before we activate the stimulator."

Smith coughed repeatedly, then croaked, "As soon as possible."

Elliot and Oshensker exchanged glances, then went to work on cleaning Smith up.

Eric turned to Nancy and Barnwell. "I guess the excitement is over."

Nancy stood. "There is nothing for us to do here. I'm sorry I let my father's condition impact our work."

Barnwell placed his hand on Nancy's arm. "It's not a bad thing to worry about your father. It means you're human."

"It's only been a couple of hours," Eric said. "I don't think the world will end because we stepped away for a moment."

Nancy looked down to Barnwell's hand on her arm. "We need to get back to work."

Eric agreed, if for no other reason than his hope that work would distract Nancy from her father's surgery. "Let's see what Karen has planned."

They made their way to the War Room and found Karen in the conference room. She glanced up as they entered. "Good. You're both here. I have the mission profile."

Nancy took her seat at the end of the table. "Proceed."

"Our asset is named Wei Dong. He's been inside Unit 61398 for almost three years." A picture of a young Chinese man appeared on the screen. "The Unit has relaxed their security. We now meet him directly instead of using dead drops. We need to ask him about the Unit and see if he knows anything about Palmer's Red Team plan."

"Sounds good," Eric said. "How many team members?"

"Two."

"Send Deion," Nancy said. "He speaks Mandarin."

"Done," Eric said.

"I have something else," Karen said. "I found a possible link between the Jade Group, the holding company that manufactured the infected ICs in the cameras from Nashville, and a shell corporation that owns the MV *Rising Star*. Both companies share an IP address registered to another holding company in Seoul called C-Tec. I can't break through their firewall, but the business has a physical address."

"Definitely worth checking out," Eric said. "Nancy, this might be an opportunity for you to get out in the world and clear your mind."

Nancy looked as if she might disagree, then nodded her head. "Perhaps you're right."

"Would you take John? He needs downtime and Korea would be a break from the last week."

Nancy raised an eyebrow. "Don't trust me alone?"

"That's not—"

"Relax," Nancy said, her mouth quirking up in a smirk. "I was … kidding. I'll get Frist, and we'll be wheels up in thirty." She stood and headed for the door. As she opened it, she turned back to Eric and Karen. "Be good," she said before closing the door behind her.

He turned to Karen. "Did she make a joke?"

Karen's mouth was hanging open. "If I hadn't seen it, I wouldn't have believed it. It almost makes her seem … normal."

"She just watched a computer insert electrodes into her father's skull. She's a far cry from normal."

"Right…"

"Look, about that guy, Dean Palmer. I want to read his report and then I want to meet with him."

"I can get you the report, but a meeting in person?"

"Yes."

"Wait, is that why you sent Nancy to Korea, so you could get back in the field?"

"No," he said, then thought better of it. "That's not *totally* why I sent her to Korea. I *do* want to meet with Palmer, though, and ask him more about Red Team."

"You know who could help with that? Valerie Simon. She helped run one of the Red Teams in 2004, before she went to Afghanistan."

"How do you know that?"

"Because I'm good at my job?"

"Karen—"

"I knew you looked into her after the thing with Nancy in Afghanistan," Karen said, "so I did a little digging of my own. She's a solid operative."

"I know. I'm thinking of recruiting her."

Karen frowned. "What does Deion think about that?"

"Does it matter? The Office could use her."

"But—"

"Besides, it's probably the only chance the two of them have together. You can't have a normal relationship in this life, not with a civilian. At least with Valerie, he stands a chance."

"You're ... starting to remind me of the Old Man. I'll get a copy of Palmer's schedule and have a mission plan on your desk in an hour."

"You can get Palmer's schedule in one hour?"

She laughed, a hearty guffaw that shook her ample chest. "I'm not Dewey, boss, but I have my moments."

* * *

Smith opened his eyes. He was in his quarters, lying in bed, and Hobert sat in a chair next to his bed.

"Checking on my well-being?" Smith asked.

Hobert snorted. "You're a damned old *fool*. I could almost strangle you."

He was still light-headed from the anesthesia, and the room spun as he attempted to sit up. "Nathan said I was fine."

"Then *Nathan* is a fool. You could have been lobotomized."

Smith glanced over at the concerned face of his friend. "That's where I was headed," he murmured. "As it is, I'm only buying time. *Assuming* it works."

Hobert glared at him, then nodded his head. "*Assuming* it works. The diagnostics appear normal. I know you're eager—"

"Not eager. My choices are limited."

"Well, he's ready to activate the probes. Are you sure about this?"

He nodded grimly. "I have work to do. You know what's at stake."

"I know that Eric is an excellent replacement. I know that Nancy isn't as … damaged … as I first believed. I know the Office will continue without you. Or me, for that matter."

Smith stood on shaky legs. "Damn it, Hob, I have to fix things with Alexandra."

"It's impossible, Fulton. Not with the time you have left, or even with the extra time this device may possibly give you. You need to—"

"I can't believe that. I *refuse* to believe that. If I can bring Alexandra home, then perhaps Nancy will finally feel … whole."

Hobert sighed in frustration. "You don't know where Alexandra is. That was part of the arrangement. You don't even have a way to contact her."

"There's an upcoming dead drop. I could message her. If I can just make Vasilii see reason—"

"*Vasilii* isn't the problem. Even if you could get him to agree, the men he works for would never allow it."

Smith wanted to shout at his friend, but he knew Hobert was only acting as the voice of reason. Numerous discussions with Hobert had not brought him any closer to a solution. "I would say it's not fair, but you know that. If I have any time left, I *must* make it right."

Hobert slumped back in his chair. "I don't know how you hope to pull it off, but I hope you can. I'll do anything to help, obviously."

Smith put his hand on Hobert's shoulder. "Take me to Nathan." He tapped the small incision on the back of his neck. "It's time to activate this thing."

* * *

"You're sure?" Elliot asked.

Smith nodded. "Yes, Nathan, I'm sure."

They were in another lab, a small room with slate-gray walls not far from the operating room, and Smith was stretched out on a hospital bed in case he suffered from seizures. Doctor Elliot held a tablet computer, watching it intently.

"Nathan?" Doctor Oshensker said. "He's ready."

"You shouldn't feel anything," Elliot said. "The amount of current being applied to the cortex is tiny, but just in case, prepare yourself."

Hobert sat on a tall stool, watching over the preparation. "Last chance to back out."

He heard the concern in Hobert's voice and the apprehension in Elliot's and knew they were worried about him. "For better or worse, I'm ready."

Elliot cleared his throat. "Applying charge."

He steeled himself, hopeful the implant would work, but terrified he might suddenly have a seizure that would send him crashing to the hard tile floor. He caught his breath but after several seconds exhaled. He felt no discernible change.

"Is that it?"

"Charge is applied," Oshensker confirmed.

Elliot turned to the display on the wall. "Telemetry shows the device is working correctly. I'm going to ask you a series of questions. Answer as quickly as you can."

They spent ten minutes going over questions designed to gauge his memory retrieval until Elliot finally raised his hand. "Stop. Your reaction time hasn't *worsened*."

Smith stared up at the acoustic ceiling tiles. For a moment, he felt a burning in his eyes, a feeling he hadn't felt in years. *Are those the start of tears?* "I was hoping for something … more."

"It's a slow process," Elliot said. "If it improves, and that's a big *if*, it will take weeks before your reaction time decreases."

He considered that. "What if it doesn't improve?"

"Then we've done all we can."

He didn't blame Elliot. The brain stimulator was a last-ditch effort, and Elliot was right—it would take time to see if there were results. "May I sit up?"

Elliot nodded and Smith sat up, then turned to Hobert. "Time to get back to work."

"You really *should* rest," Oshensker said.

Smith glanced between the two men. "Is there any reason I *need* to stay here?"

Hobert said, "Well—"

"Not really," Elliot said. "Just don't engage in any heavy physical activity, and if you start feeling faint, sit down and call us."

Smith stood on his tired old legs and folded his suit jacket over his arm, then bowed his head. "Gentlemen, you have my gratitude."

* * *

Seoul, Korea

Their flight had taken most of the day and night before they had made it to Seoul, rented a car, and reached their destination. John craned his neck to catch a good view of the darkened building in the center of the city, just south of the river. Karen Kryzowski had identified their target, a company called C-Tech, and records placed it on the eight floor.

He tried the door but found it locked. A security guard, a young Korean man in a dark blue uniform, approached them and said something in a sharp voice. Nancy nodded and answered in Korean. She removed a wallet from her purse and quickly slipped the guard a stack of cash. The guard eyed them suspiciously, then nodded and unlocked the door for them.

They entered the darkened reception area and made their way to the bank of elevators. As the elevator rose, John turned to Nancy. "You think we have to worry about the guard?"

She shook her head. "No. He'll keep his mouth shut."

"How do you know?"

She rolled her eyes. "I can tell."

He shrugged, still grinning. He was just glad to be away from the base, even if it meant leaving Kara behind. Their relationship had moved slowly, but she seemed happy taking it to a new level.

He was still confused, and he wished for the millionth time he could tell her the memory overlay hadn't held, and that he remembered bombing the Red Cross.

Then he remembered she was a soldier first. It would only take a few words from her to Doctor Elliot or even Doctor Barnwell, and then Eric would have to put a bullet in the back of his head.

As the elevator continued to rise, he wondered if Eric would feel bad when he pulled the trigger. Eric claimed to be his friend and *did* watch out for him. He wasn't so naive to think that Eric only protected him out of friendship. He represented a significant investment for the OTM, not to mention the potential use of the StrikeForce tech.

No, Eric *might* like him, but he was a beta test. Their guinea pig. A convenient way to test their technology.

The elevator slowed and the doors opened on the eighth floor. They stepped out into a dark hallway. John pointed to the directory listing across from the elevator. The names were listed in Korean and English, and their target, C-Tec, was among the floor's occupants.

He pointed to the right. "Looks like it's that way."

They walked down the darkened hallway, passing doors with brightly colored logos, until they reached the plain wooden door with the C-Tec logo in black lettering. Except for them, the hallway was empty.

He turned to Nancy. "Well?"

Nancy opened her handbag and withdrew a device the size of a cell phone. She turned it on and swept it back and forth. "No heat signatures. The office is empty."

"How are we going to get in? You want me to knock the door off its hinges?"

She rolled her eyes and pulled out a lockpick set. "It's an old-school lock." She took a key, inserted it into the lock, then withdrew a small heavy screwdriver and banged the end of the key while turning it.

There was a snick as the lock opened. He turned to Nancy and felt his jaw drop.

Nancy put the key and screwdriver back into the lockpick set, then noticed the look on his face. "What?"

"You're scary sometimes."

"Why only sometimes?"

He bit his lip. "What now?"

She pointed to the door. "You're the super soldier. You go first."

"Glad to be cannon fodder."

A genuine smile lit up her face. "I dislike you less than most. Try not to die."

"Yes, ma'am." He took a breath, then gently pushed the door open and stepped inside.

He half-expected a booby trap and was glad when nothing happened. He found the light switch and flicked it on. The office was long and narrow, with a desk at one end and a rack of computer gear at the other.

He motioned to Nancy and she entered the office and closed the door, locking it.

"Doesn't look like there's much here," he said.

Nancy pointed to the rack at the end of the room. "Karen tried to break in but couldn't get past their firewall." She shook her head. "No matter how many layers of technology you try to hide behind, there has to be a computer terminal somewhere. And *there* it is."

They approached the rack. He inspected the gear but was unable to make sense of it. "What are we supposed to do with this?"

She pulled a small thumb drive from her handbag and plugged it into the USB port of the top computer, then removed her cell phone and made a call. "It's in. You should see it momentarily. Yeah. Yeah. Okay." She hung up and put the phone back in her purse.

"That's it?"

"C-Tec is a small ISP leasing bandwidth from SK Broadband. Karen suspects these computers have been hosting IPs and websites involved with the MV *Rising Star* and the attacks in Nashville and Syria. She couldn't break in, but that thumb drive contained a rootkit that installed and took control of the computer, then dialed home via an encrypted channel. She's cloning the computer now." She removed the thumb drive and plugged it into the USB port on the next computer, waited a few moments, then continued until she had placed it in every computer in the rack. She checked her cell phone and smiled. "All the computers are talking out. Karen will soon have *everything* on these systems."

"How do you know so much about this stuff?"

Nancy grunted. "I don't, I just listen to Karen when she speaks. Osmosis, I guess. Take a look around, what do you see?"

"It looks like an office."

"Of *course*," she said, an edge to her voice. "Look closely. You've trained for this. What do you see?"

He spun around slowly. "Nothing on the walls. No pictures. No artwork. The desk is clean." He walked over and rifled through the drawers. "Nothing." He peeked over the edge. "Nothing in the trash. The office is a front for the servers and that's it." He sniffed. "Wait a minute. I smell something." He picked up the trash can and sniffed. "Smells like ... tea?"

He lifted the trash can and looked inside. There was a stain on the bottom. He tilted it so Nancy could lean in and sniff.

"Smells like green tea," Nancy agreed. "It's still pungent. It's not old. Green tea quickly loses its scent."

He raised an eyebrow. "How the hell do you know that?"

"Just one of those things. If the tea isn't old, it means a regular visitor."

"So what do we do?"

"Simple. We wait."

CHAPTER FIFTEEN

Shanghai, China

DEION WORMED THE rental car through the crowded streets of Shanghai before reaching Pudong. The city was ablaze with neon lights. He could almost close his eyes and pretend he was home in Chicago, except Shanghai had a metropolitan vibe all its own.

He kept an eye on the rearview mirror while he navigated the heavy traffic, driving past sidewalks full of young men and women wearing clothes of every color, many in shades of neon, or black leather with silver and chrome accents.

Mark Kelly noticed him watching the mirror. "How could *anyone* follow us in this mess?"

Deion snorted. "The Chinese keep a close eye on the airport. I don't *think* they have the assets to follow every car, but you never know."

"Right. So, why bring me instead of TM?"

Deion took a left. "We're trying to blend in. Two black guys on the streets of Shanghai? That's not blending in. That's a potential carjacking."

Mark guffawed. "TM is wrong. You *do* have a sense of humor."

"Don't tell Wise. He thinks I'm all business." He pulled the car to the curb and parked on a narrow side street, peering down the back alley. Their contact, Wei Dong, regularly met his handler, Robert Morrison, in the back of the noodle shop they were observing.

After several minutes, he turned to Mark. "Looks clear. Let's go."

They made their way to an unmarked door in the alley, where Deion knocked four times. An old Chinese man opened the door and glared at them until Deion handed him a paper bag full of yuan. The old man peered inside the bag, then opened the door and waved them in.

The old man led them to a storage room stacked to the ceiling with bags of flour and white cardboard boxes, nodded, then shut the door behind him as he left.

Mark raised an eyebrow. "The old man trustworthy?"

"Yu? He's worked for the OTM for years. As long as the money holds out, he's rock solid."

After a few minutes the door opened and a lean young man with greasy hair stepped in and closed the door behind him.

"Wei Dong?" Deion asked.

The young man frowned. "Who are you?," he replied in Mandarin. "Where's Bob?"

Deion didn't feel comfortable with three men parading through Shanghai, nor with Robert Morrison learning more about their mission than necessary. Even in the OTM, there were levels of operational security. "I know Bob is your handler, but we need to speak with you," Deion replied in Mandarin.

Wei eyed them suspiciously and shifted from foot to foot. "I don't *know* you."

Deion nodded. "Bob said your mother loves lilacs, but roses are her favorites."

The man stopped his fidgeting. "True," he said in heavily accented English. "What do you want from me? Things are … crazy since that bomb went off. It's all everyone can talk about."

"How crazy?"

"High security. They search us when we enter or leave."

It made sense, of course. The nuke *was* a major world event and Wei *did* work for the PLA. "We need to ask you about the data the Unit's collected. You know where it's stored?"

"Yes," Wei said. "I'm a firewall guy. I have to know where the data is so that I can protect it."

Protect it? It was stolen from US companies. "Who has access?"

"Lots of people. A team analyzes everything and rates it. If it's important, it goes to the Army guys."

"Army guys?" Mark asked.

Wei nodded. "Most of us are *hackers*. We're not soldiers. We do it for fun and for money. We're not bad guys. The Army guys? They're dicks!"

Deion smiled. "So what happens when the Army guys get the data?"

"If it has a potential commercial use, they send it to their contacts in companies across China. If it has a military use? I don't know. There's a firewall rule that allows outbound connections to an offsite Army data center." He ran his fingers through his greasy hair and smiled. "Tell me what you're looking for. Maybe I can help."

Deion glanced at Mark, who shrugged, then decided to risk it. "We're looking for a document from the EOS Corporation. Do you know it?"

"Yeah," Wei said. "I remember. It was a long time ago. They had a vulnerability in their firewall. When it crashed, it phoned home on reboot. We DOS'd the firewall until it rebooted, and intercepted the phone-home with malicious packets that overflowed the buffer and gave us root access. We tunneled back out and grabbed everything we could before they switched to different hardware."

"Can you trace the EOS data?" Deion asked. "Without getting caught?"

Wei laughed and gave them a cocky grin. "I'm the best. If *I* poke around, *nobody* will know."

Deion hoped the young man was right. If Wei was caught, there would be no second chances. "Find out. Don't write anything down and don't take anything out of the building. Memorize it. We'll meet you here tomorrow."

"If anyone can do it, I can."

* * *

Seoul, Korea

John sat on the floor of the office, watching the flashing lights from the rack of equipment against the far wall, but even the blinking lights had lost their appeal. He tried to engage Nancy in conversation but quit after numerous one-word answers.

They had been waiting for most of the night with nothing to do. He checked his watch for the hundredth time and found only a few minutes had passed since he last checked.

I should have brought a deck of cards. "Is it possible for time to stand still?"

Nancy was reclining in the desk chair. She rolled her eyes. "You're not the only one who doesn't like waiting."

"I swear, it was three forty-five two hours ago."

She snorted, stretching her arms and making fists. "I just want to hit somebody."

There was something about Nancy that reminded him of some of the soldiers he'd served with in Iraq. The way her eyes skipped over his face, the way they always seemed slightly out of focus. It was the same with the soldiers who had seen heavy combat and lost a lot of friends. *They* were the dangerous ones.

Plus, she knew the truth about him. *She's the Old Man's daughter. She has to know.*

He slumped against the wall and closed his eyes. His arm and leg still ached, and his prosthetic was still sending sharp pains up his leg. He slowed his breathing and stilled his mind, on the verge of sleep.

There was a soft rustling outside and his eyes snapped open. Nancy was wide awake, motioning for him to move. He stood and she hopped off the chair, catlike, and they pressed themselves against the wall next to the door. There was the scraping of a key in the door lock, then a click. The door swung open and someone stepped inside and turned on the light.

John blinked in the sudden glare, but as the door swung closed, he saw a short Asian man with spiky black hair in an expensive suit. The man turned, his eyes widening in surprise as he realized he wasn't alone in the office.

John didn't wait. He rushed the man, planning to tackle him to the floor and grapple with him, but the man caught his arm, rolled, and sent John crashing across the tile.

There was an explosion of pain when John's head smashed against the side of the desk, and he tasted coppery blood where he had bitten his tongue when he struck the desk. His vision swam as he struggled to sit up. He reached for the floor to steady himself and swallowed a mouthful of blood in the process.

He blinked and saw Nancy fighting the man. It was like watching two tigers in battle, all hands and feet striking and blocking.

He shook his head, trying to clear it, then staggered to his feet and lunged at the man. He caught the man's legs and they tumbled back against the door. John's head struck the wall, and there was a tunneling effect as everything shrank to a narrow black dot.

He felt himself blacking out, a warm numbness that threatened to pull him under. He shook his head, trying to restore his senses, and grabbed for the man's throat but recoiled in pain as the man's thumb rammed into his eye, forcing him to blink back tears.

This guy is going to beat me.

No, he couldn't allow it. He grabbed for the man, desperate to take him down, but it was too late. There was a zap-zapping that echoed against the office walls and his muscles locked up as electric fire surged through his body.

That bastard is tasing me!

John tried to move, but his body wouldn't respond. The stun gun stopped and the man shoved him off, then he heard the zap-zapping again, followed by a soft thud as Nancy hit the ground.

He squinted through his good eye and saw Nancy, helpless, on the floor. There was a sharp pain in his ribs as the man kicked him aside, knocking him from the doorway.

He struggled to sit as the man opened the door, then the man kicked him in the chest, knocking him back.

It wasn't anger as much as plain stubbornness that made him sit up. He wasn't about to let the man get away, not after knocking them both senseless. He only wished Nancy had allowed him to bring his M11.

It took every ounce of energy, but he managed to stand and stagger into the hallway. The man had stopped at the elevators and was frantically stabbing at the down button.

John took a limping step and the man turned to him, his eyes widening.

"Get *him*," Nancy growled from behind. He turned and saw her hunched over, following as best she could.

He pushed himself to move faster. The man saw this and turned, desperate to find a way out, but the stairwell was behind John.

He'll have to go through me to escape.

The man stopped, his face suddenly resigned, then reached inside his suit and pulled something from it.

John flinched, expecting a gun and a hail of bullets, but the man didn't point it at them. Time froze as John recognized the smooth black shape. His stomach lurched as the man smiled and pulled the pin, then held the object in the palm of his hand.

Grenade!

He turned and saw Nancy's eyes widen as he threw himself on top of her. They hit the floor in a heap. Nancy cursed but he relaxed his body, smothering her, and then a terrific clap of thunder took his breath away as the grenade detonated.

There was a steady squeal of noise in his ears. He rolled off Nancy and stared dumbly at the smoke and splattered blood on the floor and walls.

So much for light duty.

Nancy managed to haul herself to her feet and grabbed his arm, mouthing something that he couldn't make out over the ringing in his ears.

"What?" he shouted.

She screamed louder and he could finally make sense of her words. "We have to go!"

* * *

Seattle, Washington

Eric held the door for Valerie as they entered the headquarters of the EOS Corporation. The building was a thirty-story steel-and-glass triumph of architecture, and it rose like a shiny arrow to the heavens, in sharp contrast to the drab gray buildings near it. An eight-foot looped infinity symbol surrounded by a circle was plastered across the building's main floor.

Valerie tilted her head to stare at the logo. "Very tasteful."

"I thought Palmer was down-to-earth? A man of the people?"

"He was when I met him. I wouldn't have expected *this*."

He smiled and pointed to the receptionist watching them from behind the stainless-steel-and-chrome desk. The receptionist, a chipper young woman with black-framed glasses, fixed them with her megawatt smile.

"Welcome to EOS, how may I help you have a *spectacular* day?"

"We have an appointment with Dean Palmer," Eric said.

The receptionist's megawatt smile dimmed. "I'm afraid Mr. Palmer doesn't accept appointments."

Eric nodded to Valerie.

She pulled her badge from her jacket and flashed it to the woman. "The CIA begs to differ. We *do* have an appointment."

The receptionist's smile faltered. She tapped furiously on her keyboard, then looked up with narrowed eyes, her smile gone. "Simon and Wise, for Mr. Palmer." She passed them a pair of lanyards and pointed to the elevators. "Swipe these on the reader. Keep them on at *all* times."

They put on the badges and made their way to the elevator. The receptionist watched them as they stepped into the elevator and swiped their badges. The reader beeped, the doors shut, and the elevator began to rise.

"Kind of weird," Eric said.

"The man's worth ten billion dollars," Valerie said. "He probably receives a dozen threats a day. Did you notice the guard?"

"The suit wandering around in front of the windows? Former military. I could tell by the walk."

"That would be my guess."

"How did you get this appointment?"

"I called in a favor with his personal secretary. I worked with her setting his schedule during the Red Team exercises."

The elevator stopped on the twenty-ninth floor. When the doors opened, they found themselves alone in an unfinished area with bare concrete floors. The walls were concrete and steel, and the windows were visible from one end of the building to the other.

The vast expanse was littered with folding wood tables that formed a giant maze. Most were covered in desktop and laptop computers, wires neatly cabled and running to racks of switches and routers near the elevators.

In the midst of the mess, a short, portly man with a reddish-brown beard greeted them with a raised hand. "Val. Over here."

Eric turned to Valerie and raised an eyebrow, but she shook her head. They made their way through the mess until they reached the relatively calm center.

Dean Palmer wasn't what Eric had expected. He was dressed in worn jeans and a stained gray sweatshirt. He extended his hand and said, "I'm Dean."

Eric shook it. "I'm Eric Wise. I believe you know Valerie."

Palmer grinned, an infectiously warm smile that lit up his face. "I remember. I was surprised to hear from you. What's so urgent?"

Valerie looked around the floor. "We wanted to talk to you about something, but maybe we should go to your office?"

Palmer laughed, and it shook his ample belly. "This *is* my office. My executives sit on the top floor, but I kept this for myself." He pointed to the computers on the desks. "It *looks* cluttered, but I've got workstations dedicated to all my interests. Moving around helps me think."

Eric smiled. "What kind of executive doesn't stake out an office on the top floor?"

"The kind that hates *being* an executive." He pointed to an empty table. "Have a seat."

They approached the table, and Palmer handed them folding metal chairs. Eric opened his and sat next to Valerie.

Palmer sat across from them, leaning against the table. "The CIA wants to speak to me. *That* can't be good."

It was Valerie's turn to smile. "We have a few questions about the Red Team exercises."

Palmer's smile faded. "I don't know how much I can help. I mean, you were there. You know what we did. Heck, you probably know more about it than I do."

"This is about what you did after," Valerie said. "Your last Red Team exercise was in 2005. Do you remember?"

Palmer frowned. "Of course. That one got … intense."

Valerie placed her hand on the table. "We covered bioterror threats that year. You had some strong opinions."

"It hit pretty close to home. The entire purpose of EOS is to make the world a better place. Being asked to imagine ways to kill people made me uncomfortable."

"The Red Team that year had a varied skill set, but you were the only biologist."

"That's right."

"The final report had the terrorists unleashing weaponized anthrax in an airport."

"Yeah. It was one of several scenarios, but we pegged it most likely. We wrote up a twenty-point plan on how an airport could be used to infect a large population—"

"But that wasn't *your* first idea," Eric said. "You had another?"

Palmer leaned back in his chair and nodded thoughtfully. "Yeah, I had some other ideas—"

"Ideas you kept working on after the exercise ended?"

Palmer's eyes widened. "*How* do you know that?"

"You took notes, didn't you?" Valerie asked. "You wrote some of them down?"

"How *do* you know that?"

Eric cleared his throat. "You were hacked."

Palmer sighed heavily, staring down at the floor. "How could you—how did … yes, we were hacked. Almost two years ago. They ransacked our files for a month before we discovered it. They hacked our firewall and rooted our servers. We locked everything down and upgraded our firewalls as soon as we discovered it, but they had a *month*."

"Your documents were stolen," Eric said.

Palmer squinted at him. "You found the hackers?"

"Who do *you* think was behind it?" Valerie asked.

"I don't have a clue. It was sophisticated. A lot of people thought industrial espionage, but my experience has been that industrial espionage is rare."

"We suspect it was nation-state hacking," Eric said. "We read your document."

"How did you get a copy?"

Eric turned to Valerie. He had briefed her on the Gulfstream before they arrived, and he raised an eyebrow, waiting for her to take the lead.

She nodded and turned back to Palmer. "We acquired a cache of documents that were stolen from companies here in the United States. Your document was … interesting."

"You read it?"

Eric sat back in the metal chair. "I did, but I didn't understand much of it. I'd like to hear it in your own words."

Palmer sighed heavily. "I've been fascinated by the Chimera. You know, the head of a lion, the body of a goat, and the tail of a snake?"

Eric snapped his fingers. "I must have missed that in school."

"Hah," Palmer said. "Well, it doesn't matter, really, except the idea of combining things always stuck with me. So, after I started EOS, I wondered if I could combine elements, say the virulence of smallpox with another virus that attacks the nervous system. Something entirely new could be made, something never seen in nature. It spun around in my head, and I'd almost forgotten about it, until the first Red Team exercise. One of the guys on my team was Ralph Forrester, a CIA guy, and he said the Soviets worked on the same basic thing back in the eighties."

Valerie sat up straight. "I remember Forrester. He was an analyst who specialized in Soviet biowarfare."

"That's right," Palmer said. "He told me stories, well, rumors really, that came out of the Soviet Union before the Wall came down. Anyway, if you think about it, the possibilities are endless. Not for military use, mind you, but think if we could combine viruses to combat cancer? Something like the flu, but repurposed to trigger an immune response. That's much the way the BCG bacterium works. It stimulates the body to kill cancer cells in the bladder."

"That's *not* what you proposed," Eric said.

"No," Palmer admitted. "It's not. What got me thinking was bin Laden. He thought he could draw the US into an expensive war, a guerrilla campaign where Al-Qaeda could bleed the country dry. Financially, that is. I postulated a virus, like the flu, but instead of modifying it to be helpful, this one would be modified to cause meningitis. You know what meningitis is?"

"An inflammation of the brain?" Eric asked.

"The *lining* of the brain," Palmer said. "If you could induce a number of cases, say, a couple of hundred thousand, or maybe a million? You might get a few thousand deaths, but imagine the strain to the system. The intensive care alone would cost hundreds of millions of dollars. There would be panic in the streets and a collapse of faith in the healthcare system."

Eric's stomach sank. "That would do it. You also mentioned a bomb?"

"Well, just in case the virus didn't work, a small nuclear bomb would tip the country over the edge. Besides, it's a combined threat, right? The body of a bomb, the head of a virus. A Chimera."

Eric's stomach started tying up in knots. "Why would you *write* such a thing?"

"*Nobody* was supposed to see it. It was just a thought exercise. I journal all kinds of crazy ideas. Writing it down helps get it out of my head."

Valerie shook her head. "Someone read it and now they're using it as a template."

Palmer glanced between them and his face went pale. "That's … not good."

"No," Eric said, "it's not. This is on a need-to-know basis. We're only talking to you because you developed the plan."

"I didn't develop it," Palmer protested. "I told you, I journal all kinds of things. No one else was supposed to see it." He stood and began pacing around the table. "I value human life, you know? That's what inspires me. Every human life is sacred. I can't be responsible for something that would *kill* people. The entire point of EOS is to *save* lives."

"We're not saying you planned it, but it's out there and we need your help."

"Anything. Just name it."

"An unknown amount of biological material was funneled through Somalia," Eric said. "We don't know where it went."

Palmer slid back into his chair. "Somalia?"

"Yes. There was a bomb and a mobile lab."

Palmer's eyes widened. "Oh God, the bomb that went off near Somalia. I saw the president's speech on the television. That was because of me?"

"Yes. We tried to retrieve it, but it detonated. Shortly after, the mobile lab was destroyed. We lost a lot of good men."

Palmer sank back in his chair and buried his face in his hands. "I can't believe this."

"Focus, Dean," Valerie said. "We need your help."

Palmer raised his head. "Sorry, this is a lot to take in. Okay, if I were doing it, I could have cooked up the basics in a mobile lab. I could do the first stage there. But to complete the virus, I'd need a sterile environment."

"It could be anywhere," Valerie said.

"Not really," Palmer said. "See, here's the thing. There's been an explosion in high-quality equipment. Any idiot can order a commercial-grade centrifuge off the Internet, but to create a true clean room takes a lot of money. And you have to have an idea of what you're doing. There're places here in the States, but they're too well guarded. But the old Soviet Union? I can name at least a half dozen places that existed to do bioresearch. Most closed up, but the KGB wouldn't let the researchers leave. They wound up just … staying put."

"What about the condition of the equipment?" Eric asked.

"Probably out-of-date or broken, but like I said, any idiot can order gear like that on the Internet. You're the CIA, don't you monitor that kind of stuff?"

Eric stood and stuck out his hand. "Thank you for your help, Mr. Palmer. We'll be in touch."

* * *

Greg had barely gotten the Gulfstream in the air before Eric initiated the video conference with Karen. "We need to search for any signs of lab gear being bought and sent to the old Soviet Union."

"I'm on it, boss. We've, uh, got some bad news. John and Nancy ran into problems in Seoul."

Eric waited for Karen to speak, then turned to see Valerie watching their conversation. "It's okay. I'm clearing Valerie for the rest of the mission."

"They found the office and I cloned the servers. They waited around and got jumped by a guy who blew himself up with a grenade."

"Blew himself up?" Eric asked.

Karen spread her fingers. "Kablooey. Don't worry, Nancy and John are safe. They got out before the locals showed."

"What kind of people do you deal with?" Valerie asked.

"Bad people," Eric said. "Very bad people." He turned his attention back to the screen. "Did we get anything?"

"Seoul police got a name. Wong Yuan. I've finally got something to go on. If there's a record of him in any system, I'll find it."

"What about the servers?"

"The files are encrypted. I'm doing my best to break it, but it's tough stuff. I should be able to exploit a problem in the math behind the algorithm. See, it's 2048-bit, but because of—"

"It's *like* you're speaking English," Eric said, "but I can't make heads or tails of it."

"Sorry, boss. It's going to take a few days. In the meantime, I'll see what I can find on Wong Yuan."

"How's Deion?"

"He met with the asset. They're meeting again tonight. Well, tomorrow. I mean, it'll be yesterday. Wait. I *hate* dealing with different time zones."

"Does the asset know anything?"

"He's trying to find who accessed the report."

"That's quite a risk. Can he do it?"

"He thinks he's the best."

"Every hacker thinks they're the best. He better not get himself killed. We need him."

Karen cleared her throat. "I've got another piece of news. The Old Man left for Washington."

"What?"

"Dewey told me about the operation. Shouldn't he be under observation or something?"

"He's the director. He gets to make his own rules." *Apparently.* "Okay, we're on our way to Chicago to drop off Valerie."

"Gotcha, boss. I'll get back to work."

The video call ended and he turned his attention to Valerie. "Have you thought about my offer?"

She leaned back in the leather seat and eyed him critically. "I've *thought* about it."

"And?"

"My career is important to me," she said, "but I want to protect my country. Tell me how I can do that if I work for you."

"We prevent the end of the world. I'm going to read you in, right here and now. We answer only to the president. We have the authority to operate anywhere in the world, including on US soil."

Valerie frowned. "What about posse comitatus?"

"It doesn't apply to us."

"Isn't that unconstitutional?"

"Truman wasn't concerned with Posse Comitatus when he created the Office."

"Truman?"

"Yes."

"*Harry* Truman?"

"Val, the Office of Threat Management is the most powerful, most secret organization in the world. We have our hooks in the CIA, the NSA, the NRO, DHS, JSOC, and all the other agencies. We use those resources to ensure the continuation of the United States."

He saw the skeptical look on her face and continued, "Those aren't just empty words. We've prevented *many* threats over the years. Terrorist attacks. Financial manipulation that would have wrecked the economy. Crooked politicians ready to sell out the country. The scope of our influence can't be underestimated. I want you to be a part of it."

"It sounds … crazy."

"You won't be able to tell anyone that you work for us. You keep your NOC, and you'll appear to work for the CIA, but you'll have access to more resources." He grinned as he cast the last line. *Time to reel her in.* "You'll have one *other* thing. Deion."

He watched the war of emotions play across her face. Confusion, hope, and uncertainty fought for control, but determination won. "I'm in."

He remembered his own recruitment by Fulton Smith and smiled. "I *always* knew you were."

* * *

Honolulu, Hawaii

Huang Lei read the report of Wong Yuan's death in Seoul and shook his head. His enemy had found a weak spot. He sighed heavily. No matter how much wealth he possessed, it was impossible to do business without leaving some kind of footprint, some kind of path that led his enemy ever closer.

Worse, he had lost Wong Yuan. The man had been dedicated to his cause, much like Liu Kong. Wong had killed himself rather than be taken alive. He placed his hands on his desk and focused his breathing. His enemy was crafty, with significant resources, and would soon have access to the data on the servers. Somehow they would find a way to trace it back, and the next connection would be Liu Kong. He turned to his computer and initiated the video call.

Liu Kong answered promptly. "Have you read the report?"

"It is a great loss. Wong Yuan was a good man."

"I'm afraid the plan might fail."

"It is possible," he allowed, then shook his head. "But unlikely."

No, it *had* to succeed. All his work couldn't be for nothing. Not after everything they had sacrificed. Not after everything his *father* had sacrificed. "They will come for you."

"I know. I am preparing for our enemy. They will not best us so easily."

He bowed deeply. "I trust you to handle this affair."

"If I should fail," Liu Kong said, "*you* must be prepared."

Huang Lei glanced around at his office. It was the center of his power, but it was only a space he occupied. Even the painting on the wall was just a physical thing. Things could be replaced. "Fear not. I shall *never* stop."

CHAPTER SIXTEEN

Washington, D.C.

THE PRESIDENT WAS waiting for Smith in his underground bunker. "Tell me it wasn't us." The president tapped his fingers nervously against the desktop, the edges of his eyes tinged with red.

Smith shrugged. "Mr. President? I have no idea of what you speak."

"I *did* as you asked," the president said. "I went out during the press conference and played dumb. This morning the CIA director called me to ask about a suicide in Seoul. Tell *me* that *wasn't* us."

"Would you rather *not* know?"

The president sagged back in his chair. "Damn it. I was *hoping* it wasn't us. What happened?"

"That man was involved with the nuclear bomb. We were following an information trail, but he killed himself before we could question him. Sir?"

The president's face filled with dread. "Yes?"

"We suspect there might be ... more to the plan than just a bomb. There may be a biological component."

The president soaked in the information, his face pale, before finally giving way to weary acceptance. "What can I do?"

"We're working the intelligence."

"Should I alert DHS?"

"No. They would likely get in our way. If we need their resources, we have ways of acquiring them. We'll mitigate this threat, I promise you." He hesitated, then decided it was time to broach the subject. "Mr. President? There's something else."

The president groaned. "Haven't we had enough?"

"It isn't a new threat, sir. I've mentioned Eric Wise is to be my replacement?"

"Yes, yes, of course," the president said. "Are you saying you're ready to step down?"

"That day is quickly approaching. I'm not a young man anymore, not like yourself or Eric. He's a good man. His will be a steady hand to lead the Office."

"What about your daughter?"

Smith had forgotten how perceptive the young man from Chicago could be. "I love my daughter dearly, but she's not a … viable candidate to lead the Office."

The president started to speak, caught himself, then nodded. "It's your decision, Mr. Smith. If there's one person I trust, it's you."

Smith offered the president a rare smile. "Thank you, sir. I'll keep you informed of any updates."

He turned to go and was almost to the massive bunker door when the president stopped him. "Mr. Smith? What's that on the back of your neck?"

Smith absently fingered the bandage, forcing the smile back on his face. "Just a small skin biopsy," he lied. "A young man like yourself doesn't have to worry about such things, but old men like myself need to keep a keen eye on our health."

"Take care of yourself, Mr. Smith. So much depends on you."

"Thank you, Mr. President."

He keyed open the steel door with his badge, then took the electric tram back to the underground parking deck. He thought about the president's concern for his health, but he actually felt better than he had in years. His thoughts were sharper and words came to his lips quicker.

Since the stimulator had activated, he'd felt twenty years younger. Mentally, at least. He was upbeat and felt he could take on the world, a feeling he had long been missing.

He sniffed as the electric tram rolled through the tunnel. He detected the smell of ozone from the motors, a sharp, pungent odor he hadn't noticed before. No, that wasn't correct. He hadn't noticed it for many years, not since the electric tram had been installed in the seventies. He could even detect the faint hint of grease from the axles.

It was as if his senses had dulled through the years, then suddenly sprung alive, awake again after a long hibernation. His body was still old and aching—especially the arthritis in his hands that had swollen his knuckles and limited his movement—but the ache didn't wear him out.

It had been less than two days since the implant and he felt alive again. A growing hope filled his heart.

Perhaps there's still time.

* * *

Smith was impressed with the speed and precision of the attack. Robert was turning the Lincoln north at the intersection of G Street onto Twentieth when four black Chevy Suburbans surrounded them. Robert hit the brakes and the vehicles came to a stop.

"Sir? What should I do?" Robert asked quietly.

Smith shook his head. "If they wanted me dead, they would have shot by now."

"I don't like this," Robert said.

He knew Robert carried a SIG Sauer, and he had his ancient Colt M1911 service weapon in his metal briefcase, but that would be no match for whatever firepower was most likely contained in the big SUVs. Behind them, horns began to blare as traffic backed up.

Two Asian men emerged from the lead Suburban, one old and withered and one young and alert. Both wore suits, and he had no doubt the young man was well armed under his jacket. The young man stopped at Robert's door while the old man stepped to the back and tapped a fingertip gently against the window.

"Mr. Smith," the old man said. "We must speak."

The old man's voice was rough with age, and Smith guessed the man was Chinese, given his heavy accent.

"Robert, if you will let the young man drive, I believe we will soon be safe and sound."

Robert turned to him, his face hard. "Give the word, sir, and I'll take as many with me as I can."

Smith smiled. "That won't be necessary."

They did a careful dance amid the honking and blaring traffic. Robert exited the Lincoln and the young man took his place, casually closing the driver's door. The old Chinese man pointed to Robert and nodded. Robert took the young man's place in the lead Suburban.

The old man opened the rear door and carefully slid inside next to him. "Mr. Wang," the old man said to the man in the driver's seat, "if you would?"

The young man honked the horn twice and the vehicles accelerated as one. They passed the International Monetary Fund to the east, and every Suburban but the lead vehicle turned west onto H Street at the next intersection. Their driver continued to follow the lead vehicle as they navigated through the heavy D.C. traffic.

Smith turned to the old Chinese man. The man's suit was well tailored, but not exceptionally so. His face was bland, with deep wrinkles that hinted at concern or amusement. He didn't know the man's name, but he had a sneaking suspicion that he knew his role. "You wanted to speak?"

"You're an *interesting* man, Mr. Smith," the old man said. "You don't exist. Not electronically. Do you know how rare that is?"

Smith said nothing. If this man was who he suspected, he would learn more by remaining silent.

"Your apartment is not in your name," the old man continued. "Your apartment and the other apartments in your building are rented to people who don't exist, and they have been since the building was constructed. Your office is much the same. You have no phone, no television, no bank account or credit cards. You've never held a mortgage or owned a home. You've never owned a car."

The old man paused and looked around the Lincoln. "Even this does not belong to you. It is registered to a private company that has no address, phone number, or record on file. Tell me, does your driver know who you are?"

Smith said nothing.

The old man chuckled, eyes twinkling. "Do not worry about your driver. He will be unharmed. I thought it time we finally meet. You understand why?"

Smith shrugged but again said nothing.

"Of course you do. I know who you are, and I know what you do. I know this because I've watched you for fifty years. I was assigned to Washington as a young intelligence officer. It was a *great* honor. I was quite good at spycraft, but I began to suspect there were others who were better. I discovered a most *interesting* secret. There were shadows within shadows, and one could spend a lifetime looking through them. The deeper one looked, the deeper one *could* look, but no matter how deep, there were always more. No, there had to be another way. I began to look for *nothing*. Much to my surprise, when I looked for *nothing*, I found *something*."

The old man's piercing gaze rested upon his. "I was nothing," Smith said.

"Quite correct," the old man said. "Only a man of importance leaves no trail. *That* is how I found you. There were others, of course, but none so totally removed from the world as yourself. I spent years tracking your movements. Bugs were planted and removed. Any attempt to track you met with failure. So, I applied the same lesson. I didn't look for where you *were*, I looked for where you *were not*. Again, success!"

Smith couldn't help but smile. The old man seemed delighted to tell the story, but Smith had learned over the years that sometimes the most *important* story wasn't the story being told—it was the story that wasn't. "This conversation is fascinating. Please, continue."

The old man beamed at him. "By now your men in Shanghai have realized their hacker friend will not be returning. An *unfortunate* necessity, but a *fortuitous* discovery. You are a smart man with a keen mind. Tell me what you have learned from our conversation. I have a valuable piece of information, but only if you tell me a story *worthy* of such a gift."

Smith laughed, one of his first hearty laughs in more years than he cared to remember. "I *like* you, sir. You play a fantastic game. You would like to hear my story?"

The old man bowed his head. "Please."

Of course you would, because you can learn how I think and take my measure by how much I've gathered from you. "The Chinese government had nothing to do with the bomb. Or the virus. I knew that much. It's too direct, too crude, and far too … indelicate."

"Continue," the old man said with approval.

"You knew about the PLA hacking program, but you weren't aware of Mr. Palmer's report. Someone else, someone not affiliated with your government, is behind this. You know their identity."

"Just so. I was not wrong about you. Your mind is as sharp as ever. Spycraft has many elements, but its core is intelligence. This amazing age we live in? Is it not wonderful? So much information. So many avenues to exploit. Yes, I knew of the hackers and their work. Old men such as us have learned to adapt to these modern times. So much information brings ... considerations."

"Of course," Smith said. "You sat on it."

"Quite right. No, the report you speak of was filed away, never to be read. How, then, did such a small piece of information in such a vast sea of data become problematic?"

"You were hacked," Smith said softly.

The old man's face contorted into a mask of rage, so sudden it was as if the good humor had never existed. "Some men do not understand their place," he spat out. "It is an *affront* to the game to allow such men to meddle in affairs beyond their reckoning."

Smith nodded. "You want *me* to do your dirty work. Normally I'd be offended, but in this case? I accept."

The driver glanced up in the rearview mirror. Smith realized they had driven in a big circle and were almost to G Street, next to the Eisenhower Building.

"Yes, Mr. Smith," the old man said. "The man you seek is named Huang Lei. I believe you knew his father."

Smith rocked back. He hadn't heard the name for many years. He pursed his lips together. "I—" He stopped, unsure of what to say, then realized the old man probably knew everything of importance. "I knew Huang Jin. He had a son. I never knew what happened to him."

"Huang Jin was very unhappy with your decision to stop his research," the old man said. "He fled America. Many in my government were unwilling to trust him. A Chinese, born in San Francisco, who worked for *your* government? He was taken to Tianjin, along with the boy. Years were spent learning everything we could from him."

The old man stared intently at him, and Smith realized the old man was waiting for him to speak. "He wasn't allowed to continue his research."

"Of course not. The risk was too great." The old man bowed his head, his sudden anger evaporating. "I do not claim to be a perfect man. I know we had many programs that were equally … barbaric. Huang Jin's work was terrifying. I understand why you chose to stop."

"There are certain lines that should not be crossed," Smith said. He meant it. The things Huang Jin had proposed danced near the edge of madness. Plagues the like of which the world could not imagine. Virulent diseases spliced together that could kill every living being. The means to eradicate all life on the planet. He shuddered at the memory.

"There are lines that should not be crossed," the old man agreed. "Huang Jin died a broken man, his anger directed at the United States and the men who halted his precious work. Huang Lei was seventeen. He listened to his father rage about the United States. It changed him."

"He wants to destroy the country that killed his father."

"What you must understand about the boy is that after his father's death, he set himself a task. He acquired great wealth and power. His fortune allows him great influence. His agents have approached us many times with plans to strike America. We have always refused. He believes us weak."

Smith nodded at the old man. "You take a long view of the game. Why risk something so dangerous when you have all the time in the world?"

"*You* understand," the old man said agreeably. "This young man threatens the world. He *must* be stopped."

The driver followed the Suburban around a corner and pulled in behind it next to the International Monetary Fund. The left rear door of the Suburban opened and his driver, Robert, stepped out and approached the car. The young Chinese man turned to them, bowed his head, opened the door and stepped out.

"I believe our meeting is at an end. Good luck, Mr. Smith. No one knows Huang Lei's location or even what he looks like. He hasn't been seen in public in twenty years. Perhaps you will find a way to locate him?"

Smith bowed his head as the old man got out of the Lincoln. "Perhaps I will try looking where he is *not*, instead of where he *is*."

Robert slipped in behind the wheel and glanced back, then turned to watch in the mirror as the old man carefully closed the rear door.

The old man tapped the glass and Smith fumbled with the button until the window lowered. The old man leaned in and eyed him shrewdly. "You *are* a clever man."

* * *

Area 51

Nancy's computer dinged when the decryption finished working on the last of the server's files.

She opened the first folder and started reading. Soon she was awash with data, thousands of records that she couldn't begin to cross-reference.

Why can't there be a flashing red arrow pointing to a plot to bomb or poison America? She shook her head. It had been an hour and she still didn't have anything to show for it.

DEWEY, she IM'd.

She waited for several minutes before she got her answer.

WHAT'S UP? YOU WANT TO COME WATCH TELEVISION?

CAN'T, she typed. BUSY. GOT A QUESTION.

U ONLY HAVE TO ASK.

I HAVE NEW DATA, BUT I CAN'T MAKE SENSE OF IT.

There was a pause. I'M GOING TO INSTALL SOMETHING ON YOUR DESKTOP.

She sighed. There was no sense in arguing with him. She watched as he assumed control of her workstation and installed a new link.

THIS IS A DATA ANALYTIC PROGRAM I WROTE. CLICK ON THE LINK.

She clicked on the link and a web page loaded. There was a single button on the top. She clicked the button and it opened a folder dialog box.

POINT IT TO THE TOP LEVEL OF EVERYTHING YOU WANT TO ANALYZE.

She clicked the folder dialog and pointed it to the location of the decrypted servers. A progress bar appeared and slowly filled until completion.

WHAT DOES THIS DO?

THERE'S A RUDIMENTARY AI THAT LOOKS FOR PATTERNS IN THE DATA. IT'S THE BASIS FOR THE THREAT-SCANNING SOFTWARE I WROTE FOR THE VIDEO CAMERA SURVEILLANCE PROGRAM.

When the upload finished, a graphical representation of icons began to swirl, each icon linked by a spiderweb of black lines.

HOW LONG WILL IT TAKE?

A FEW HOURS. FEED IT MORE DATA AND YOU'LL GET BETTER RESULTS.

She thought about that for a moment, then directed the program to another folder containing the search data for bio equipment. The progress bar slowly filled and the program continued to churn.

THANKS, DEWEY.

* * *

The program finished with a soft chime and Karen clicked on the link to expand the results. When the picture finished loading, her mouth dropped.

The program worked.

She pored over the results, becoming more excited as she dug deeper, until finally messaging for Eric to meet her in the conference room with Sergeant Clark.

She stood and walked through the War Room, concentrating so hard on the output of Dewey's program that she almost walked into the glass door.

"Karen?" Clark asked. "You okay?"

She turned and found him standing behind her, face full of concern. "I'm fine."

"You almost smashed your face into the door, and you're not even holding your coffee cup," Clark said before opening the door and holding it for her. "*Something's* up."

They entered the conference room and were soon joined by Eric. "Please tell me you found something," Eric said, looking haggard as he took his seat.

"What do you know about Biopreparat?" she asked.

He squinted, then his face lit up in recognition. "The Soviet bioweapon research company? I've heard of it. They shut down years ago."

"That's right," Clark joined in. "They closed up in the nineties. My first job for the Office was tracking the closure of their facilities."

Karen had worked for the Office for almost seven years, much of it spent working hand in hand with Todd Clark, but she often forgot that his service with the Office predated her own.

The man rarely spoke of himself. He was an omnipresent inhabitant of the War Room, calmly guiding the analysts in their work and the ongoing missions, neatly attired in his Army uniform—unusual, since most in the underground base preferred fatigues—his light brown hair neatly trimmed. She liked Sergeant Clark, but more importantly, she *respected* him.

"Did you hear of a facility in Feofilivka?"

He thought for a moment, then shook his head. "That doesn't sound familiar."

"Officially it never existed," she said. "It's in the eastern Ukraine, near the border. The Ukraine has no love for the Russians, not after the split, and they weren't eager to advertise a weapons lab. I checked the records and there were only vague hints of Feofilivka. It wasn't doing major research like the ones in Yekaterinburg or Stepnogorsk. The facility was abandoned and never received money or attention from the US, not like the others. The scientists there weren't the cream of the crop, so there was no attempt at recruitment by terrorist cells. It just ... faded away."

"Let me guess," Eric said. "It's active."

"Truckloads of equipment have recently been delivered. Some of the former scientists started regularly depositing small sums of money. The Office never noticed. It was all done through shell corporations, but with the data we recovered from the servers in Seoul—"

Eric smiled. "You found the trail of bread crumbs."

"There's *more*. I have a name. It was buried in sales records in Europe, but the organizer of this mess is named Liu Kong."

"Liu Kong? What do we know about him?"

Karen typed on her keyboard and a profile soon emerged on the wall screen. "Liu Kong. He's Chinese. I found a passport entry from 1998 where he entered Australia with—and get ready for it—Wong Yuan. Nothing since. He's probably been using assumed names. If the age on his passport was correct, he's now thirty-four. The records weren't digitized. We have no picture. I expanded my search and found Liu Kong is listed as the CEO of a dozen companies, all shells."

"What about Feofilivka?"

"It's been refurbished."

"You're sure?"

"The shell corporations purchased centrifuges, refrigeration units, spectrometers, DNA sequencers, and racks of computers … everything they need to do heavy-duty bioengineering. I ran the equipment list past Doctor Elliot. He said if they did basic prep on the MV *Rising Star*, it would only take a few days for them to complete their work, depending on what they were brewing up."

Eric shook his head, his face hard. "Sergeant Clark, tell Taylor Martin I want wheels up in thirty. First stop is Chicago. Valerie Simon has accepted my offer to join the Office. Next, we'll pick up Deion and Mark in China, then on to Seoul to get Nancy and John before we arrive in the Ukraine."

Clark stood and saluted, then left the conference room to make it happen.

"You're going, aren't you?" Karen asked before she could stop herself. Eric turned to her and she felt a warmth through her body. She wanted nothing more than to sleep with him, one last time, but she saw the way he looked at her.

Eric was becoming emotionally involved, and it would end badly for him. He approached until he was close, and she felt the heat radiating from his body. She shook her head and said, "That's not a good idea," before he could touch her.

Surprised, he took a step back. "Why?"

"You need to find someone you can love, someone who'll love you back. I'm *not* that woman."

His jaw clenched and he shook his head. "I don't see how you can be so unemotional."

She sighed. *It's definitely time to call it off.* "Boss, you need your head in the game. I thought I was helping, but I think I was distracting you."

"You *were* helping," Eric insisted. He turned and sat down heavily in his chair. "This place is—well, stressful is too light a word. When we're together, it relaxes me. I *think* more clearly."

She smiled. "I'll always be here for you, boss. You know that."

"I know, but it doesn't mean I have to *like* it."

CHAPTER SEVENTEEN

Washington, D.C.

SMITH ANSWERED THE video call. "Yes, Eric."

"Hello, sir. How are you feeling?"

Smith leaned back in his chair. He glanced around his office and for the first time noticed it was utterly bare. He had grown used to the slate-gray walls and the matching industrial carpet, and he had shipped his ancient wooden desk to Area 51 after he'd taken over the underground base. His current desk was a modern high-density fiberboard with laminated gray top, and it still reeked of plastic. The foul stench was the only thing of note, the only hint of personality in the room. "I'm well. Better than I've felt in *years.*"

His young protégé nodded. "I think we've found something. We have a name. Liu Kong. He's involved with the MV *Rising Star*, as well as the infected ICs from Korea. There's been activity at an old biolab in the Ukraine. A city called Feofilivka. I'm leading a mission there."

Smith took a moment to digest that information. "I *also* have a name. Huang Lei."

"Who is Huang Lei?"

Smith wondered how much to tell Eric but finally settled for, "A ghost from the past. I would like Mr. Green to investigate Huang Lei. Dewey has a knack for finding the unusual."

"Yes, sir."

"Will Nancy be on this trip to Feofilivka?"

"Yes, along with my men, and Frist, of course."

"Of course." Smith smiled. "When shall you leave?"

"Soon," Eric said, then frowned. "Why do you ask?"

His heart was beating faster, the start of an idea forming in his head. "I need to make certain preparations."

"What preparations?"

"Nothing you need concern yourself with. Eric?"

"Yes?"

"Tell Mr. Green to look for where Huang Lei *isn't*, not where he *is*."

Eric's face grew puzzled. "What does that mean?"

"I suspect Mr. Green will understand."

* * *

Robert dropped Smith off at the National Mall again, and he quickly made his way around to the old man in the unfashionable suit who waited for him by the reflecting pool. "Vasilii."

"Fulton. We meet so soon?"

"New information, my friend. I've identified the party behind our latest problem."

"Why so pleased?"

Smith paused. If this worked, he might finally reunite his family before his mind faded completely. "The disgruntled man is a third-party actor. A phantom from our past. Yours and mine."

"Tell me his name," Vasilii muttered. "I will send someone to eliminate this *stain* on humanity."

Smith continued walking. "I don't think so."

"And why not? Is this some game?"

He smiled lazily. "I've been reminded, quite recently, that's it's always *been* a game."

Vasilii glared at him. "I do not care for this. Why have you called me here?" The old man's gaze intensified, and the faintest of smiles appeared. "Ah. So, that's it?"

Smith laughed, loud enough to cause tourists to turn and stare at the two old men as they walked along the pond. "Feofilivka."

"You joke."

"Afraid not."

"That is history. No one cares."

"They will. Your country never acknowledged Feofilivka."

Vasilii shook his head. "How will this help? You think to threaten us? Bah. Old ghosts, my friend. Old ghosts."

"Even old ghosts can kill. Especially if they are used to generate a new threat."

"I stopped that," Vasilii said. "We *agreed*."

"Huang Jin's son. He's planning something. He's behind everything. Feofilivka is active again."

"Huang Jin?" Vasilii asked. "He disappeared and took his son with him. I searched for him. I would have executed him. Anything to keep that man's work buried."

"The Chinese. They took him, along with his son, Huang Lei. The father died. The son hates us."

"He means to lay waste to you and blame us?"

"Yes."

"Not bad plan," the old man admitted.

"The boy is clever."

Vasilii shook his head. "I still don't see how this helps with Alexandra."

"My daughter and her team are en route to Feofilivka. They will clean up this mess and then they will find Huang Lei. They will keep this quiet." He turned to the old man and raised an eyebrow.

"This?" Vasilii said. "This … might be possible. Perhaps," he said, turning to stare at the dirty brown water of the reflecting pool, "if I push, if I talk to right people. If I do this thing for you, *perhaps* Alexandra could return." He spun on his heels. "Why?"

"Because she never deserved this," Smith said, searching for some sign of understanding in Vasilii's face. "She never meant to betray her country. She never meant to get pregnant. You *know* this."

Vasilii stared at him, his face finally softening. "After all these years, I have come to believe you speak truth."

"You'll support me in this?" Smith's heart soared. It seemed too good to be true. After all the years spent searching for a way, the love of his life was finally within his grasp.

Vasilii stuck out his hand, and Smith took it, shaking it firmly.

"Perhaps she has suffered enough," Vasilii said. "If your daughter can prevent Feofilivka from becoming public knowledge, I do what I can."

* * *

Boryspil, Ukraine

John sighed as his hand holding the cordless screwdriver banged against the bumper of the Ford transit van. He worked with Taylor Martin, putting fake plates on the vans. They were in an aircraft hangar at the Boryspil International Airport, southeast of Kiev, preparing for their mission.

He turned to Taylor. "Just once I'd like to travel as a tourist, you know? Sample the cuisine? Buy some postcards?"

"Nobody buys postcards anymore," Taylor said. "They just share every little fart on Facebook." He grunted as he finished attaching a license plate to the other van and eyed it critically. "Looks good."

John tightened the last screw on his van. "Yep. No one will suspect two vans full of Americans who work for a secret government organization coming to kill anyone trying to release a deadly virus."

"You're in a mood."

John shook his head. He was still upset about the suicide bombing in Seoul that had almost killed Nancy, and hadn't been thrilled hiding out at the airport while waiting for the C-17 to arrive from Area 51.

"Cooling my jets with Nancy for a day wasn't exactly *fun*, know what I'm saying? She wasn't good conversation."

Taylor stood and stretched his tall frame before offering John a smirk. "Could have been worse. Could have been stuck with Deion, like Mark. When he found out Eric recruited Valerie?"

Taylor was right. Deion could be prickly even under the best conditions. *Eric recruited Valerie?* He had seen Valerie on the plane and wondered what role she would play, but hadn't realized she had been recruited. He shuddered. *Deion is going to be even more of a pain in the ass.* "When are we leaving?"

"Soon as they want us to know, they'll tell us."

"Battlefield philosophy?"

"Practical experience."

Mark Kelly carried plastic cases of gear down the ramp and carefully packed them with the rest in the back of the vans. "Are you two done goldbricking?"

John rolled his eyes and let loose a mock groan. "Now what?"

"We're leaving in five. It's a hundred and twenty miles, so hurry up and wait. We'll be sitting on our asses for the next couple of hours."

"That's why I joined the Army," Taylor said, "so I could go to strange foreign lands and kill people, but slowly. Very damned slowly."

As Taylor finished speaking, Nancy, Eric, Deion, and Valerie exited the C-17. John saw Valerie's eyes focus on him, and he knew, somehow, that Eric had briefed her on the StrikeForce technology. From the way her eyes darted away, he suspected that Eric had also briefed her on his history. He wanted to grab her and shake her, screaming that he wasn't that person anymore, but he knew it wouldn't make a difference.

Some sins can't be forgiven.

"All right, people, let's get rolling," Eric said. "Valerie, you're with Deion and Mark. Nancy and Taylor are with John and me."

They left the airport and headed toward Feofilivka. True to Mark's word, the drive took several hours. Eric and Nancy rarely spoke during the trip, except to offer directions. Once they were well away from Kiev, the roads were barely more than one vehicle wide, and by the time they reached Mais'ke, the roads had turned from concrete to dirt.

They proceeded through Mais'ke, turned left at Stepne, and soon entered the almost-abandoned town of Feofilivka. Eric pointed to a dirt road that led north. "That way."

Taylor nodded and turned, driving carefully over the dirt road. Mark followed close behind in the second van. They approached a small lake and Eric pointed to a stand of trees to the west and said, "The facility is through there."

Taylor nodded and pulled the van close to the tree line.

"Valerie and I will stay with the vans," Eric said as they got out, shooting Nancy a quick look. "Heh. Beat you to it."

Nancy frowned. "You shouldn't be here."

"Well, I *am* here. Everybody suit up. We don't expect any contamination, but we're not taking chances. Wear your JLISTs and your M50s."

They nodded and began suiting up. John took a deep breath. The smell of pines reminded him of a trip he had once taken with his parents, north of Pasadena. The mountains were beautiful, the trees majestic. The old forest in the Ukraine had the same earthy scent.

If only I had time to enjoy it.

He opened the plastic crate, stripped to his briefs, and strapped on the Battlesuit. He noticed Valerie watching and tried to put it out of his mind as he fiddled with his prosthetic. The Battlesuit would offer moderate protection against contaminants, but nothing like the JLIST. He stared at the VISOR, then felt a clap on his shoulder.

"You'll have to get by *without* the VISOR," Eric said, standing beside him. "Doc Elliot said it would interfere with the M50."

"How are you going to run things from back here without video?"

"The earpieces will do. We're easily within range of the facility, so we'll have coverage. It's not the same as the VISOR—"

"I'll get by," John said. He glanced longingly at his M11s nestled in their case. "I'll miss *them* more."

Eric smiled and patted him on the back before leaving to check the others. John continued putting on his JLIST before strapping the M50 mask to his head. He pulled the top of the JLIST tightly over the back of his head and tightened the clasps.

He picked up his spare HK417, a replacement for the one lost in the Gulf of Aden. He checked it, then strapped extra magazines to his belt. He wished he could wipe the sweat trickling down his neck, but there was no way to reach the skin with the JLIST sealed. He fumbled with the pack that held the M50's carbon filter and the hose that connected the filter to the mask, making sure it was tight and out of the way of his rifle.

He turned to find Nancy, Taylor, Mark, and Deion already wearing their JLISTs, standing around, their weapons at the ready. His earpiece crackled. "Okay," Eric said, "we've got a Sentinel overhead. It will give us a good read on radio chatter, but we have minimal visual and *no* thermal."

John shook his head. They were going in almost blind. "You sure about this?"

"The intelligence is as good as we're going to get," Nancy said, the barest hint of edge to her voice. "We don't *have* to like it. We just have to do the job."

* * *

The team shuffled down the dirt path, the afternoon sun obscured by dense tree cover. John led the way, glancing at the path as they went. The ground was soft and spongy and had recently been disturbed. "There's been trucks through here," he said. He dropped to get a closer look, then pointed so the team could see. "Tire tracks. They haven't filled back in or weathered away."

He couldn't take the credit for his tracking skills. Eric had taken him to the mountains in Colorado for high-altitude training and taught John everything he knew about mountaineering, orienteering, and tracking. Eric assured him it was a time-honored set of skills that Delta Operators learned in their first year, handed down from the first Delta members.

The skills had been useful since, but not as useful as he now found them. "Eric, we've got signs of multiple trucks, none too heavy. More than three or four, but less than a dozen."

There was a pause, then Valerie's voice came through the earpiece. "It wouldn't take much to outfit the lab. I've got a list of the equipment that Kryzowski tracked. It would easily fit in half a dozen panel trucks."

They continued and in less than five hundred feet came to a clearing. A white concrete box, ten feet square, stood in the center.

John squinted. The white paint was dirty and discolored from years of neglect. The gray steel door to the complex was covered in rust stains. He raised his hand, and everyone stopped.

"Do you see something?" Deion asked. He stepped forward, but Mark put his hand on Deion's shoulder.

"Let me and TM take the lead," Mark said.

Deion nodded, and Taylor and Mark joined John at the front. "What do you see?" Taylor asked.

"Nothing," John said. "It's weird. If this place is active, shouldn't there be guards?" He pointed to the clearing. "There's the entrance to the lab."

"Estimates put it at thirty thousand square feet," Taylor said.

He inspected the clearing and guessed the base to occupy the same footprint. "They must have dug up the ground and built it before covering it back up."

His earpiece crackled. "There's multiple levels," Eric said, "but Taylor is right. There are air vents hidden in the trees, and the underground power lines run near where you're standing."

"It just doesn't feel right," John said.

"Listen to your instincts," Eric urged. "If they're telling you something's wrong, then something *is* wrong."

"Excuse me," Nancy interrupted, "but at this point it doesn't matter. We have to move forward. The Ukrainians know the C-17 is at the Boryspil Airport. Sooner or later, they'll send someone to investigate. We're also near the border, so the Russians will know as soon as the Ukrainians. If we're going to find Liu Kong, we *have* to risk it."

John turned and glanced at Nancy. She held her HK416 at the ready. He turned to Deion, who nodded, but before he could speak, his earpiece crackled again.

"She has a point," Eric said, "but if John's worried, maybe we should scout first. You could—"

Eric stopped so suddenly that John thought his earpiece might have quit working. "Eric?"

"Wait." There was a long pause, and then Eric continued, "Okay, we have orders from the Old Man. John, head for the bunker. Everyone else, fall back and take cover."

John sighed. "Got it." He turned to Taylor and Mark. They shrugged, then led Nancy and Deion back the way they had come before fanning out and taking positions behind the trees.

He glanced at the entrance to the underground lab. *Might as well get going. Staring at it won't make it any better.*

He walked slowly through the dirt lane that led through the clearing. "Eric? Maybe you better activate the Implant."

There was a pause. "Activating now."

John felt the sudden rush of adrenaline, his heart skipping in his chest. He paused for a moment and let the effects of the drugs settle down. His fear and hesitation fell away, and the world sharpened.

He could taste the stench of the M50 mask, stale and oily, and almost laughed at how ridiculous he must appear in the camouflaged green JLIST.

He was on the verge of laughing when the forest erupted in gunfire.

CHAPTER EIGHTEEN

JOHN DROPPED TO the ground and gasped for breath. It felt like a pair of hammers had struck him in the chest.

"Fall back," Nancy yelled.

"John's down," Taylor screamed.

"Sitrep?" Eric asked.

"Hostiles, repeat, hostiles," Mark said calmly. "More than six, I'd guess. John is twenty yards from the lab entrance."

Gunfire echoed through the trees, a pop-pop-popping that reverberated weirdly as it bounced around the trees. John sucked in air, trying to get his wind back. The Battlesuit's liquid body armor had absorbed the bullets, or he wouldn't be breathing. That didn't stop his chest from hurting or his heart from jackhammering.

"I'm good," John said. "The Battlesuit's armor absorbed it."

"I'm cranking up the Implant," Eric said.

Every nerve ending in his skin activated as the influx of drugs roared through his body, like a hot iron burning through him. He jumped to his feet, ready to take on the world.

"I'm engaging tango." There was a man hiding behind a bush to the west, and John ran toward him, his feet practically flying over the thick grass. Everything around him slipped out of focus as he concentrated his attention on the target.

There were singing noises around him, and he knew that bullets were whizzing past his body. He didn't care. The only thing that mattered was taking out the target.

"Suppressing fire," Taylor screamed, and the team's HK416s began steadily crack-cracking.

The man looked up and tried to aim his AK-47, his black eyes widening in surprise, but John squeezed the trigger on his HK417. He had trained extensively with Eric in shooting while running, and it finally paid off as he saw the man pitch forward, unmoving.

The man was dead, or soon would be, and was no longer a threat.

He turned to the right and saw another man with a blue wool cap and a bandanna across his mouth crouching near one of the giant firs. The man's gun barked, but it was higher-pitched and sounded soft, an AK-74 firing 5.56mm rounds. The rifle's suppressor eliminated most of the muzzle flash, but there was still a bright flicker as the man fired wildly.

"We've got activity at the van," Eric said.

John heard pop-popping over his earpiece, but he couldn't worry about it. Bullets chewed up the ground near his feet as he ran at the man with the wool cap until he felt an impact in his left leg.

His left foot fell from under him as he realized the man's lucky shot had caught him in his prosthetic. He hit the ground hard and rolled, protecting his HK, then came up and carefully shot the man in the face.

The man slumped forward, the blue wool cap falling to the twigs and pine needles, and John sprang to his feet as the bullets continued whizzing past his head.

He made it to the nearest tree, a dark fir as big around as a barrel, as the bullets came closer. He took cover behind the tree, and there was zinging and cracking as the bullets found their mark, gouging chunks of bark out of the old tree.

Screw this.

The JLIST and M50 mask were constricting his movements. He yanked the M50 from his face and threw it into the forest, then removed his gloves and JLIST, which quickly joined the M50 among the dirt and moss.

Time to go on the offensive.

* * *

Eric turned to Valerie. Her face was pale, and she was waiting for him to speak. He heard gunfire in the distance, but there was another sound echoing around the inside of the van, a pinging that made his stomach churn.

"They're shooting the van." Before Valerie could speak, he continued, "Don't worry. The vans have the same armor as John's suit. Otherwise, we'd be dead by now. We're good for a few minutes, but enough rounds *can* degrade the armor and then we're in trouble."

"What do we do?"

"We have no intelligence and no way of knowing how many are out there." He opened John's Battlesuit case and withdrew the VISOR, staring at the flat black helmet. "I'm going out. You stay here. Deion would never forgive me if I got you killed."

"I can protect myself," she said fiercely. "Don't worry about *me*."

He smiled. *She's a fighter.* He handed her an HK416 and a stack of magazines. "When I run to the tree line, I want heavy suppressing fire. Full auto."

She nodded, then grabbed the HK and jammed in a magazine before cycling the bolt and chambering the first round.

He popped the release on the VISOR's helmet and it clamshelled open. He placed it on his head and was immediately plunged into darkness. He had a moment of claustrophobia before the electronics blazed to life.

A female voice spoke softly in his ear. "Unknown user."

"Eric Wise. Activate secondary profile."

"Voiceprint confirmed," the AI said.

He had trained for such a possibility, using one of the spare VISORs to create a backup profile tuned to his thought patterns in case John was incapacitated.

He lacked John's enhanced musculature and carbon-graphene-sheathed skeleton, and he had no Implant to give him an adrenaline-fueled edge or painkillers to allow him to finish his mission.

What he *did* have was years of training and the desire to save his team.

He took an HK416 and a nylon belt full of magazines, strapping the belt across his chest. He turned to Valerie, amazed as always by the VISOR. Her skin practically glowed in the LCD. "Ready?"

She nodded confidently. "I was *born* ready."

* * *

John peeked around the tree, looking for signs of the enemy. Gunshots echoed through the trees, and he tried to guess how many fighters were hidden among them. He came up with a number close to a dozen. "Deion, I'm holed up on the west side of the clearing, but I can't make it to your position."

"We're working our way back to the van."

"Hold your position," Eric said. "I'll meet up with you."

"What about Val?"

There was the sound of fully automatic gunfire on the other end of the earpiece before Eric responded. "She's safe."

John breathed a sigh of relief. Even though Valerie had watched him with apprehension and dread, he still liked her. He took another peek around the thick fir as enemy gunfire stitched across the front of the tree. "I'm pinned down."

"Roger that," Eric said in a hoarse voice. "I'm coming from the east." There was a long pause. "I count four enemies on the east side of the clearing. They don't see me."

John heard a crack-cracking from across the clearing.

"Two enemies to the east," Eric said, "and *now* they know I'm here."

John ducked around the tree and fired off several rounds before he heard another crack-crack.

"Still two enemies to the east and they're on the move, heading south," Eric said.

"I'm flanking," Mark said. "I'll be on your six."

"Deion, take Nancy and Taylor and meet up with John on the west," Eric ordered.

"On our way," Deion said. "There's two men between us. I finally have eyes on them."

"I'm heading south to meet you," John said. He ran, using the trees for cover. The incoming gunfire had thinned down, and he estimated there were only one or two men left to the north. He weaved between a pair of trees and saw the brown camouflaged back of a man twenty yards away, facing south, peppering Deion's position with gunfire.

He carefully aimed and put two bullets in the man's back and was rewarded when the man collapsed onto the soft forest floor.

There was a muzzle flash to his right and he dove to the ground, rolling up next to a rock as the man's partner unleashed heavy fire at his position. "There's one to my three."

"We see him," Deion said. There was the sound of multiple rifles to the south, a steady crack-crack-cracking that suddenly went silent. "He's down."

There was the sound of rifles firing to the east and then Eric spoke. "Enemy clear to the east."

John stood and saw Deion and the rest of the team approaching, running in a half crouch, using the trees for cover. There was still gunfire to the south, and he assumed someone was still firing at the vans, but the north had gone silent.

He ran to meet Deion, who appeared angry. Nancy appeared even angrier. Taylor took cover behind a tree and scanned to the north, then said, "Steeljaw, we have no enemy to the north. Copy?"

"I see one heat signature. He's one hundred yards away and moving."

Heat signature? It dawned on him that Eric was using the VISOR, and he felt a stab of jealousy. The VISOR was part of the StrikeForce tech and *he* was the StrikeForce tech.

"You have a plan?" Deion asked.

"Valerie is safe for the moment. The VISOR's acoustic modeling says there's two distinct rifles to the south. We head north, eliminate that threat, then circle—"

There was a tremendous whump and the ground shook like an earthquake.

John turned to Taylor, who looked toward the clearing. The concrete entrance to the underground lab had shifted and there was a crack on the side running from the ground to the roof.

"There went the lab," Nancy said with disgust. "This site's been burned."

* * *

Eric felt the ground tremble and guessed instantly what had happened. He turned to Mark, who was looking at him with widened eyes.

"They blew the site," Mark said.

Damn.

The sound of gunfire faded to the south. "They're pulling back," Eric said. "Everyone back to the van."

Mark nodded and headed south, careful for enemy movement. Eric ran to the body of the first man he'd killed. The man was on his stomach, face pressed into the soft pine needles. He rolled the man over and brushed the debris from his face. The man had a large, crooked nose and boxy ears, with a white scar that sliced across his chin.

Eric concentrated and activated the VISOR's internal camera. "Clark?"

"Yes," Clark said from half a world away.

"Analyze that photo."

There was a long pause. "Karen's on it."

He ran to the next body and repeated the procedure, taking another high-quality photo. "This one too."

There was a pause as the photo uploaded. "Got it," Clark said.

Eric concentrated and the thermal and infrared overlay appeared. He swept left and right and waited for the VISOR's computer to read the imagery.

There were no heat signatures nearby.

He left the woods and ran through the clearing until he reached the concrete box. The rusted metal door was ajar and smoke billowed from around the edges. He wanted to yank the door open but caution got the better of him. There was no telling what pathogens—if any—were in the underground bunker, and he had no idea whether they were now airborne.

He hesitated. If there were anything below that could help find Liu Kong or Huang Lei, he would regret leaving. On the other hand, it wouldn't do the OTM any good if he died before he made it back to the surface.

He looked over the door and the thermal vision showed it solid red. He placed his palm on the door, felt a scalding heat, and yanked it back before his skin could blister.

The lab is gone.

He sighed and ran south across the clearing. Soon he caught up to the rest of the team. They were standing at the tree line, watching the van, which was now peppered with holes through the white paint.

Deion turned to him. "Anything?"

He scanned the trees with the thermal vision but there were no human heat signatures. "Nothing. We've been had."

* * *

The long drive back to Boryspil almost drove Eric crazy. They stopped south of Stepne and patched the bullet holes in the vans with white epoxy, but they couldn't do much for the spiderweb of cracks in the windows. The armored tires still provided traction, although several had taken gunfire.

Someone anticipated our arrival.

The sun had turned the horizon a dark orange when they reached the airport. They had received a few curious glances from passing cars and motorcycles, but there were no checkpoints to navigate, no authorities to dodge.

They reached the hangar and stowed the vans in the C17. Mark and Taylor helped the Loadmaster strap them to the floor of the plane before takeoff, giving Eric time to talk to Nancy, who was sitting in the front of the cargo hold.

"They *knew* we were coming," he said.

Nancy glanced up. "We had eyes on us before we left the airport?"

"It's probable."

"Liu Kong or Huang Lei?"

"Does it matter?"

She turned and her eyes came to rest upon Deion and Valerie, sitting across from her. "It could have been worse. We survived."

She had a point. They were still alive and no one was hurt, except for John, who limped onto the plane and took the seat next to them.

"Those assholes shot me in the foot," John said, pulling up his pant leg to expose the prosthetic. There was a chuck of metal missing from it and John frowned. "They caught me right between the armor."

Eric slapped him on the back. "You got lucky. They could have shot you in that big head of yours."

Nancy turned to John and gave him an awkward smile. "That's twice you've saved my life in the past two days."

John stared at the deck of the plane, his face turning red. "Just doing my job."

Deion stopped talking to Valerie and glanced across the plane. "You did good, man."

Eric felt a twinge of pride. For all John's past, he had turned out to be an exemplary soldier. He wished Deion and the rest could see that John succeeded in *spite* of his past. On the other hand, if he told anyone that John remembered bombing the Red Cross, it would probably end with John's execution.

His earpiece crackled. "We have a match on the photos," Clark said.

"Who were they?"

"Karen says Ukrainian mercenaries. Vladimir Miroshnychenko and Petro Andrushko. We're checking their accounts—"

"How?"

Clark cleared his throat. "Probably best you don't know. Karen said it might violate international law. She expects recent significant deposits."

"Thanks, Sergeant. We're readying for takeoff. We'll be wheels up in ten."

"Understood. We'll contact you if we find anything else."

He turned back to Nancy. "The men I photographed at Feofilivka were mercs. Locals."

"Liu Kong hired them?"

"Does it matter? We're back to square one."

CHAPTER NINETEEN

Atlantic Ocean

LIU KONG SLAMMED his fist against his burled walnut seat tray, causing his laptop to shake. The trap in Feofilivka had failed.

He stared out the window at the dark ocean below. Luck had been against them the entire operation, handing the Americans victory after victory.

The Americans. Always the Americans. Huang Lei held a dim view of them and believed them an uncivilized force that must be stopped for the good of humanity. But that was Huang Lei, and Huang Lei was a great man.

Unlike Huang Lei, Liu Kong *hated* the Americans.

They were oafish beasts—full of rank emotions and bravado—without serious reasoning capacity. They lacked Huang Lei's magnanimity. Since Huang Lei had rescued him from the streets of Tianjin, he had come to believe that Huang Lei wasn't just a mere mortal, but the reincarnation of Yuanshi Tianzun, the Jade Emperor, who had fashioned humans from clay.

He owed the man his life. He would do anything—pay any price—if it meant helping Huang Lei. He tapped on his laptop and initiated the video call.

Huang Lei answered. He appeared calm, but Kong read the concern in the older man's face.

"You have news?" Huang Lei asked.

"The trap failed."

"It is of no concern. They cannot stop us now."

Kong smiled. He would not let the Jade Emperor down. "I will arrive soon. We are on the cusp."

Lei nodded, his face softening. "You are like a brother, Kong. All that I have and all that I have achieved, I owe to *your* support. Together *we* are on the cusp, and together we will remake the world."

* * *

Area 51

Karen navigated through the maze of tunnels, finally reaching the door to Dewey's office. She knocked softly and entered when Dewey called out.

His office was strangely clean. She looked to her right and found all his extra equipment stacked neatly against the wall.

"Dewey? What the hell?"

Dewey paced in front of his wall of monitors. He turned to her, dark bags under his eyes, hair stuck in sweaty patches. "Hey, Karen. What's up?"

She took the seat next to his desk and watched him pace across the tile floor. "What did you do to your office?"

He turned to stare at the equipment. "That? I needed to clear my head. I'm trying something."

She sniffed the air and raised her nose. "When was the last time you took a shower?"

"Yesterday? Why, do you want to shower with me?"

"No, I do *not*. Dewey, you can't live down here like a troll. You have to take care of yourself."

He smiled. "Hey, did you ever see *Troll 2*? What a piece of crap."

"I don't care about some stupid movie. What are you working on?"

"Another project for the Old Man. I guess there's no rest for the wicked."

"What does he have you working on this time?"

He pointed at his wall of monitors. "I'm searching for where a man *is not*, not where a man *is*."

It was the most absurd thing she had ever heard from him, and he had once quoted an entire episode of an obscure television show called *Cop Rock*. "What's *that* supposed to mean?"

"Beats me." He grabbed his office chair and flopped down on it. "I'm looking for a man named Huang Lei."

"I heard. He's tied to the bomb and the virus. What have you found?"

"There's a bunch of Huang Leis in the world. I've found an actor, a doctor, and an engineer. Hey, that reminds me of a joke—"

"Could you focus? It's like you're getting worse."

He bowed his head. "It's hard for me to concentrate, you know? Anyway, I've found so many Huang Leis I don't even know where to begin." He stood and began pacing again. "Look for a man where he *is not*, not where he *is*. I wish I knew what that meant."

Karen sighed. "Did you speak to Nancy after the Old Man's surgery?"

He stopped pacing. "She sent me an email from Seoul. We are no longer to engage in sexual activity, and she wishes me well. What does *that* mean? I read their mission report—she's with that guy John Frist, the one Doc Elliot experimented on. You don't think she's having sex with *him*, do you?"

"How many times have I told you to *stop* hacking other people's stuff? You're not supposed to know about the StrikeForce technology, Dewey."

"How could I *not* know about it? I wrote software for the VISOR and the Implant."

"How did you know it was implanted in Frist?"

"Well ... I might have read it somewhere—"

"Damn it! Didn't we *just* talk about this a few days ago? You're going to get yourself locked up if you keep doing shit like this!"

"But ... that was *before* we had that conversation. I read it, like, years ago."

The look on Dewey's face softened her anger. He truly didn't understand what he had done wrong. "Don't ever mention that part about Frist again, understand?"

"I understand," he said solemnly. "But you don't think Nancy dumped me for Frist? I mean, he bombed a bunch of people—doesn't that mean he's a psychopath?"

"Dewey!"

"Right. Sorry. I'm sorry. But you don't think...?"

She shook her head. "I *highly* doubt it. It's probably the work you did on the Old Man's implant. Maybe she just got tired of you."

"Does that happen?"

"Sex with the same person *can* get boring. Or sometimes the relationship goes too fast. Or not fast enough. Sometimes it's just in a couple's best interests to end the relationship."

"I'm glad you're here to explain this stuff to me. It's not like television *at all*. I don't understand how people work. It's not like Boolean logic—"

She saw the funny look on his face. "What?"

He closed his eyes and turned his head as if reading an invisible display. "It couldn't possibly be that simple," he muttered. "I'd have to be a complete *idiot* to have missed that."

"What, Dewey? To have missed *what*?"

He opened one eyelid. "Is that friend of yours still working on financial manipulation?"

"Brenda? Yes, she's been working on a new algorithm to replace the Altman Z-Score so that she can see if there was a single player behind the worldwide financial collapses of the past decade."

Dewey spun around in his chair and began typing so fast his fingers were little more than a blur. "Where does she keep her research? Under her own directories or under a shared directory?"

Exasperated, she said, "What did we *just* talk about?"

He stopped typing and grinned. "Don't worry, I'm not poking around because I'm bored. I *might* have an idea. Well, the *beginning* of an idea."

* * *

Karen entered the cafeteria, nodded to a few coworkers, then poured herself the largest cup of coffee she could find. At the counter, the short blond-haired woman in green camos smiled. "Been one of those days?"

She smiled back, in spite of herself. "You know me, Vicky, it's always one of *those* days." She took a seat near the entrance and sipped at her coffee.

Watching Dewey work was taxing, because of both the speed at which he flipped through data and his poor explanations. She was used to processing large amounts of data, but Dewey was in a league all his own. He read faster than she could keep up, and the deeper he engaged in the problem, the less he spoke.

He probably hasn't even noticed I left.

She sipped the coffee and found it good. She was trying to cut back, to please Eric and get Todd Clark off her back, but it was her *one* vice.

Well, that and sleeping around.

She sighed. Listening to Dewey talk about Nancy had given her something to think about. She hated to admit it, but Nancy *had* matured. *That, or she's become a better liar.* She felt bad for Dewey. His view of the world was one of childlike wonder, filled with constant distractions. He lacked any kind of social boundaries, but he made up for it by having a kind heart.

And by being one of the smartest people among a whole base of smart people.

She worried that Nancy might have used Dewey, but it terrified her that the Old Man had assigned Dewey special projects. She vowed that when the current mission was complete, she was going to grill Dewey about what *other* things he might have done for the Old Man.

How would anyone know? Who would he tell besides me? All he does is hide out in his office and watch stupid TV shows.

He explained once that television made sense, that there weren't the uncertainties and tangled communications that came when dealing with people. It had taken her years, but she finally understood what he was trying to tell her.

His office is his safe place, and his TV shows take the place of human contact.

Then Nancy took an interest in Dewey. In their own weird way, they were alike—both incapable of normal human relations.

Except Nancy is a trained killer, and Dewey is just … Dewey. What am I going to do with him?

Her cell phone beeped and she read the message from Dewey, then ran out, her coffee cup forgotten on the table.

* * *

Atlantic Ocean

Eric checked their location with the pilot. After refueling in England, they were nearing the United States. The team had spent most of the trip writing after-action reports and doing their hot wash. With the reports complete and nothing else to do, the final leg from England to Area 51 was the longest part of the trip.

He went back to the cargo bay and found the team scattered about. Nancy sat by herself, reading from a laptop. Deion and

Valerie were sitting with Mark Kelly, engaged in a spirited debate about the pros of Valerie visiting Deion's father again in Chicago.

John was in the back, behind the last van, stretched out across several of the fold-down seats. His prosthetic foot was on the deck next to him. His eyes were closed, but he would occasionally answer a question from Taylor Martin, who was sitting on the other side of the plane.

Nancy didn't look up when he passed, but he nodded at Deion, Valerie, and Mark, then walked to the back and took a seat next to John. He glanced down at the young man. "Feeling okay?"

Without opening his eyes, John responded slowly, "My foot hurts."

Surprised, Eric asked, "Your right foot?"

"Nope. The left."

"How can your left foot hurt? You don't even *have* a left foot."

John opened one eye. "Doc Elliot says it's normal. Says it's all in my head, but damned if doesn't still hurt. It's like an itch I can't scratch."

Eric glanced over to Taylor, who shrugged and pointed to the prosthetic. "I *never* get used to seeing him take that thing off."

John opened his other eye and rolled his head to glance at Taylor. "When we land, I'm going to chase you around the plane with it."

Taylor laughed. "You'll be hopping on your good foot."

"Just you wait and see," John said, waggling his eyebrows. "I'm going to freak you the hell out."

It was good to hear John make a joke. The young man was under a tremendous amount of stress, and the missions over the past week hadn't helped. "How's your arm and leg?"

John shrugged. "It's going to scar like crazy." He paused, then ran his fingers through his short brown hair. "I guess a scar is better than losing them."

Eric's phone vibrated and he held up his hand. "Hold that cheery thought." He put in his earpiece and answered the call. "Go for Wise."

A woman's voice came through the earpiece. "It's Karen. We have information you need to hear."

"Who's we?"

"Dewey found it—"

"Again with that guy?"

"The Old Man asked for his help. You won't believe what he discovered. Dewey says that he looked for where Huang Lei *wasn't*, not where he *was*. He wrote this new software and was trying to correlate patterns of behavior—"

"I'm not going to understand any of this from a phone call, Karen. Can you just highlight the details?"

"There are dozens of companies—big companies—that don't appear to be owned by anyone. Their net worth is staggering. High-tech companies, software companies, pharmaceuticals, biotech—"

"Biotech?"

"Yes. They're *all* owned by the same type of holding corp that ran the Jade Group. Most holding corps eventually track back to publicly or privately traded stock. No matter how deep we dig, we can't find the owners of *these* companies. It's all designed to obfuscate the owner."

John and Taylor watched him curiously, and he felt his pulse quicken. "*How* did we not find this before?"

"There are so many layers to this, it's amazing we found it at all. If these belong to Huang Lei, then he's one of the wealthiest men in the world. At least in the top twenty."

Eric nodded to himself. It made sense. Only someone with really deep pockets could have purchased a nuclear bomb from North Korea, let alone delivered it to Somalia. The software embedded in the video camera hardware showed Huang Lei possessed cunning and foresight. The use of the portable biolab on the MV *Rising Star* had taken considerable planning.

No, Huang Lei was proving a formidable opponent. More than that, the man seemed bent on causing mass causalities to the United States. "Wait, did you say pharmaceutical companies?"

"Yes, that's what worries me. How much do you know about syringe production?"

His stomach flip-flopped. "I'm afraid you're about to fill me in."

"There are only a handful of syringe manufacturers in the world," Karen said. "It's one of those things where there's not a lot of profit. Because of safety concerns, most syringes in the US are made at a plant outside of Nashville."

"You've *got* to be kidding."

Taylor and John were sitting up now, watching with great interest.

"It gets worse. Because of the upcoming flu season, the biggest single production run is happening now. They start shipping this week."

"Liu Kong. That's where he's going." It wasn't a question. After all the threats, after all the missions of the past week, it made perfect sense.

"Yes. Dewey used the same software to track flights entering the United States, and he found a Gulfstream registered to the Serpentine Group."

"Serpentine? Never heard of them."

"Serpentine is a group of rocks, sometimes referred to as *false jade*. Here's the kicker—the Gulfstream's point of origin was the Boryspil International Airport. It departed shortly after your C17 arrived."

* * *

Nashville, Tennessee

The wheels of the C17 chirped as they touched down. It was almost dawn when the big aircraft taxied toward a hangar the OTM had rented while still in flight.

The team members were strapped in next to him. Eric turned to them and said, "Everyone clear on the mission?"

There were nods all around.

"Okay, let's make it happen."

The aircraft came to a halt, and the Loadmaster opened the rear of the plane. Several black Suburbans were waiting as they stepped onto the tarmac and into the crisp September air. The lead agent stood, ramrod straight, waiting for them.

"Agent Waverly," Eric said. He hoped John Waverly wouldn't cause him any more grief than he had the last time they were in Nashville, but the Office needed the FBI's help. "I see your request to open a field office in Nashville was finally approved."

Waverly's eyes narrowed. "The request was submitted over a year ago, and then it suddenly got approved in the past two days. Are you implying *you* had something to do with that?"

Eric raised an eyebrow. "How could DHS expedite a request for the FBI? Probably just a coincidence."

Waverly turned to each of them, and Eric could almost see the man's brain churning, taking their measure. "Do you think I'm incompetent? This is supposed to soften me up? I know you don't work for DHS. I asked around. Nobody knows you." He turned to the C17 and pointed. "This? Don't insult my intelligence. Tell me what the military is doing here and why you need my help." The man's bushy eyebrows suddenly furrowed. "Unless this is some CIA black op."

He is *sharp.*

No amount of cover story would lower the man's suspicions, so he decided to take the direct route. "John. Can I call you John? We're on the same side. Right now we have a serious threat to national security. We need the FBI's help, but this can't be on book." Before Waverly could speak, Eric continued. "I know you're a good agent. I've read your sixty-seven file. Now you have a choice. You can do things *by the book*, or you can *throw the book out* and help us stop an imminent attack."

Waverly ran his fingers through his thick black hair. "I still don't trust you, but what do you need?"

CHAPTER TWENTY

JOHN QUIETLY APPROACHED the Gulfstream V. The plane was on the east side of the airport, fifty yards from the Citation parked next to it. Its white hull was clearly visible, even though the sun wouldn't rise for another two hours. He activated the VISOR's thermal vision and swept over the plane.

"I can't tell if anyone's home," he said.

The black Battlesuit made him harder to see, but he knew the mercury vapor lights from the hangars to the south were bright enough to make him visible if anyone looked.

"The FBI has this side of the airport barricaded," Eric said. "According to the airfield manager, the pilot is still on board."

John concentrated and keyed up audio. As the different waveforms appeared on the LCD, he concentrated again, and the noise from the airport began to disappear as the VISOR's computer canceled out the noise.

Soon, the roar of arriving jets had faded. He could still feel the rumble in his chest, vibrating within him like a drum, but the sound was effectively washed from the VISOR's audio. Then, the sound of vehicles in the distance. Soon there was only a creaking from the Gulfstream's airframe as someone on board walked the length of the plane.

"I've got movement."

"Go," Eric said.

John drew his M11s from his hip holsters and approached quickly. He didn't need the Implant for this. His prosthetic still ached, but not enough to keep him from making it to the plane's hatch as it opened.

The pilot of the Gulfstream stared at him in shock. His cap fell from his head as he stumbled back on the steps, a heat bloom spreading across his genitals as his bladder released.

"Jesus, don't shoot," the pilot begged. "I'm not armed. Don't shoot!"

* * *

John stood in front of the pilot, Ron Lipfield, in a hangar south of the Gulfstream. Lipfield wasn't talking, and Eric was arguing with Nancy and the FBI agent, Waverly.

"We don't have time for this," Nancy said.

"She's right," Eric said. "We need answers, and we need them *now*."

"I'm an agent of the law," Waverly said. "I won't be party to any CIA dirty tricks."

"We never said we were CIA," Nancy said. "I'll get the information out of him. Just stay out of my way."

Lipfield sat on a metal chair, and John watched his face. The man stared at him in abject terror. John didn't disagree. He had seen himself in the mirror when dressed in the Battlesuit. The smooth face of the VISOR betrayed no emotion.

He looked fearsome. Monstrous.

I look *like an inhuman killing machine.*

The funny part was, Lipfield wouldn't be wrong. The OTM had made him into something more than human, with almost unbreakable bones and vastly improved reflexes, and he used those enhancements to hurt people.

All in all, I'd rather be back with Valerie in the C17.

Lipfield's eyes darted from him to Nancy, who was quickly approaching. Waverly and Eric followed Nancy, and Taylor, Mark, and Deion brought up the rear.

Nancy stopped in front of the pilot. "We need answers. Tell us about your passenger."

"I don't have to tell you anything," Lipfield said. "I have rights. I want to speak to my lawyer."

"Do you even *have* a lawyer?" Nancy asked. She leaned forward and John saw her hand flexing. "Why do you think we're here? What are you trying to hide?"

Buddy, if I were you, I'd answer.

"I don't know what you're talking about," Lipfield said, his voice cracking. "I haven't done anything wrong."

Nancy sighed. "You're boring me. John, shoot him in the kneecap."

For a brief moment, John wondered if she was kidding, but the tone of her voice was matter-of-fact. He knew that when she spoke like that, she was definitely *not* kidding.

He pulled his M11 and fired one round. It echoed inside the warehouse, and the man screamed, his face going white, and then fell out of the chair and writhed in pain on the hard concrete floor.

"*Jesus*," Waverly yelled and pulled his gun, training it on him. "You can't just *shoot* people!"

John stood perfectly still. He knew Waverly's Glock stood little chance of penetrating the VISOR or his Battlesuit. He also knew that Waverly *didn't* know that.

Eric started to speak, but Nancy cut him off.

"Mark," Nancy said, "if Waverly shoots, put him down."

Mark Kelly nodded and aimed his HK416 at the tall FBI agent, his sad brown eyes betraying no emotion. "Yes, ma'am."

Nancy turned to Deion and Taylor. "Get this asshole back in the chair."

Deion started to argue, but he clenched his jaw and with Taylor's help got Lipfield back in the chair.

Lipfield did not appear well. He gasped for air, obviously in great pain. The sound of his wheezing breath and constant moaning filled John's VISOR.

"Would you like to try again?" Nancy asked.

"You *shot* me," Lipfield croaked. "Who *are* you people?"

"Who was on your plane?" Nancy demanded.

"Mr. Kong," Lipfield said. "His name is Liu Kong. He's the CEO of the Serpentine Group."

"Anyone else?"

"No, just Mr. Kong."

"Why weren't you answering our questions? Did Kong tell you not to talk?"

Lipfield shook his head. "It's because I've ... I've got a record."

"We didn't find evidence of any arrests," Eric said.

Lipfield looked down at his knee. Blood slowly oozed from the bullet wound and soaked his black slacks. "Mr. Kong made it go away. I got caught with some coke a few years back. No commercial airline will hire you with *that* on your record. Mr. Kong offered me a job. Said he could get my conviction buried. Look, I'm not a criminal. I just had a problem, that's all. I never did anything wrong!"

"Where did Kong go?" Nancy asked. "Was he carrying anything? Did he have any luggage? Packages?"

Lipfield bit his lower lip. "He had a big box. A plastic case." He held his hands apart, as wide as his shoulders. "About this big. He left with that case and his laptop. He was going to Nolensville."

* * *

John was sitting in the back of Waverly's Suburban as the FBI agent led the other vehicles south along Haley Industrial Drive, passing several manufacturing sites and warehouses on their way to Sakra Limited.

The morning sun was just beginning to dawn over the hills to the east, casting shades of orange and blue that looked almost neon in the VISOR's display. Waverly and Eric were in the front, talking in hushed tones.

The FBI agent was *not* happy.

They had argued the whole five miles from the airport. Waverly was appalled by the gratuitous violence that Nancy had used questioning Lipfield, and Eric was explaining the threat from Liu Kong and how sometimes the end justified the means.

He hated to agree with Eric—he certainly hadn't enjoyed shooting Lipfield—but in this case, Eric was right. They *were* faced with an imminent threat. Every life lost because they refused to make the hard choices would be on them.

The line of Suburbans pulled into the last parking lot before the road dead-ended in a turnaround. Sakra's parking lot was empty except for a silver Toyota at the front.

Too early for the morning shift?

"This is it," Eric said.

They climbed out of the vehicles and soon a handful of agents wearing jackets with giant yellow FBI letters joined the OTM members.

He saw the FBI agents' curious glances and wondered what they thought of his armor.

Probably the same as Lipfield.

"Okay, our target *should* be in this building. There will most likely be a security guard monitoring the plant. Agent Waverly, if you would direct your men to barricade the parking lot? John," Eric said, pointing at him, "will lead the way."

Waverly shook his head. "We don't have a warrant."

"We don't *need* a warrant," Nancy said.

"I thought you said you *weren't* CIA?"

Eric shook his head. "DHS doesn't need a warrant in a case of imminent threat."

"You're *not* DHS," Waverly muttered under his breath. He turned to the dozen agents standing around, watching the exchange. "You heard them. Get that barricade up."

A pair of FBI agents positioned two of the Suburbans across the entrance to the parking lot, stringing yellow tape between them while the other agents helped the OTM unload their gear, and soon both OTM members and FBI agents were wearing bulletproof vests.

Eric turned to John. "We're ready when you are."

* * *

They approached the building and stopped at the glass-walled visitors' entrance. A heavyset man in his thirties wearing a guard's uniform was sitting at the front desk, his nose buried in a paperback copy of *Harry Potter and the Deathly Hallows*.

John turned to Eric, who shrugged and tapped on the glass with his HK416. The guard didn't look up, and John realized he was wearing earbuds. He kicked the glass door with his prosthetic foot, hard enough to shake the frame as well as the glass to each side.

The guard jerked and glanced up, did a double take at the sight of the FBI agents and OTM members, and dropped his book on the desk. He stood on shaky legs and stumbled to the door. He turned the lock, hesitated, then opened the door.

"Uh. Can I help you?"

Eric grabbed the man, yanked him through the door, and shoved him to a waiting FBI agent. "Go, John."

John nodded. He stepped through the entrance and made his way to the door in the back. He opened it carefully and looked down a short hallway. There was a heavy steel door at the end. He concentrated and keyed the VISOR's audio to maximum, but there was nothing except for the gentle hum of the building's HVAC system.

As he walked down the hall, he half-expected the door at the end to burst open, but it remained closed, the building quiet.

When he reached the door, he turned and found Eric was right behind him. "The door *could* be rigged."

"Good point," Eric said. "Maybe we should find another way in."

Several thoughts ran through John's head—a picture of him stepping through the door and the flash of an explosion. The sight of the Ryder truck exploding in front of the Red Cross and the shame he now felt. The image of bodies, lined up like firewood, in makeshift hospitals, their eyes hollow.

"Step back," he said.

"Are you sure?"

John pointed to the door. "I'm tired of this. Liu Kong is in there. I'm going in to get him."

"You sure?" Eric asked again.

Behind Eric, Deion nodded. He saw Taylor and Mark give him the thumbs-up, and even Nancy had the beginning of an approving smile on her face.

"I'm sure."

Eric and the rest of the OTM and FBI agents retreated to the entrance and John turned around, twisted the handle and kicked the door.

The steel door slammed open, and John finally saw what lay beyond. The floor of the manufacturing plant was empty, the lines of gleaming silver equipment silent, the day's run of syringes not yet started. He stepped past rows of complex machinery whose function he couldn't begin to guess. The bare floor was as clean as an operating room.

He turned left and passed a bank of injection molding machines, ready for the day's production. The room was still eerily quiet, but when he made the next right, he finally found Liu Kong.

Kong sat on a metal stool, his face impassive, watching him.

It was the black plastic case on the floor in front of Kong that caused John to freeze.

"I have waited for this moment," Kong said. "Welcome."

There were footsteps behind him, and John raised his hand. "Don't come any closer," he warned Eric and the rest. "Something's not right."

The footsteps stopped. "What's he playing at?" Eric asked.

"I don't know. He's just sitting there." To Kong, he said, "Whatever you have planned, it won't work. We have the building surrounded."

Kong bowed his head. "My faceless enemy has no face."

John wracked his brain, trying to figure out what Kong meant, then realized he meant the VISOR. "We are *not* your enemy. Whatever Huang Lei has told you—"

"Huang Lei is beyond your mortal ken," Kong said blandly. "You cannot defeat him."

"We stopped the bomb," John said, taking one step forward, "and we're going to stop you. Huang Lei has already *been* defeated. Tell me where he is."

"You will *never* find him. He is more than a man. He is the Jade Emperor."

John recognized the gleam in Kong's eyes. Kong wasn't a terrorist. Kong was a fanatic. "There's only one way this ends," John said. He held up his right hand with the M11 pistol. "Either you come willingly, or I'll be forced to shoot. You're finished. Get on the ground."

A smile played across Kong's face, and then the man bowed his head again. "I *am*."

In that instant, John knew what Kong intended. He knew why Kong had waited so patiently for them to enter the plant. He turned to his team and saw their eyes widen.

"*Get out!*" John screamed.

It was too late. The impact slammed into him like a giant's hand, rattling every bone in his body, so violent that he saw a bright flash of light behind his eyelids before the darkness claimed him.

CHAPTER TWENTY-ONE

Pacific Ocean

HUANG LEI SANK back into his leather chair, watching the coastline far below as his plane banked, heading for the open ocean. The waves formed in lines of white, breaking neatly parallel before pounding the beach with frothy foam.

He sighed. He would miss his office, but there were many others around the world in many different cities and under many different names. He would disappear, and his enemies would find only an empty penthouse.

Kong was most likely dead. If the plan had succeeded, his enemy was now infected. The Americans would not have time to find a cure to keep the sickness from spreading. Soon, America would be on its knees, finally stepping back from the global stage.

Finally, the Americans would *know* their place. He only wished the Russians had suffered an equal fate, but he still had plans for them.

Liu Kong's death would not be in vain. The world would soon be on a new path. A greater path.

After hundreds of years of America's failed experiment in government, sanity would be restored.

* * *

Area 51

Eric sat up slowly. The room spun, and he shook his head, trying to clear the wooziness. John stared back from the bubble across from his, then raised his hand and waved. Nancy was still asleep in her bubble, but Taylor, Deion and John Waverly were awake.

Taylor listened to an MP3 player, and occasionally his voice would join in on some old country song before John would holler for him to shut up. Deion lay on his hospital bed, reading quietly. John Waverly played cards on a table in his bubble, hardly speaking to anyone.

They had turned one of the spare aircraft hangars under the mountains of Groom Lake into a quarantine area, and men and women in white containment suits worked on the last bubble in the line, the one containing Mark Kelly.

Eric's laptop beeped and he answered it. Nathan Elliot smiled back at him. "Feeling better?"

"Yes," Eric said. "I'm still weak. How much longer before we get out of these things?"

"You're just lucky I have been working on a viral component for the next version of the StrikeForce technology. If we hadn't installed dozens of fourth-generation DNA sequencers—"

"Yeah, *real* lucky. How's Mark?"

Elliot frowned. "Not well. He's the only one of you to suffer such ... drastic consequences. I'm afraid he might not be the same."

Eric's stomach sank. "What are you saying?"

"The swelling in his spinal column was severe. He may not walk again."

Eric cursed under his breath. "That's unacceptable."

"Do you understand how lucky you are?" Elliot asked, his rumbling voice rising in pitch. "Not just that we managed to quarantine you all. Not just that we stopped Kong from infecting millions of flu shots. For whatever reason, the virus wasn't designed to be lethal. If it had been, you'd all be dead. As it is, you'll be back to normal in a day or two, but Mr. Kelly is going to require intensive care."

"I'm sorry, Doc. I *am* grateful. I'm just not used to sitting around doing nothing."

"We're doing our best," Elliot said. "There's something else. John's blood tests."

"The virus?"

"No. Something *else*. We've detected free-floating cancer cells."

"I see. How much time does he have?"

"I don't know." Before Eric could speak, Elliot continued. "I'm not just saying that. Even the best oncologists in the world can't accurately predict how much time a patient has left. I'm sorry, Eric."

"Me too," Eric said, then closed the laptop, cutting off the connection.

He had no reason to complain. They had stopped a potential pandemic, at a heavy cost to Mark Kelly. They had quarantined the people exposed to the virus and sterilized the Sakra factory before burning it to the ground.

John was a different matter. The tech inside his body was killing him. He glanced over to John's bubble, where John rested peacefully.

He was going to have to make a decision about John.

Soon.

He only wished the team Smith had sent to Hawaii had found Huang Lei instead of an empty office. But the OTM would never rest until they had captured the bastard who had almost killed them.

＊ ＊ ＊

Washington, D.C.

The president stared at them. "How did this happen?"

Smith shook his head. "Your predecessors were committed to certain types of research. One of the men, Huang Jin, was instrumental in creating some of the worst known to man. He became distraught when I stopped his research, and he fled to China with his son. I can only imagine how he poisoned the young man's mind."

"You caught him?"

Eric started to speak, but Smith raised his hand. He was proud of his young protégé and glad Eric had bounced back within the week.

Unfortunately, Mark Kelly had not been so lucky and was still adjusting to his wheelchair, trying to make do without the use of his legs and arms. The swelling in his brain had reduced Kelly to a quadriplegic. The OTM members were there, helping, and offering moral support, but Kelly was deeply depressed as the full extent of his injury sank in.

"I'm afraid not," Smith said softly.

"You mean he's still on the loose?"

"Yes," Eric said. "We've seriously degraded his ability to cause harm. We're following the money trail. We've recovered thirty companies worth over five billion dollars in assets."

"Five billion dollars? How could he have amassed that kind of money?" The president slammed his fist on the table. "Is that even possible?"

"He was a *bright* young man," Smith said. "Dedicated. Idealistic." It was a shame Huang Lei was so misguided. Given more time, perhaps he could have redirected the young man's energy. *Alas, it was not meant to be.* "The facility in Feofilivka has been sanitized."

The president sighed. "Why the Russians? What did this man hope to accomplish?"

"The Russians acquired his father's research," Smith said.

"You mean they *stole* it."

Smith nodded. "The Chinese would not allow Huang Jin to continue his work. When Jin found the Russians were continuing with his research, it only drove him further toward madness."

"So this Huang Lei wanted to unleash a deadly virus?"

Smith shook his head. "Far from it. The Chimera virus wasn't designed to be lethal. It is more insidious. Perhaps forty percent of those infected would suffer flu-like symptoms—"

"The flu? That's it?"

"The flu kills fifty thousand Americans each year, Mr. President," Eric said. "It can be deadly."

"In smaller numbers, this virus also causes a severe form of meningitis," Smith said. "Imagine five hundred thousand Americans suddenly paralyzed by an inflammation of the brain and spinal cord. No, Lei planned to infect the syringes used in the influenza vaccine. Imagine as word spread that the flu vaccine was causing deaths, and in some cases, paralysis. There would have been mass panic. Then, if it was discovered to be an engineered virus, created at a Soviet facility?"

The president slumped back in his chair. "It would have been mayhem. Putin thinks he's still fighting the Cold War. He would have assumed we did this to ourselves as a cover for pushing closer to his borders. I can only imagine Congress would have voted to deploy more interceptors for the missile shield."

"I believe you understand," Smith said. "I don't think Lei intended to kill millions. He is more cunning than that. Why kill millions when thousands will do? Why start wars when sowing discontent accomplishes the same thing."

"What *is* he trying to accomplish? What is his strategic plan?"

Eric cleared his throat. "We can only guess, Mr. President, but we believe he wants to cripple both the US and Russia. China and India are chomping at the bit to fill that gap, especially China."

"You have no idea where he went?"

"He had time to prepare," Eric said. "He had the money and the means to escape. We're still searching. When he reappears … and make no mistake, he *will* reappear … we will be there."

The president sighed heavily. "Thank you, gentlemen. I know I sound ungrateful, but I understand what you've done for your country."

"No thanks are necessary," Smith said. "It's what we do. Now, we have another matter to discuss."

Eric turned to him. "We do?"

"Mr. President, effective immediately, I'm turning over the day-to-day operations of the Office to Eric. I have a few things to finish up before my retirement, but Eric will now run the Office."

Eric swallowed hard. "I … thank you, sir."

"Don't look so shocked," Smith said, finally allowing himself to smile. "You knew this day was coming. Mr. President, it's been an honor."

The president stood, glanced between the two of them, then snapped off a passable salute. "Mr. Smith? No words can acknowledge the service you've performed for your country."

Smith saluted back. For a moment, he felt like the raw young recruit called to speak with Truman in the basement of Davis House. "Mr. President? It has been *my* pleasure. Come, Mr. Wise, it is time we leave the president to his business so we can attend to ours."

Eric followed him out of the bunker and through the tunnel connecting the White House to the Eisenhower Building, and soon they were in the back of the Lincoln, with Smith giving directions to Roger to drop them off near the reflecting pool.

As the Lincoln slowed, Eric asked, "Who are we meeting?"

"You'll understand soon enough."

Roger pulled the Lincoln into a parking spot and Smith got out with Eric in tow, and they walked through the throngs of tourists until he saw Vasilii standing by the pool, staring across the water.

"Vasilii?" Smith said.

The old Russian turned to him, his face registering surprise. "You bring someone after all this time?"

"Eric, meet Vasilii Melamid. He occupies roughly the same position that you do." He saw the shock on both their faces. "Yes, the Russians have an equivalent to the Office," he said to Eric, then turned to Vasilii. "And, yes, I'm stepping down."

Vasilii nodded, but there was a twinkle in his eye. "Is good. A man of your years must get rest. Or perhaps be put in one of those nursing homes I see on television?"

Smith laughed. "You're not that much younger, you old bear. Soon your country will be calling *you* home. Eric, you can trust Vasilii." He saw the surprise on Eric's face. "Oh, not completely—he is *still* the enemy, but occasionally there are … overlaps. Places where it is of mutual interest to work together. Vasilii understands that it does no good to win the war if it means the extermination of the human race. Compromises *can* be made."

The old Russian eyed Eric shrewdly. "Fulton placed much trust in you. You are good man?"

Before Eric could speak, Smith interrupted. "He's good enough to keep you on a tight leash."

Vasilii nodded and stuck out his hand, which Eric shook. The old man bowed his head. "A pleasure, young man, but now I speak to Fulton."

Eric's eyes narrowed and Smith could practically feel the gears turning in the young man's head. "I'll meet you back at the car," Smith said. "It's quite all right. Vasilii and I have unfinished business."

Eric nodded and headed back toward the car, leaving the two men alone.

"Thank you for cleaning up mess in Feofilivka," Vasilii said. "It could have been … problematic."

"That's one way to describe it. Now, about that other matter."

Vasilii glanced away. "I'm sorry, old friend, but was not enough. They will not allow it."

"I thought you were going to push for this? I thought you were going to help?"

Vasilii shook his head sadly. "I tried. What Alexandra did? The way she left? They say it cannot be forgiven. I am sorry. I *did* try."

He wondered if Vasilii *had* tried. No one had been hurt more by Alexandra's betrayal than Vasilii, and his sudden reversal on her position had come too easily. "Did you?"

"Even against my better judgment," Vasilii said quietly. "I do not wield your power. I still answer to superiors. I used every bit of influence. It was not enough. You understand? *It was not enough.*"

Smith felt his anger rising, not at the old Russian, but at himself for thinking he could reunite his wife and daughter. He turned to stare at the murky water in the reflecting pond. "All my power? It's not enough to give me the one thing I desire."

Vasilii turned to join him and together they stood, two old men, looking out across the water, lost in their thoughts.

* * *

Smith stood next to the intersection, calmly watching the traffic rumbling through the heart of Washington. It had been two weeks since Liu Kong had released the virus, but the Office was slowly recovering. He had one last piece of business to complete and it would soon be over.

He squinted, looking to see if he could make out the forms of the snipers positioned on the rooftops along G Street.

His earpiece crackled. "You're good, sir," Taylor Martin said.

"Thank you, Mr. Martin." Martin and the newly recruited Bill Burton were armed with Barrett sniper rifles, although he didn't expect them to be needed. But recent events had reminded him that careful preparations made *all* the difference.

His earpiece crackled again. "Your target is approaching, over," Dewey Green said from his office in Area 51. "I picked them up on the traffic cams two blocks from your location, over."

He bit back laughter at Dewey's absurd speech patterns. "Thank you, Dewey."

He glanced down G Street. Traffic was heavy, but it wouldn't interfere with his plan. He waited patiently until he saw the black Chevy Suburban, between a Nissan Sentra and a Toyota Camry. As the Nissan passed, he stepped into the street and turned to the face the driver of the Suburban.

The SUV screeched to a halt and the young Chinese driver stared at him with wide eyes.

Smith smiled at the young man, slowly walked past the driver's door, and tapped on the rear window.

There was an old man's voice inside, then the doors opened and two burly men climbed out. They glared at him but remained silent. He nodded at them, then slid in next to the old man in the backseat.

"Please continue, Mr. Wang," Smith said over the sound of blaring horns.

The young man watched them in the rearview mirror until the old man finally nodded. The Suburban accelerated, heading west on G Street.

The old man turned to him, his face a frozen mask of indifference. "I believe Americans call this a *reversal of fortune.*"

Smith tilted his head. "One good turn deserves another. Huang Lei is missing."

The old man said nothing. Smith continued, "We stopped his plan, but I believe it is a temporary setback."

The old man finally nodded. "You felt the need to tell me in person?"

"I followed your advice. I looked for where he *wasn't.* Thank you."

The old man offered him a faint smile. "You are most welcome."

"You offered your help to prevent the PLA's hacking operation from coming to light and to keep China from suffering an international incident. You knew Huang Lei had hacked your data center, but you didn't go after him yourself. You used *us* to fix *your* problem."

The old man bowed his head. "As I said, you *are* a clever man."

"We *will* find him," Smith said. "No one can hide from us forever. Neither him … nor anyone else. Do we understand each other, Mr. Chen?"

The old man's eyes widened, almost imperceptibly. Smith might not have caught it before, but his senses were keener than they had been in years. It warmed his heart and he smiled, baring his teeth.

"I believe we do," Mr. Chen finally said.

"You may pull over, Mr. Wang. I'll be getting out here."

The driver nodded and the Suburban pulled to the curb. Smith opened the door and stepped out. Then, before he closed the door, he turned back to Mr. Chen. "You are also a *clever* man."

Before Chen could speak, Smith slammed the door shut. The Suburban's tires squealed as it took off, but Smith didn't care.

"Sir?" his earpiece squawked. "Are you okay?"

"Yes, Mr. Martin. I'm heading back."

"Do you want us to pick you up?"

"No, It's a pleasant day. I'm going to enjoy the walk."

"Roger that."

He nodded and strolled casually down the street, enjoying the last of the warm September sunshine on his face and the smell of autumn in the air.

ABOUT THE AUTHOR

Kevin Lee Swaim studied creative writing with David Foster Wallace at Illinois State University.

He's currently the Subject Matter Expert for Intrusion Prevention Systems for a Fortune 50 insurance company located in the Midwest. He holds the CISSP certification from ISC2.

When he's not writing, he's busy repairing guitars for the working bands of Central Illinois.